A Lot Like
LOVE

A Lot Like
LOVE

JENNIFER

USA TODAY BESTSELLING AUTHOR

SNOW

Entangled Publishing, LLC
10940 S Parker Road
Suite 327
Parker, CO 80134
Visit our website at www.entangledpublishing.com.

Amara is an imprint of Entangled Publishing, LLC.

Edited by Liz Pelletier
Cover design by Bree Archer
Cover art by JACOB LUND/Stocksy,
Paperkites/Gettyimages,
LUNAMARINA/Gettyimages,
Cavan Images/Gettyimages,
Interior design by Toni Kerr

Print ISBN 978-1-64937-024-2
ebook ISBN 978-1-64937-037-2

Manufactured in the United States of America

First Edition July 2021

AMARA

ALSO BY JENNIFER SNOW

A Lot Like Love is a sweet, small-town romance that is full of hope and heart, but there are images and themes that might be triggering to some readers. Widowhood, death, and mentions of WWII and prisoner of war camps appear in the novel. Readers who may be sensitive to these elements, please take note.

To "Ronnie from L.A." and Marla W. Carpe Diem!

CHAPTER ONE

This was how she was going to die.

With her lower body dangling below the splintered landing on the spiraling staircase of the B&B, Sarah Lewis supported her weight as best she could on the broken wood around her. She'd fallen through and had been hanging there for almost seven minutes, and according to her Apple Watch her heart rate was reaching a dangerous level.

Her *inheritance* of Dove's Nest B&B felt more like punishment the longer she was stuck there. The ominous water damage bubble on the ceiling above her head looked ready to pop any second, and the yellowing of the ceiling tiles in other areas suggested it wasn't the first warning sign that the place needed a new roof.

She tried pulling herself out of the hole, but each upward motion of her body caused spikes of wood to dig into the exposed flesh at her waist. She winced, squirming to get more comfortable as the wood threatened to impale her. Glancing down through the opening in the shards was terrifying. She couldn't go up…could she go down? The drop was only about twelve feet…

She could survive the fall, but her body was literally trapped. Up or down required significant bravery that she simply did not have right now.

Her cell phone taunted her from a position on the lower step, just out of reach of her fingertips. Her boss's number lighting up the display for the third call in seven minutes had her freaking out more than her current predicament.

What the hell was she going to do?

Risk a broken ankle or the death of her career?

She closed her eyes tight.

Here goes nothing.

But a knock on the B&B front door saved her from the split-second decision of letting go. "It's open!" she yelled, her voice echoing through the large open foyer. Luckily, she'd left it unlocked.

A slow creaking sound was like something out of a horror flick before heavy footsteps resonated on the hardwood floor below. "Hello?"

Oh no. Anyone else but him.

The familiar voice from her past made this situation a million times more mortifying. Maybe she should stay quiet. Maybe he'd leave again without noticing her legs dangling above his head.

"Hello?" Wes Sharrun called out again.

Sarah sighed. He was not her first choice for rescue, but he may be her only one. "Hi... Up here," she called out.

A moment later, she could see Wes's face looking at her through the cracks in the shards. "Sarah?"

Was it the sight of someone stuck in a staircase that made his voice rise in surprise or the fact that it was her? "Yep, it's me," she said, her cheeks burning. Thank God she wasn't wearing a skirt.

"What happened?" he asked.

"Isn't it obvious?" she asked, catching a glimpse of

him through the shards.

He put his hands on his hips as he smirked up at her. "You know, I'm actually not surprised to find you this way."

Great, her past reputation as…accident prone hadn't been forgotten when she'd left town. "Do you think you could help? I'm starting to lose feeling in my lower half."

"How long have you been there?" Wes asked, slowly ascending the staircase.

Long enough to miss three calls from her boss.

Gail Woodrow, CEO of Digital Strategies in L.A., didn't believe in leaving messages. She simply called until Sarah answered. Which was usually immediately.

"Too long," she said. "Be careful."

If he fell, too, she would be stuck in a staircase with her high school crush, who looked even better in person than he did in his Facebook photos. In tight, faded, dirty denim; work boots; and a black T-shirt with white paint splatters on the chest, he would have caused her heart to race any day, but right now, the embarrassment and fear of falling were all she could think about.

This was not the way she had envisioned running into him when she'd gotten the call about her grandmother's passing and had made her plans to return to her hometown of Blue Moon Bay.

She was a successful professional now with an amazing promotion pending and a rent-controlled apartment in downtown L.A. Not the gangly, dorky teen he must remember.

Yet, here she was…falling right back into her old

awkward ways.

"Stay still. I'm going to get you out." He headed back down the stairs, and less than thirty seconds later, he returned wearing his tool belt, which would normally be a sight fit for a fantasy, but he was also holding an ominous-looking tool in his hands.

Her eyes widened. "What's that?"

"A skill saw."

"Are you sure about this?"

"Do you want to live in the stairs?"

"Maybe there's another way to get me out." She'd always been deathly afraid of anything sharp. The sight of needles made her feel faint. This saw thing brought an instant rush of sweat and had her mouth salivating as though she were about to throw up. It was going to require a shit ton of trust on her behalf to let him use that thing so close to her body—and trust was not something that came easily to her.

Especially not with him.

"Do you have another idea?" he asked.

"How about you stand beneath me and I'll let go?"

He looked amused by the idea. "Serve as a crash mat?"

"Or, more heroically, you could catch me."

"Tempting, but no. We'll do it this way." He started the saw, and her palms went slippery against the wood, making it even harder to hold on.

"Fine." She squeezed her eyes shut as she heard the loud buzzing of the death machine draw nearer and he carefully cut the wood around her. Pressure at her upper body eased, but so did the grip of her forearms on the wood. "I'm slipping," she said, opening her eyes. It would be just her luck to survive the saw just to fall anyway.

Wes grabbed her arms. "Ready, on three... One... two..." He pulled, and her body lifted from the hole. Wood shards scraped against her stomach, but at least she was free, with just a few scratches and deep embarrassment to show for her ordeal.

He quickly shifted his weight between two lower stairs as he settled her in a safer spot at the top landing on the third floor. His hands on her body seemed to burn into her flesh, so she brushed them away and quickly moved out of reach.

She did not need him touching her. In her somewhat fragile current state, who knew what she'd do next? Cry on his shoulder, maybe? Those broad, muscular shoulders...

Nope. She was a strong, successful, independent woman. She could handle this latest disaster fine on her own. Now that he'd freed her from the stairs, anyway. "Thanks," she mumbled, avoiding his gaze.

He nodded. "No problem. I saw the rental car parked outside and thought maybe a guest was trying to check in or something, but I hear you're the one who inherited the place."

There was a hint of disbelief in his voice that mirrored her own. She'd been just as stunned when her grandmother's will was read the day before, naming her as beneficiary. "I guess news travels fast in a small town," she said, forcing several deep breaths to calm her anxiety.

"Did your grandmother hate you, by any chance?"

"I'm starting to think so."

"You're not staying here, are you?" Wes asked.

He meant at the B&B, but Sarah had just been wondering the same about Blue Moon Bay. She'd been back in her hometown for two days, seven hours, and—she checked her watch—twenty-nine minutes, and already her stress was escalating. She needed to get back to the city, back to her office. She'd only put in for three days of holiday time, but it looked like she'd need to stay a bit longer.

Her grandmother's funeral two days before had been a beautiful celebration of Dove Lewis's life. The intimate gathering of Dove's two children, their spouses, and her grandchildren to spread the woman's ashes over the bay in front of the B&B was exactly what her grandmother had wanted.

They had followed her wishes precisely.

Everyone had arrived, said a private farewell, and then, after a nice dinner and rare family photo taken on the beach, they had all returned to their lives. Even Sarah's parents had only stayed long enough for the funeral and the reading of the will before flying back to Phoenix that morning.

A will that had Sarah prolonging *her* stay in Blue Moon Bay.

Sticking a FOR SALE sign on the lawn and heading back to L.A. was the smartest thing to do. Collect whatever she could from the run-down establishment and be free of it.

No one would fault her for it. The rest of her family had looked relieved when she'd been the one named as the new owner. The cost of the renovations or the headache of disposing of the property weren't anything anyone wanted to take on.

"I've been sleeping in the living quarters part of the house the last two nights," she said. "It's better maintained than this side." At least she hoped the queen-size bed in the master bedroom wouldn't collapse through the floor during the night.

Grandma, what the hell were you thinking keeping this place so long?

"Okay, well, I'd stick to that side and watch your step," Wes said. "I'm sorry to see the place in such bad shape." He glanced at the open-concept entry as they carefully stepped around the broken landing and descended the stairs, staying close to the wall. "It really used to be something special."

"It sure was." Sarah scanned the original dark-wood frame of the impressive foyer. Twenty-foot ceilings and spiraling staircases on either side of the large check-in desk gave the appearance of elegance, packaged in a cozy, inviting beach house. The old three-story Victorian home, built in the late 1800s, had hosted vacationing celebrities and families alike, and her grandma had treated everyone like extended family. Her warm, caring personality had once turned Dove's Nest into the best place to stay in Blue Moon Bay.

Unfortunately, no one had stayed there in a long time. Her grandmother had closed the doors to the B&B five years before at age ninety, deciding she was too old to run the business alone, and no one else in the family had stepped up.

Sarah had been building her own career in L.A. and had never entertained the idea of moving back home. She loved her grandma, but the B&B had been Dove's dream, not Sarah's. Dove loved entertaining, and every guest became a friend. Sarah was more of an introvert, preferring a few close friends and intimate gatherings. She enjoyed the security and distancing that working online provided. That was her comfort zone. And her grandmother was the first one to encourage everyone to follow their own passions.

So why she'd left *her* to deal with this, Sarah couldn't figure out.

Wes's cell phone rang, and he glanced at the caller ID. "Sorry, just a sec," he said before answering. "Hey, sweetheart, I'm on my way…"

Must be his daughter. Sarah had seen photos of her on Facebook over the years.

"No, you have soccer practice tonight. Yes, you have to go… Because you gave the team your commitment."

Sarah felt like she'd gone back in time as she listened. How many times had her own father said those words to her? Despite her being clumsy and allergic to basically everything in nature, her parents had insisted that she at least give team sports a try. They gave up when the coaches begged them to stop forcing Sarah to participate. Apparently, it only took scoring on your own net a few times to get the coach to put in the plea.

"Okay, see you soon," Wes was saying.

As he disconnected the call, Sarah shook her head. "I still can't believe you're a dad." The Wes in her memories was a smart-ass jock who thought he was too cool for school. A childhood hearing problem that developed after a terrible ear infection seemed to make paying attention in school more challenging for him.

As the school's football star, he used his athletic body and her tutoring skills to help get him to graduation. Going pro had always been his dream, and he'd gotten drafted by the NFL after college, but an injury had taken him out of the game—literally and figuratively—after three seasons. So now he was running his own construction company in their small hometown. Or at least that's the information her Facebook stalking provided.

She'd also learned that Wes's wife, Kelly, his high school sweetheart, had lost her second battle with cancer five years before, and he was raising their daughter alone. Sarah's chest tightened, her sympathy for him overshadowing the cold shoulder she'd been intent on giving him when and if she ever saw him again. "Sorry to hear about…"

Her voice trailed, and he nodded. "Thank you." He paused. "So, what do you plan to do with the place?"

"I can't sell it like this, can I?"

"I wouldn't recommend it. You wouldn't get close to what it could be worth with some structural and cosmetic renovations," Wes said.

Ugh. That might require staying in town.

Her cell phone rang, and seeing her office number, she winced as she sent the call to voicemail. Her boss was going to kill her, but she did not need an audience when she was on a call with Gail. Asking for more time off wasn't going to go over well. "I'm not sure I'm prepared to take that on," she said.

"I did an estimate for Dove a few years ago," Wes said. "I'd be happy to send that to you."

Sarah hesitated. "I don't know, Wes. Dumping money into this place seems kinda futile."

"Look, I'll send you the quote and you can think about it. Don't do anything too quickly. It would be a shame to lose this place," he said.

A shame for him, maybe. But this inn, or rather the ocean in front of it, had been the scene of Sarah's most embarrassing high school moment, just weeks before she'd escaped town. She didn't blame the incident on the inn, but it had lost some of its appeal for her after that night.

And she *did* blame the guy standing in front of her…

He checked his phone. "I have to go, but I'll get the quote to you tonight."

Sarah's nod was noncommittal as she followed him outside. Renovating the place could take weeks or even months. She could possibly oversee the work from L.A., but this was just a headache and a distraction she did not need right now when she was up for a promotion.

"It's good to see you," Wes said, and his gaze held a note of appreciation as it swept over her.

Heat rose to her cheeks, and irritation overwhelmed her. Was it? Was it really?

Based on his casual, awkward-less demeanor, he obviously didn't remember the past like she did. The way his rejection had broken her young teenage heart.

She squared her shoulders. She'd moved on. They were adults now. No need to rehash the past.

And besides, she'd basically sabotaged her plan of the kind of reunion that would have him regretting his actions years ago by being found in a staircase. "Sure. You too," she mumbled.

He waved as he climbed into his truck, and Sarah tested the strength of the deck railing before leaning against it. Several planks of the worn, weather-beaten wood had needed to be replaced years ago. In fact, the entire wraparound deck should have had a full teardown and rebuild. She had spent almost three days at the B&B, and everywhere she looked, something needed fixing or replacing. She didn't need a contractor to explain to her the extent of the repairs needed to rehab the entire inn, and she wouldn't even think about how much it might cost.

Selling it in its current state and leaving its fate to the new owner was the logical thing to do.

The sound of waves lapping against the shore and the familiar salty ocean-scented air did nothing to settle the uneasiness in her chest as the truck's taillights disappeared from sight.

"Why me, Grandma?"

A question she'd never have answered.

CHAPTER TWO

Sarah Lewis had inherited the inn.

Wes wouldn't have bet his truck on that one. The friend he remembered from high school was book-smart bordering on genius, but she wasn't exactly comfortable in social situations. The year they'd graduated, she'd won the award for Most Klutzy and, while those old awards seemed rather cruel in hindsight, it appeared she might still be in the running for it at their ten-year reunion.

Stuck in a staircase. He chuckled.

He'd always found her awkwardness endearing. And it had helped him not feel so intimidated by her when he was forced to endure the embarrassment of needing her tutoring to graduate.

Her grandmother must have had her reasons for choosing the one grandchild least capable of running an inn, but Wes wasn't so sure the old lady had chosen correctly if she hadn't wanted the place torn down.

Sarah had looked ready to drive the bulldozer herself.

Watching the inn deteriorate and then sit abandoned when Dove moved into a retirement facility had been heartbreaking. The B&B was located on the most easterly coast of Blue Moon Bay. Breathtaking views of the ocean at sunrise and sunset made it the perfect tourist destination for travelers looking for some R&R. The mild surf in that area of the beach was ideal for swimming and sunbathing, and a small alcove made it feel private and remote. There was even a shallow area for young kids to play without their parents needing to worry about a strong current or undertow.

Jagged cliffs in the distance gave a magnificent backdrop over the sandy shores, and the acres of green grass and lush vegetation surrounding the property required a lot less maintenance than the building itself. With the right renovations, Sarah could easily flip the place for a better price and the inn could live on.

If he had the money to buy it himself, he'd readily take it off her hands. Five years ago, when Dove had closed the inn, he'd been about to make an offer. Then Kelly had gotten sick, and things had changed so fast.

Before his wife's fight with cancer, their lives had finally been headed in the right direction—after a few slight detours, including a failed pro football career. At least he'd made enough from his three seasons playing for the Rams to start his own construction business. Plan B wasn't the dream, but buying his first property—a run-down vacation rental to fix up and flip—had been surprisingly easier than he'd thought, and it'd paid off.

That first successful venture had renewed his confidence in himself after the crushing setback. The success of the company also made it possible for Kelly to stay at home to raise Marissa, and they'd been talking about adding to their happy little family.

Then Kelly got sick.

Between the medical bills and paying for someone to look after the house and Marissa, the expenses increased while his ability to earn decreased as he spent more and more time with Kelly at the hospital. He'd missed opportunities, and his company's reputation had taken a hit. He'd struggled the last five years trying to pay off those bills and get back the clients he lost when he was unavailable. Marissa was now nine, and being both mom and dad was challenging. He had her future to think about as well, so he had to find a way to turn things around and soon.

Pulling into his driveway, he climbed out of his truck and headed inside through the kitchen door. He stepped over boxes and sucked in his body as he wiggled past the small desk in the corner of the already cramped kitchen. His assistant/aunt Carmen was on the phone, and she glanced up in time to catch her coffee cup from spilling as his hip hit the desk.

"Sorry," he whispered.

This definitely was not ideal working conditions. He desperately missed having an office. Moving them into his kitchen was supposed to have been temporary when he'd lost the lease on his office space, but it was going on three years now, and there were no concrete plans to move out of his home anytime soon.

"I'll schedule you in for a quote next week," Carmen said, rummaging through the papers on her messy desk to find a pen.

Next week? What was wrong with this week? Tomorrow, even. He grabbed a piece of paper on her desk and wrote: *Why next week?*

Had a new job miraculously popped up that would keep him booked until then?

She took the pen and wrote back: *The illusion of being busy.*

More like a delusion, if anyone in town believed that.

If he was busy, he wouldn't be coaching every Little League team in town and teaching surfing lessons during the summer months to camp kids. There were tons of small jobs around town—deck repairs, painting, roofing...but he couldn't bring himself to charge his friends and neighbors enough to be profitable after cost of supplies and paying his crew.

He was great at construction work. Not so great at the business side of things. Everyone in town still treated him like the local football star he used to be, and maybe he wanted to preserve that image somehow. Still feel that rush of being the guy everyone could depend on...if in a different way.

"Great. Looks like he has an opening on Tuesday at nine a.m.," Carmen said. She disconnected the call and turned to him. "How'd it go at Mrs. Miller's?" She stood to write next Tuesday's job on the whiteboard behind the desk.

She'd sent him to pick up a check from the eighty-year-old widow for the work he'd done on her fence the week before. "Let's just say her payment was delicious." He'd eaten six of the chocolate zucchini muffins already that day.

Carmen wagged the dry-erase marker at him. "Stop letting them pay you with baked goods. Baked goods, homemade knit scarfs, signed author copies of their self-pubbed books, these things don't pay bills."

"I know, I know," he said, running a hand through his hair and over his face. He reached for the coffeepot and poured the lukewarm liquid into his cup that was still sitting on the counter since that morning.

All the breakfast dishes were still sitting there, too. Marissa was supposed to have filled the dishwasher. He sighed. She didn't do it to disobey him; she was just absentminded. No doubt she'd forgotten about her chore the moment he left the house.

Carmen took his mug from him and put it in the microwave. She struggled with the door that was refusing to shut lately and hit the Reheat button.

"Mrs. Miller was good for gossip, though," he said, knowing she'd appreciate that, at least. Small towns thrived on their gossip for excitement, and Blue Moon Bay was no exception.

Sure enough, his aunt raised an eyebrow. "Oh yeah?"

"Turns out, Sarah Lewis inherited Dove's Nest."

Carmen looked confused. "Good heavens, what was Dove thinking? What on earth could that girl do with it?"

"Says she's thinking of selling it in its current state."

"That's a horrible idea. Whoever buys it will just tear it down." His aunt retrieved the cup and handed it to him.

"That's what I said." He took a sip of the bitter liquid and grimaced.

Carmen nodded slowly. "Do you think you can talk her into renovating?"

Obviously, she was thinking about the possibility of a

decent project and payday for his company, as well as preserving the inn that used to mean a lot to the community and Blue Moon Bay's tourism.

"I'm going to try," he said, kissing her forehead. Though he wasn't sure how successful he'd be. Sarah hadn't exactly been thrilled to see him. She'd actually seemed a little standoffish, and the way she'd practically batted his hands away from her body once she was on safe ground had warned him not to go in for a "long time, no see" hug from his former tutor and friend.

But maybe it was the circumstances that had her on edge.

"Where's Marissa?"

Carmen raised an eyebrow above her oversize glasses—the same pair she'd worn since Wes was a kid, only now they were suddenly stylish again. "Where do you think?"

Her bedroom. Sitting in front of her computer screen. "Has she been outside at all today?"

"Only when she thought the mail carrier was delivering her new chemistry kit."

Wes left the kitchen and headed down the hall to his daughter's bedroom. On the door was her Do Not Enter—Science Experiments in Progress sign.

He knocked anyway. "Marissa."

"Come in!"

He entered the messy room and forced a calming breath. The dishwasher, the bedroom…she was ignoring every task on her summer daily chore list.

"Hey, Dad," she said quickly before turning her

attention back to the computer screen where she was typing a bunch of code he would never know how to read.

He opened the closed window blinds, and sunlight cast across the screen. She squinted and held up a hand as though he had blinded her. "Ah, my eyeballs!"

"It's called sunlight, and let me introduce you to fresh air," he said, opening the window. A faint smell lingered, and he'd bet there was food or a wet swimsuit left in a backpack somewhere.

She shot him a look only a nine-year-old going on forty could deliver. "The UV rating today is an eight. Do you know how dangerous that is?"

"So is vitamin D deficiency. Wear sunscreen and a hat," he said, tossing her a baseball cap that said STEM on it. "Come on, you have to get ready for soccer."

"Can I just finish this code?" She folded her hands in a pleading motion, and he almost caved. Being a single dad, he was always struggling to find that balance between being a parent and allowing her independence. The first year after Kelly died had been the hardest. He found himself giving in to everything and anything Marissa wanted to compensate for her tragic loss, but he quickly realized that setting boundaries was in the little girl's best interests. Or at least that was what all the parenting books Carmen kept giving him said.

"No."

"Dad! It's important."

"So is movement and fun and seeing friends."

"I hate soccer," she said with a pout, but she reached

under a pile of clothing—dirty or clean or a mix of both, he wasn't sure—and retrieved her soccer cleats.

"It's more fun when you actually try."

Connecting with her had never been this difficult before. It didn't seem that long ago when they had picnics in the backyard with her dolls or when pushing her on the swing was met with squeals of delight as she swung higher. Now she was into science and math and all this computer stuff he just did not get. He'd wrongfully assumed he'd have at least a few more easy years before Marissa's teenage hormones made things challenging. After all, what did he know about teenage girls? If every discussion now was a challenge or a negotiation, what would it be like when he had an actual teenager to deal with?

She sulked as she tied the laces of her cleats and he flicked through the pile of clothes for her soccer jersey. Number 7. His old number when he'd played professionally. Now he wore whatever number the beer leagues gave out.

"Hey, um...did you give that camp any more thought?" she asked, trying to sound casual, but he heard the eagerness in her voice.

Marissa had been asking about the STEM summer camp since first learning about the science and technology program during spring break, when the school had hosted a free week-long session.

But that had been different. This two-week sleepaway camp cost $1,500 and was three hours away: $1,000 more and not local like the Girl Guides camp she would be attending in Blue Moon Bay next month.

He hesitated, looking at her hopeful face. "Still thinking about it." Wes wasn't at all comfortable with letting his nine-year-old go that far away from home that summer but right now he did not have the heart to break hers with the truth.

CHAPTER THREE

Googling "wood rot" and seeing the photos of termites was all it took to have Sarah reconsidering her free accommodations at Dove's Nest. The wood tunnels around the baseboards in the downstairs main bathroom looked like the perfect home for these insects, and they weren't exactly the guests she wanted to share a B&B with. Sitting on the deck, she was about to call the local five-star hotel's reservations desk when a car turned into the circular driveway.

She smiled for the first time that day, seeing her best friends, Jessica and Whitney, climbing out of Whitney's banana-yellow Miata convertible. Whitney had bought the car a month ago, and it was perfect for the spirited, upbeat woman. No one would dare mention that it lacked a back seat for all the kids Whitney's fiancé, Trent, insisted they wanted.

Sarah put her phone back in her pocket and met them at the top of the deck stairs. "I thought I wouldn't see you guys until tomorrow," she said, hugging them both at the same time. They had wanted to give her time with her family while they were still in town for her grandmother's funeral, but seeing them now brought a rush of tears. Growing up, Jessica and Whitney had been more than friends; they were her sisters by heart. It was tough the last few days being in town and not seeing them, but they were here now, and she wasn't sure if the tears were joy at seeing them or at finally being able to let go and grieve her grandmother. Maybe both.

"We couldn't wait any longer," Whitney said.

"And when we got your text that you'd inherited Dove's Nest, we wanted to make sure you didn't walk straight into the ocean," Jessica said.

She didn't admit that for a heartbeat or two, she had contemplated doing just that. "It's tempting," she said. "What's with the bowling shirt?" Jessica's shirt was white with bold red sleeves and a single red stripe down the front, with an embroidered logo on the left-hand side that read BAY'S SINGLES.

"She joined a coed league," Whitney said, the eye roll implied in her tone. "As if dart club and competitive ax throwing weren't extracurricular activity enough."

Jessica shot her a look. "It was supposed to be a singles team, but apparently, 'single' just meant 'not married.' So now I'm stuck carrying an awful team with two actively *not single* couples and Bert Elliott."

"The hardware store guy?" Bert had worked the paint counter for years. "Isn't he married?"

"Recently separated. Again, not exactly single," Jessica said as Sarah led the way to the outdoor seating on the side of the house. She wasn't sure if the deck could hold all three of them without another hole-in-the-floor fiasco. The sun was getting low in the sky and the furniture on the patio was positioned around a stone fire pit. Despite needing a fresh coat of paint, the Adirondack chairs were in surprisingly good shape. Given what she had seen so far of the rest of the furniture in the B&B, the patio seemed the best option for a visit with her besties.

"You'd date a sixty-two-year-old man if he was?" Whitney asked Jessica, hanging her purse over the back of a chair and removing her gray suit jacket.

"Hey, Bert is a sweetheart, and he always makes sure I have a cold bottled water at each game. That's about the most attention I've had from a man in a long time."

"That's just desperation talking." Whitney rolled the sleeves of her silk blouse and undid the top button. Her golden, sun-kissed skin was enviable.

"Hey, if I date Bert, I could get Sarah a discount on paint," Jessica said.

Sarah laughed. "Who said I was doing any painting? A sledgehammer might be useful, though."

The familiar banter helped remind her of how much she'd really missed them. They kept in touch with weekly FaceTime chats, but when they were together like this, she realized how that barely seemed enough. They had all gone to school together since kindergarten, but they really became friends in the fifth grade when Jessica had started a "single child club." The three of them had bonded over their joint disappointment that their parents hadn't given them the courtesy of a sibling.

Jessica and Whitney still lived in Blue Moon Bay and saw each other frequently. Sarah struggled with feeling like the third wheel or the one left out, but she had her busy job in the city as a consolation. Her friends understood her lack of availability.

"Wineglasses?" Jessica asked, taking a bottle of red from her oversize purse, followed by a box of cream-filled pastries from her bakery, Delicious Delicacies.

Sarah's mouth watered, and she wasn't sure which she craved more—the alcohol or the carbs. "I'll see what we have. Save me something covered in chocolate," she said, hurrying inside. She grabbed three of the largest glasses she could find, washed them quickly, and carried them outside.

Whitney had the bottle open already. "So, how bad is it?" she asked as she poured.

Should she mention her near-death experience? Probably best to keep the embarrassing story to herself. Her friends already had plenty of adventure stories with her as the leading role of klutz. She had spent years trying to rewrite that narrative, plus they would worry about her. Best to keep that story for another time.

"Bad," she said simply. "And Wes Sharrun had the nerve to try to guilt me into renovating." "Guilt" may be a strong word. He'd simply suggested she think about it. But she did feel guilty, and it was partly his fault.

Her friends exchanged looks.

"What?" she asked, biting into a chocolate pastry. The combination of cocoa and sugar made her eyes close as she savored the burst of flavor dancing on her tongue.

"Wes was here?" Whitney asked.

"A few hours ago."

The two women stared at her as though waiting for her to elaborate.

"Well, how was seeing him again?" Jessica asked, tying her dark, wavy hair back from her face as the early-evening breeze off the ocean picked up.

Sarah waved a hand. "I see him all the time on Facebook. It was no different."

Except that it was totally different. Her former crush was no longer a cute athlete who she'd tutored for two years and never had a chance with, given he and Kelly were the school's famous couple. Now he was a hot-as-hell business owner, widower, and single dad. One who had encouraged her to invest a ton of her savings into restoring an old family property she wanted nothing to do with.

"That's a lie," Whitney said, sipping her wine.

"That was a schoolgirl crush I had on him years ago. And I've totally forgiven him for the incident that we're never to discuss." Maybe telling her friends what had happened that night years ago or her revenge fantasies since then was a bad idea.

"Okay, we'll pretend to buy that," Whitney said, kicking her feet free of her sandals and folding her long legs under her on the chair. At five foot nine and 120 pounds soaking wet, her blond bombshell of a best friend had missed her calling as a fashion model. Instead, she was head of marketing and tourism at the mayor's office in town.

"So, what do you plan to do?" Jessica asked.

"I don't know," she said honestly.

"So many hotel chains have been after this amazing location for years; you could reach out to one of them," Whitney said.

"Grandma always said no to their offers."

"She loved this place," Whitney said softly. "Even if

keeping it wasn't in her best interest."

Sarah heard her friend's unvoiced warning. Would she be repeating her grandmother's mistake if she kept it and renovated in the hope of saving it?

"How was the funeral?" Jessica asked, changing the subject as she reached out to squeeze Sarah's hand.

The comforting gesture was something she hadn't realized she'd needed. The last few days had been busy with the funeral and will, and she really hadn't had time to mourn the loss. "Nice. Private. The way Grandma would have wanted it."

Her grandmother spent her life opening her door to strangers, but her heart had been reserved for family. She always knew everything about everyone within minutes of meeting them. People loved to open up to Dove, but the older woman had always kept her own secrets close to her chest.

"Everyone's gone already?" Jessica asked.

Sarah nodded. "We did manage to get a family photo before they left, though." Unlocking her cell phone screen with her thumbprint, she flicked to the photo and handed the phone to Jessica.

"Aww…this is a nice one," she said, tilting the phone so Whitney could see. She squinted, peering closer. "Who's the guy in the background?"

Whitney dragged her finger and thumb across the screen to enlarge the view of the beach. "Isn't that the old guy who lives down near south pier? He's always out there on the beach with his metal detector. I've never seen him around here before, though."

"He doesn't have a metal detector here," Sarah said, looking at the photo. She hadn't even noticed him on that side of the beach that day.

"Friend of your grandma's, maybe?" Jessica suggested.

Sarah shrugged, taking the phone back. "Maybe. He didn't talk to us." Most likely just a stranger strolling the beach that morning. She could crop him out if she decided to frame the picture.

"Did your grandmother leave a note or anything, explaining this?" Whitney asked, gesturing around them.

Sarah nodded, reaching into her pocket for the ambiguous five-word sticky note she'd been trying to figure out all day and handed it to Whitney.

"A Post-it? That's it?" she asked.

"Grandma kept things brief," Sarah said, gulping her wine.

"You'll know what to do," Jessica read over Whitney's shoulder. They looked at her. "Do you?"

"Nope. Other than selling it, what else can I do?" She checked her phone. She'd left three messages for her boss, who was now ignoring her calls, and Sarah recognized the power move that said she was on thin ice. "I really need to get back to L.A."

"Have you heard about your promotion yet?" Whitney asked.

"Not yet. Being here isn't exactly helping." She bit her lip. Her boss was a workaholic. She never took time off and didn't love the fact that she was expected to give her staff holiday time. This time off was the first "vacation" Sarah had taken in four years. She loved her job at Digital Strategies, where she worked developing new apps for long-distance communication and teleconferencing. And with the promotion, she'd be working directly under the VP of development, a position she'd been busting her butt for, hoping it would give her more freedom and flexibility to work on projects she was passionate about.

"Staying in town for a while wouldn't be so bad. We love having you here." Jessica nodded. "And you can help us plan Whitney's *wedding*."

As one of the bridesmaids, Sarah would be heavily involved in her friend's big day...if Whitney ever committed to a date. A year since she'd gotten engaged, Whitney turned a shade paler whenever anyone asked when the big day would be.

Like now.

"Do we have a date yet?" she asked.

Whitney squirmed on the chair. "We're getting closer to nailing down a day..." She sipped her wine.

"So...fall?" Jessica asked.

"Maybe fall...maybe next spring," Whitney said, unfolding her legs and sitting forward on her chair. "Right now, we're dealing with Sarah's dilemma."

Sarah suspected Whitney had good reason for putting them off, and she respected her friend's privacy, so she shot Jessica a look that said, *Let it go for now*.

Her cell chimed with a new notification, and she dove for it.

But she frowned, seeing the Facebook message. "It's a Facebook message from Wes."

I've attached the quote for renovations based on the inspection we did months ago. Let me know what you think.

"It's a quote for renovations," she told her friends.

"How much?" Whitney asked.

Sarah lowered the phone and shook her head in disbelief. "You know, that guy has a lot of nerve just assuming I'll do what he wants. I told him I didn't know what I planned to do yet."

"How much?" Whitney repeated, sending her a look that suggested her past grudge was showing.

Sarah sighed as she skipped the list of things needing repairs and found the price at the bottom. She squinted to look at the dollar amount. "Could that be right?" She'd estimated at least double what he was quoting. She quickly responded, asking Wes if there was a mistake.

Seconds later came his reply: *Incentive pricing to give the inn a second chance.*

She sighed.

"What did he say?" Jessica asked.

Sarah showed her friends the message.

"Well, the price to fix this place up couldn't possibly be better, and you could work from here, right?" Jessica said.

Her office *did* do most of their work remotely with just weekly meetings or pitch presentations in the office... Sarah stared at the old house. Could she do it? Obviously her friends wanted her to, but putting her own life on hold didn't exactly appeal to her. But then neither did seeing a historic building and her grandmother's legacy disappear.

"I think I need more wine for this decision," Sarah said, picking up the bottle. Three drops trickled out.

"Is there any in the cellar?" Whitney asked.

Sarah's eyes widened. "I'd totally forgotten about the cellar. Let's go check." They stood and followed her inside. "I feel like I should ask you to sign waivers before entering," she said, stepping over a loose floorboard in the entryway. "Be careful on the stairs." She hit the light on the wall above the curving, concrete stairwell heading down to the cellar. The dim lighting and low ceiling made her shiver.

"This is creepy at night," Jessica said, echoing her thoughts.

"It's kinda *Phantom of the Opera*-ish," Whitney said. "You could totally use this staircase in pics for the sale brochure."

They reached the big wooden crescent-shaped door with its iron ring handle. When they were kids, the cellar used to make the best hiding place. She hadn't been down there in years, though, and it was no doubt just a castle for spiders and mice by now. She shivered at the thought as she pulled, but the door wouldn't budge. "It's stuck."

"Grab the ring," Jessica told Whitney.

"On three…"

They pulled, and this time the door flew open.

Sarah entered, feeling along the wall until her hand hit the switch. As the space illuminated, her breath caught. Wall-to-wall, ceiling-to-floor wine racks were full of dusty bottles.

"Holy shit," Whitney said, entering. She approached a rack and picked up a bottle, then blew the dust away. "This is a 1987 merlot." She picked up another one. "This one is from '79."

"These are all vintage, too," Jessica said from the other side of the rack. "There has to be thousands of dollars' worth of wine down here."

"Everything is organized by type...and date." Unexplainable excitement rose in Sarah's chest as she continued scanning the rows of liquid gold.

Jessica rejoined them, a bottle of wine in each hand. "I think this is a sign."

Sarah shook her head. "You think everything is a sign."

"This cellar would be an amazing draw for a potential buyer, if they could get past the deteriorating exterior," Whitney said, then held up her hands in defense of Sarah's look. "Just sayin'."

Sarah released a deep breath as she stood in the middle of the cellar. This cellar was a treasure, and the price to renovate was reasonable. She'd make the money back after the sale. And she didn't really need to be on-site to do her job. She could drive into the city whenever necessary...

Whitney and Jessica continued to stare at her expectantly.

Sarah sighed. "Fine, Grandma—you win. Here goes nothing," she said, taking her cell phone from her pocket. Opening the message from Wes, she typed quickly before she could change her mind: *When can you start?*

CHAPTER FOUR

There were worse ways to wake up in the morning.

Maybe she was still dreaming. Sarah blinked several times, but the sight of Wes's six-pack abs was real outside the bedroom window.

Those certainly hadn't been there in high school.

He'd always been athletically built, but more lean and cut from a young metabolism and all the cardio playing football. This new muscular body was the product of his hard, laborious days. A tanned chest and the hint of oblique muscles appearing at the top of his jeans were almost enough for her to forgive the unmerciful hammering he was doing at... She rolled to look at the clock on the bedside table.

Ten fifteen?

Shit.

She sat up quickly. Too quickly. Her head throbbed, the pounding inside her brain keeping time with the pounding against the roof. Too much wine the night before.

The muffled sound of her cell phone ringing coming from somewhere among the bedsheets and pillows, her boss's ringtone, had her moving all her electronics off the bed to try to locate the phone. She'd been awake until two a.m. working on the proposal for SmartTech Kids. Their new potential client needed an app aimed at kids and teens, and if Sarah had a shot at the promotion, she needed to push herself beyond her comfort zone of telecommunications and show her boss she could handle different kinds of accounts.

Finding the cell phone, she took a deep breath and tried to sound as wide awake as possible as she answered. "Gail! Hi!"

"Is there no cell service out there?"

Her boss's chilly tone made her shiver. "So sorry, Gail. Yesterday was…eventful." She'd spare her the details; Gail wasn't one for water cooler chitchat. Her employees' personal lives were of zero interest. Sarah knew absolutely nothing about her boss besides her hard-nosed business persona. She'd never met a spouse at any of the corporate events the company held, there were no family photos in her boss's office, and her expensive suits were always pet-fur-free, so Sarah could only assume the company was Gail's life. Unless there was a goldfish or something…

"I received your email last night with the revisions to the first proposal…"

Sarah held her breath. These revisions were the fourth round that her boss had requested. She was running out of ideas for ways to design the kid app the company was looking for. Not having kids, it was difficult for her to determine what they'd even use an app for in the first place. So far, she'd focused on practicality—a messaging system to connect with friends, a safety GPS locating system…but the company wanted the app to appeal to kids, not necessarily to their parents.

"It's still not wowing me," she said.

Not much wowed Gail. Almost impossible to impress, but there was such a sense of accomplishment and pride to be had whenever Sarah *was* able to garner any kind of praise from the woman. "I'm still coming up with ideas."

"You're thinking with your adult head. You need to think like a kid. What did you wish you had an app for when you were ten years old?"

To beam her out of Blue Moon Bay. Same thing she'd like an app for right now.

She repressed a sigh. Staying upbeat was the only acceptable attitude with Gail's critiques. "You're right. Absolutely. I'll work on it again today."

"Here at the office? I'll meet you there for a brainstorming session."

Sarah cringed. The last brainstorming session had been sixteen hours long, and they hadn't even ordered in food. Her desperation for sustenance had somehow miraculously led to an idea Gail was happy enough with. Obviously her creativity thrived on survival mode. "I've actually hit a snag. Nothing too serious," she said quickly. "Just something I need to deal with for my grandmother's estate…I'll need another day here."

Silence.

Gail always gave employees time to revise their final answer. "I mean, not a full day, of course." It was already after ten. "I'm sure I can wrap this up and be back in L.A. in a few hours."

"I'll expect you at the office around four."

She better hope not to hit traffic on the way back

into the city. "Thank you so much for understanding, Gail. And I'll work on the—"

Silence. Gail had hung up.

Tossing the bedsheets aside, Sarah ran to shut the blinds (after another peek at Wes's body). She could ogle *him*, but there was no way he was seeing *her* first thing in the morning.

Hurrying into the bathroom, she undressed, turned on the shower, and stepped into the spray. She quickly lathered her hair and ran the soap over her body.

Think like a kid…

What would a kid want to do with an app? Play games? There were enough of those available already. The design she had so far could already post photos and videos to the internet. What else did kids do with technology?

She was coming up blank, and she needed something new to offer, otherwise she'd be at the office with Gail that evening until sunrise tomorrow morning.

Come on, Sarah! Think!

Freezing-cold water hit her back, and her breath caught in her chest. She scurried away from the stream, grabbing the curtain to use as a barrier from the spray. She slipped on the wet, soapy bathtub floor and clutched the fabric frantically, causing the rod to come loose from the wall.

What the hell?

She cranked the tap higher and tentatively reached a hand forward.

Still cold.

Shaving her legs would have to wait, even though it really couldn't, but she needed to wash the suds out of her hair at least. She hung the suction-cup rod back in place; then, taking a deep breath and summoning all the courage she could muster, she ducked her head under the freezing water.

Her breath came in a succession of short gasps as the drops cascaded down her back. Dancing from one foot to the other, she struggled to stay beneath the stream, but fear of hypothermia had her shutting off the taps within seconds. Goose bumps, the size of golf balls, appeared on her skin, despite the sweltering heat in the un-air-conditioned bathroom.

Shivering, she wrapped her towel around herself and slid her feet into a pair of slippers.

Her hair, soapy and flat to her head, the strands dripping down her back, she rushed downstairs and out onto the front deck. Making her way to the side of the house, she stopped when Wes's ladder came into view, propped against the side.

"Wes!" Damn, this was embarrassing. It might have been better to let him catch her in her pajamas, but she needed to finish her shower and hit the road as soon as possible. "Wes!" she called louder over the hammering.

He stopped and bent his head lower beneath the awning to see her. "Good morning."

"Nope. Not even close," she muttered. She gripped the towel tighter at the top of her breasts with one hand and tried to yank it lower with the other, suddenly aware of how small it was. A warm ocean breeze blew across her legs, reminding her of how long it had been since she'd shaved them.

Damn. Could he see how hairy they were from that distance?

His gaze drinking her in made her wish she'd braved the cold water a little longer. The hot sun beating down on her wasn't to blame for the heat rushing through her core. It wasn't lust or desire in Wes's eyes scanning her, but a hint of amusement.

No doubt he was thinking that she hadn't changed a bit since high school. So much for trying to rewrite the local perception.

"There's no hot water," she said.

"Oh shit, sorry. I thought you'd be done by now. The plumber arrived and needed to shut the hot water off to do some repairs. As promised in the quote, we're replacing the hot water tank with a higher efficiency unit."

She'd appreciate that once she was dressed and dried off and all the soap was out of her hair, perhaps. "Can he turn it back on just for a few minutes?" She hadn't exactly been prepared for him to start the renovations that day, but she vaguely remembered agreeing to it after the second bottle of wine the evening before.

She'd been afraid she'd back out if she slept on the idea.

"Sorry, Sarah, no can do. He's on the clock, and we need to come in on budget." Wes grinned as he descended the ladder.

Nope. Go back up there.

She shielded herself as best she could as he walked toward her, then tugged at the top of the towel while trying to drag it lower on her thighs, but the fabric would only go one way or the other.

Why are these towels so small?

His amusement seemed to grow as he witnessed her struggle, his blue eyes even more intoxicating when his smile reached them. She'd always been a sucker for that smile. How many times had she falsely assumed that his smile meant something more? Hoped that maybe their friendship could develop into something deeper? She'd been so drawn to him years ago that she hadn't even given a second glance to any other guy at school. But Wes had only ever been interested in her ability to help math make sense.

"The ocean's warm. You could go for a dip," he said casually.

She cocked her head to the side. "In my towel?"

"Or naked," he said, putting his hammer in his tool belt. "It's not like you haven't done it before."

Her mouth dropped; then she snapped it closed. "We were silly teenagers, and we were never supposed to speak of it again." That night almost fifteen years ago had been filtered through her memory so many times over the years, she'd almost convinced herself it had never happened.

Unfortunately, the sting of humiliation lingered, assuring her that moment was real.

It was his last tutoring session before final exams. They'd been studying on a picnic bench on the beach in front of the inn, almost unaware that the sun had set until they couldn't see the math book anymore. Wes had been teasing her about the fact that she'd insisted they study on a Friday night. Of course he was meeting friends after their session…while her big plans had consisted of studying for her chemistry final.

Somewhere along the way, he'd dared her to run into the ocean. Naked.

"I got two math problems in a row right…a third and you have to go skinny dipping," he'd said.

"I'm not following your logic. Why would I have to do that?" she'd asked, her teenage hormones aflutter. Wes Sharrun wanted to see her naked?

Naked? Or humiliated? Or just whether or not she was brave enough to do it?

He'd shrugged. "A reward?"

He was still teasing her. And testing her. But just once, she wanted to prove that she wasn't simply the bookworm, the clumsy nerd they all thought she was.

So she'd accepted the challenge. "Fine. But this is a tough one," she said, sliding the practice problem his way.

Her heart thundered as he lowered his head over the paper. Did she want him to get it right or not?

He'd grinned as he'd slid the paper back toward her seconds later. "I guess this means you have to take your clothes off."

Dang. He'd gotten it right.

Okay, she wouldn't back down from the challenge. But not with him watching. "Turn around."

His look of surprise revealed he'd never expected her to actually go through with it. But she refused to walk away from a bet or a dare or any kind of challenge. Everyone thought she was a shy, quiet nerd, but she had a fun side, too.

As Wes turned away from her, she hid behind a garbage can on the beach and removed her shorts and tank top, then her bra and underwear. A deep breath for courage and she was running into the waves before he could turn around.

His expression when he'd seen her in the ocean revealed she'd definitely impressed him. She'd impressed herself, actually. And when he'd climbed out of his swim trunks and joined her in the moonlight waves, she'd almost taken the leap, almost asked him on a date...a real one, one without their math books. And she'd been almost certain that he would have said yes. That night in the water, there had definitely been a spark between them.

Then Kelly and several of his friends had appeared in their car on the beach and honked their horn at him, and after just a second of contemplation, he'd abandoned her for them. She'd been left bobbing naked in the ocean, the sound of her classmates' laughter echoing in her ears.

"Sarah?" He waved a hand in front of her face.

"Sorry, what?"

"I said, you could drive to my place to finish showering if you want." He pulled his keys out of his pocket, but she shook her head.

"That's okay. I'll figure something out," she mumbled.

The sound of a lawn mower in the back had her peeking around the side of the house. An older man, wearing a set of noise-canceling headphones, was cutting the grass along the fence. "Who's that?"

Wes shrugged. "Not one of my guys. He arrived about fifteen minutes ago and said he used to do the landscaping for Dove."

Sarah bit her lip. "I hope she didn't pay him much." She'd hate to have to let him go, though she could barely afford these renovations. But how did she fire a senior citizen? From that distance, the guy looked to be about a hundred years old. His slow pace made her hope he didn't charge by the hour. "Could you try to find out who he is?"

"Sure thing."

"Great...thanks. Um, I'll be leaving in a few hours. I'll just give you the keys to the place, and you have my cell number..."

Wes frowned. "You mean you're going back to the city?"

"Yes."

"I thought you were sticking around while the renos were being done."

"Why would I do that?" The edge to her voice had him retreating slightly. As though he couldn't possibly understand why she'd want to leave and get back to her life. Why being back in a hometown that never fully understood her could be causing her anxiety. Or how seeing him and remembering the past might have her itching to once again distract herself with long hours at work. "I'm needed back at the office."

"Yeah, no, I get it," he said. "So I assume you've added the inn to your homeowner insurance already?"

She frowned. "I rent."

"You have no coverage on the place? I know Dove let it expire."

Damn it! "Don't you have insurance and workers' comp?" She eyed the men on the roof.

"I do. But that covers my ass. What if someone stumbles in here when we're not around and gets hurt?"

Sarah sighed. This place was already a headache. "I'll figure it out." She was not staying here another day. There had to be a way around this. Preferably a quick way.

She turned to go back inside. Now more desperate than ever to get the shampoo out of her hair and figure this out.

"Oh, and Sarah?"

She stopped and turned back. "What?"

"That towel is really see-through."

. . .

Wes hadn't expected that sight this morning.

Sarah Lewis in a towel, wet hair hanging down her shoulders, long legs coming out of the towel from one end and an amazing view of her cleavage above the other had nearly made him fall off the ladder. Her body was insane. She'd always been an attractive girl in her understated way, but she'd definitely grown into the long, lanky build and filled out in all the right places. The sexy collarbone and the soft-looking skin at her chest had his mouth going dry, and the hourglass figure hugged by the barely there towel had him struggling not to envision the body beneath.

He shook his head as he climbed back up the ladder. What the hell was wrong with him? It was Sarah. Sarah didn't make his body react this way. She'd been his smart friend, his tutor, the quiet, introverted girl who watched the fun from the sidelines.

So why was he now dealing with a semi-hard-on while he worked in the sweltering mid-morning heat? The instant he'd seen her standing there soaking wet, he'd been transported back to that night in the ocean.

His dare was one he'd thought she'd never take him up on, but she'd surprised the hell out of him. Discovering that she had a wilder, less reserved side had him wondering what else he was missing when he looked at her. What other qualities was she hiding from the rest of the world? He'd found himself intrigued by her that night in a way he hadn't expected.

Then, when he'd joined her in the dark ocean waves, illuminated by the moon, there had been a moment. Just a quick one…

He shook his head. That was in the past. Nothing had happened between them then, and nothing would now. He'd never really thought of her that way, and it had to be just the sexy body she'd grown overnight that had him reacting like he was.

But damn, what a body.

It had been a long time since he'd been with a woman. Since Kelly. He wasn't interested in dating or one-night stands. He had too much responsibility and too much on the line to mess around. It had been five years, but he wasn't sure there was a time limit on grief. Just because a significant amount of time had passed and it was okay to move on, Wes couldn't jump into a new relationship if he wasn't ready. If his heart wasn't in it. It wouldn't be fair to himself or to the woman or to Marissa.

His daughter was his priority, and he wasn't ruling out the possibility of another relationship in his future, another shot at happiness, but to take a chance, to take that leap, it needed to be worth it.

Unfortunately, he couldn't deny that something had stirred in him just now seeing Sarah. He hadn't been tempted by someone in a long time, and he'd certainly been tempted looking at her.

He hammered several tiles into place, desperate to shake the image of her, to shake the uneasiness in the pit of his stomach, but both lingered.

And that worried the hell out of him. Good thing she planned to leave right away.

Hearing her stressed-out voice inside her room, he stopped hammering. She must be on a call.

"It's going to cost how much?"

Obviously checking out the insurance.

"No, that's fine. I really don't have a choice. Please send me the paperwork as soon as possible," she said.

He heard the regret in her voice, and a slight pang of guilt hit him. He'd basically convinced her to do the renovations and had purposely started them before she could have a change of heart. He hadn't meant to cause her more headache, but he really didn't want to see Dove's Nest torn down and replaced by some big hotel chain resort.

"It's going to take how long?" he heard her say. "Can't I sign the documents electronically or something?" A long pause. "So I'm basically stuck here guarding the place until the paperwork goes through?"

An unexpected twist in his chest he couldn't quite define had him even more uneasy. Obviously Sarah wasn't able to make the quick escape she'd been hoping for.

And he wasn't sure just how he felt about that.

CHAPTER FIVE

"What do you mean, you're staying?"

"Believe me, Gail, if there was any other way around it…" Sarah rubbed her chest as she paced the bedroom an hour later after boiling water to rinse her hair and sponge bathe her body.

This was a nightmare. She should never have agreed to these renovations. She'd back out now if she hadn't already received the huge fruit basket from Mayor Rodale's office thanking her for being such an amazing community member. She couldn't return it—she'd already eaten all the grapes.

"Can't you just put barricades around the property and no trespassing signs?" Her boss clearly thought this was the least of Sarah's priorities right now.

"Apparently, I'll still be liable if anyone gets injured." She closed her eyes and took a deep breath. The call to the insurance company had not gone as planned. They needed copies of new ownership, which Sarah needed to apply for from the city with a copy of Dove's will, and then the application could take a few weeks to process, with their prehistoric way of filing paperwork with actual paper!

"How long do you think you'll need?"

Sarah heard the warning in her boss's voice. She shut her eyes tight and prepared for an earful. "A few weeks?"

"Are you asking me or telling me?"

"I'm sorry, Gail. I know the timing isn't ideal. But don't worry, I can work remotely, and I'll be back in the city in plenty of time to present the proposal to Smart-Tech Kids."

"It's *not* ideal, Sarah, but you do have the holiday time banked," she said begrudgingly.

Sarah's shoulders sagged in relief. "Thank you."

"I'm expecting great things with the next version of the proposal."

Sarah winced. "Absolutely. Already have some new ideas." The lie wasn't convincing anyone.

"And make sure you use our existing clients' software we've developed for them for any technology upgrades you're planning," she said.

Sarah frowned, then her eyes widened. Upgrades! That was a brilliant idea. "I definitely will," she said. "Thank you," she added before disconnecting the call.

If she was stuck renovating the inn anyway, why not do it her way?

An hour later, her list was growing.

Starting at the check-in desk, she made her way through the old house and was almost vibrating as the ideas came to her. Dove had never upgraded to an online reservation and check-in system. Dove's Nest had a website that Sarah made years ago in high school and that had been sufficient for her grandmother. Dove had still preferred that guests call to make reservations— said she could always get a vibe about them from the phone call and was able to tailor their experiences to suit them. Quiet, shy guests were treated to more privacy, and outgoing travelers were the ones Dove would deliver breakfast in the room or plan afternoon teas in the library.

She really knew how to read people. It was one of her gifts.

But any potential buyers would be expecting an online system and computerized check-in, not the paper ledger books her grandmother still kept in banker boxes in the attic dating back fifty years or more.

Moving into the den, she made a note to add a computer station with scanner and printer. Guests might want the access to check in for their travel plans and flights after their stay, and some might need to log in for business purposes.

The library she'd leave as it was…besides updating the furniture. The old sofas and chairs were worn and the fabrics faded. But she would ask Jessica for her help with that. Her friend's parents collected antiques and old furniture for their store on Main Street, and Sarah would replace the furnishings in this room with antiques in better shape. Her intent wasn't to modernize every room in the inn, just ensure guests were as comfortable as possible.

She ran a hand along the bookshelf, along the dusty spines of old classic novels. As a kid, this was one of her favorite rooms in the B&B. She'd read so many of these books and in later years, she'd study in the library, which was often quiet and underutilized. Her grandmother would bring her snacks, and they'd sit and chat for hours sometimes. Dove had led a fascinating life from the stories she told, but more often she listened more than talked and Sarah always had a feeling that there were things—secrets, parts of herself she kept in a special place, locked away.

She paused, seeing an old journal at the end of the shelf. The hair rose on the back of her neck, and a shiver ran through her as her thoughts manifested. Picking it up, she turned the old, weathered leather book over in her hands and recognized her grandmother's initials embossed in the cover.

It was locked by a tarnished latch on the side, and there was no key attached or on the shelf... What should she do?

If Jessica were here, the lock would be picked by now, but something gave her pause. These were Dove's secrets, her private thoughts. Would she want Sarah to read them? Leaving something so personal lying around seemed awfully trusting. Then again, now people used social media as their diary, so there was no real privacy anymore.

She ran a finger over the initials *D. L.*, then she carried the book to the old mahogany desk near the window and placed it in a drawer before picking up her upgrades list and continuing on her mission through the inn, the old journal lingering in the back of her mind.

• • •

Using his discarded T-shirt, tucked into the top of his jeans, Wes wiped his forehead the next morning. It was just a little past eight a.m., but already the blazing summer sun in the cloudless sky beat down on him. It was going to be a scorcher. Perched on a ladder, haphazardly propped against Mrs. Granier's old oak tree on her lawn, Wes hung her latest bird feeder. Next to the seventeen other bird feeders in the tree.

All of which he'd hung for her.

He wasn't at all fooled into believing Mrs. Granier was an avid bird-watcher. He knew she chased squirrels out of these wooden, multicolored painted boxes more often than not. Her request for his assistance always oddly enough coincided with her weekly breakfast book club.

Right now, six little old ladies sat sipping their tea, watching him work.

He descended the ladder and, folding it, he carried it under one arm toward the storage shed. He waved to them as he passed. "How's the book?" he asked with a chuckle, nodding to the Oprah's book pick, sitting untouched on the table in front of them. The same one as last time.

Mrs. Granier flushed slightly. "Oh, you know, lots of hype…" She waved a hand.

He put the ladder away and climbed the deck. "Well, enjoy your new bird feeder."

She reached for her wallet, but he stopped her. "It was my pleasure, Mrs. Granier." He took her hand and kissed it quickly. The older woman looked like she might faint, and the gaping mouths around the table had him hiding a grin. "Ladies, nice to see you all again.

Until the next bird feeder," he said with a wink as he headed back to his truck.

He pulled on his shirt as he climbed back inside the cab and a moment later, he headed down Main Street toward the inn. This time of day was quiet along the otherwise busy street. Most offices didn't open until nine and the shops around ten. The pace of small-town life suited him just fine. He waved to Jessica, seeing her load her delivery van outside Delicious Delicacies, and she smiled back at him as she worked. She must love having Sarah in town for a while. Jessica, Sarah, and Whitney had been inseparable through the school years. They were all so different personality-wise that they seemed to complement one another. Balance one another out. Jessica was the bubbly, optimistic, friendly one who was as sweet as her baked goods. Whitney was a determined go-getter with a fierce loyalty to her family and friends. And Sarah was the quirky, lovable, slightly self-deprecating optimist often masquerading as a pessimist.

Or at least that's who she used to be. He couldn't really claim to know her anymore. After high school, she'd left Blue Moon Bay for college and had never looked back. They were Facebook friends, but he wasn't a fan of social media, so he hadn't really used the platform to spy on old acquaintances.

Wes slowed the truck as he approached the vacated office space on Main Street that used to house his office. The FOR LEASE sign had gone up on the property again the week before. Pulling to the side of the street, he got out. Cupping his hands around his face, he peered in through the front window. The thousand-square-foot space was small, but it suited his company perfectly. A comfortable reception area, two offices, a boardroom, bathroom, and kitchenette. Nothing fancy, but at least it wasn't his kitchen. A law firm had moved into the space after he'd vacated it three years before, but now it was available again.

If there was any way…

The inn renovations might be enough to secure first and last month's rent on the space, but he'd need to generate more future business to ensure he could sustain the payments. Real estate on Main Street was higher than other parts of town, but the visibility was worth it.

His goal was to expand his company from repairs and renovations to new construction projects, new developments on vacant property around town. Unfortunately, he needed the money to invest to get started, and so far there was nothing on the horizon.

Climbing back into his truck, he headed home.

"Morning, Carmen," Wes said, entering the kitchen twenty minutes later, the smell of banana bread making his mouth water. "Something smells amazing," he said. He really didn't deserve Carmen. She not only kept track of the books, she cared for Marissa and insisted on spoiling them with her delicious baked goods.

He'd always been close to his only aunt. His parents had both been workaholics, climbing corporate ladders for big corporations in town, and therefore his aunt had stepped in to help raise him over the years.

She peered at him over the rim of her glasses as she

held up an unpaid invoice that had been sitting on her desk for weeks. "Did you tell Mrs. Sampson that you wouldn't charge her for painting her deck?"

Wes opened the fridge for a bottle of water, avoiding his aunt's disapproving stare. "Mrs. Sampson is eighty-six years old."

"And she's using her age to take advantage of everyone in town," Carmen said, waving the invoice at him.

That might be true, but no one could call the sweet old woman out on it. A former elementary school teacher, Mrs. Sampson had taught Wes in the fourth grade. She volunteered on all the committees and was just as much of a landmark as the statue of the town's first mayor in the center of Main Street. "The deck was small. It only took a few hours."

"Every few hours of work adds up, and no one should expect you to work for free." Carmen sighed. "Look, honey, I know you have a good heart, but no more freebies, okay?"

He nodded. "You're right." It wouldn't be easy to start charging all the familiar faces in town, but if he didn't, he wouldn't have the business much longer. He couldn't keep making plans to build his company if he wasn't proactively taking the right steps toward success. "I should take a shower and head out…" He wanted to get an early start on the inn. Overhearing Sarah's conversation the day before with her boss, he needed to ensure the renovations were done as soon as possible.

Getting her out of town quickly had nothing to do with the fact that his body's reaction to her the day before had him slightly freaked out.

"Hey, honey, any chance you could bring Marissa with you today? I forgot about a doctor's appointment I have this afternoon," Carmen said.

Wes frowned. Doctor's appointment? Those words stopped his heart these days. Since so much of Kelly's last year had been spent at hospitals and medical clinics, Wes tried to avoid them at all costs. Whenever Marissa so much as got a sniffle, he was on high alert. "You okay?" It was probably none of his business, but he couldn't not ask.

She nodded as she reached for the oven mitts. "Just fine, honey. Yearly check-up, that's all. Nothing to worry about."

He swallowed hard. Kelly had said the same thing after the first couple of appointments. She hadn't admitted she was sick—really sick—until she'd had no other choice but to tell him. "Okay. Well, yeah, of course I'll take Marissa. I'll get her."

"Great. I'll package some of this to go," she said, setting the banana bread on top of the stove.

"Thanks."

"Oh, and Wes," she said as he turned to leave the kitchen.

"Yeah?"

"You need to tell Marissa she can't go to that science camp this year. Time's running out," she said, cutting into the loaf.

Shit. His aunt was right. He needed to grow a set and be honest with his daughter.

CHAPTER SIX

The delivery truck was right on time. Bringing the B&B into the twenty-first century made sense. Sarah could still preserve its charm and uniqueness, while transforming it into a property people would want to buy. She wasn't installing virtual reality or anything... not yet anyway. Just the basics that guests expected from other vacation properties.

She'd done her research. Countless searches and online tourism review sites had provided all the data she'd needed to finalize a list of upgrades that would make Dove's Nest more appealing to travelers and help establish it as the place to visit along Highway 1.

A few rush overnight order shipments had cost more than she'd originally planned on spending, but adding these elements to the renovations were increasing her confidence level, and they would only help her secure the best price when the time came to sell.

"What's this?" Wes asked, coming up behind her. He wiped his dirty hands on his jeans, and his bare chest glistened with sweat. As usual, his half-dressed state had Sarah's heart pounding. How was she supposed to have a conversation with him when she was continually distracted by the toned, sculpted, tanned muscles?

Could she make it mandatory for her hired workers to wear shirts? Then again, she'd really only be hurting herself. This daily viewing of Wes's hot body was the only "action" she was getting or had gotten in a long time.

"Just some stuff I ordered," she said casually. She suspected he'd be annoyed by her plan, and she'd already decided to take care of most of the work involved with the upgrades herself—like installing the TVs in the bedrooms and internet modems, projectors and screens in the large meeting rooms, and the like. She would only need Wes and his crew for the big stuff...

He squinted to read the boxes the delivery men unloaded from the back of the truck. "Flatscreen televisions?"

"I decided the B&B could use some upgrades."

His hands on his hips only drew her attention to the oblique muscles disappearing beneath the low-hanging denim, weighed down even farther by his heavy tool belt.

How did one even get stomach muscles like that?

"Dove never wanted televisions in the guest rooms."

Sarah sighed. Her grandmother hadn't watched television a day in her life. She never owned one herself and insisted that guests on vacation didn't need one, either. No one ever complained, but that was before Yelp reviews gave everyone a public voice to share their opinion.

"All rental properties have televisions," she said. It was a basic expectancy.

"The inn was great the way it was," Wes said tightly. His jaw was tight, as though he were clenching his teeth. But this wasn't his decision to make.

"In your opinion," she said, waving to the delivery truck driver. "The front door's open. Just bring them inside."

"I thought you were trying to keep the reno costs low?"

Sarah averted her eyes and shrugged. She had dipped further into her savings than she'd planned, but with a quick sell, she'd recoup the extra expenses. "Let me worry about that," she said, taking a list out of her pocket. "And you can worry about these." She handed him her new list of construction improvements, and he lifted his sunglasses over his dark hair to read.

Sarah stared at the soft-looking, messy locks. What would it feel like to run her hands through his hair? She'd always been tempted to. He'd always had great hair. He hadn't buzz cut it like most of the other athletes in high school and he hadn't let it grow long like the stoner, surfer kids. It was always clean-cut but just long enough to fantasize about.

Fantasies that had just left her heartbroken. Time and distance hadn't changed the fact that Wes had only ever seen her as his tutor. After that night in the water, they'd barely spoken, and once school had ended and she'd moved away for college that September, they hadn't kept in touch. She may be stuck there longer than she planned, but that didn't mean she had to get sucked right back into old habits and unrealistic hopes and dreams.

"Solar panels…" he was saying, as though she were asking for spaceships to be installed on the roof.

She waited. He was going to love the next one.

"You want to put balconies off the rooms?" His eyebrow rose as he glanced up at her. "All of them?"

She'd considered only adding them to a few of the bigger rooms but then decided to go all in. Even if she wasn't going to be running the inn herself, she wanted Dove's Nest to be special for everyone who stayed there, not just the guests who booked premium rooms. She knew her grandmother would approve of that choice as well. "Yes. The rooms have an amazing view of the ocean. Both sides. It's a shame that there isn't a place where guests can sit and enjoy the view with their morning coffee or evening glass of wine." The reviews online had been significantly higher for resorts and hotels that provided that extra outside comfort.

"That's why they leave their room and go to the beach or sit out on the existing deck," Wes said, folding the list and handing it back to her as though her requests were never going to happen.

Which just fueled her fire even more. Sarah took a deep breath. "And I'm sure most guests still will, but I'd like to give them an option. It's their vacation. They can choose if they want to go outside or watch Netflix all day."

Wes winced, as though that sounded like a horrible vacation to him. Well, not everyone was into surfing and swimming and beach volleyball. Some people went on vacation to relax or get away or be alone. To catch up on binge-watching shows their demanding, fourteen-hour-a-day jobs didn't give them the opportunity to enjoy. She didn't expect an extrovert like Wes, who had the freedom to make his own work hours, to understand.

"These decks are a lot of work," he said, obviously

attempting to sway her with a more logical approach. "We'll need extra support beams, and depending on the dimensions, you may need to get a building permit."

She shook her head. "I've already checked into that with the mayor's office." Thanks to Whitney. "As long as the decks don't extend farther than the existing wraparound deck on the lower level of the house, no extra permits are needed."

"Wow, you did your homework," Wes mumbled. "But, Sarah, I don't think you understand how much extra work is going to have to be done in a short period of time. My quote was for the work I'd discussed with Dove."

She refused to let him discourage her. She'd watched episodes of *Flip This House* and *Love It or List It*. Under pressure, things could get done fast. "Can you do it?"

"I can, yes," he said through gritted teeth, "but I don't want to."

Damn, he was hot when he was annoyed. The stern expression with the tight jaw combined with the slightly reluctant look that said he knew he wasn't going to win this battle only made him that much more attractive.

Not attractive enough for her to back down. "Okay." She shrugged. "I'll hire someone else," she said, turning to head inside. *One, two, three…*

"Sarah, wait."

She hid a grin as she turned back and waited. The first person to speak in a negotiation lost.

His chest heaved as he sighed. "I'll get you a new

estimate by tomorrow. But I'm warning you, you're not going to like how much this is going to cost."

She walked back toward him and handed him the list. "It will be worth it." Once she made her improvements to the B&B, the place was going to look amazing and be even more functional than before. Someone would definitely want to buy it.

Her gut twisted slightly at the thought, which was ridiculous. She did not want to keep the place. Letting it go would be easy. It would not be hard to leave her hometown the longer she stayed.

Or the hot-as-hell man scowling at her.

. . .

Upgrades. What the hell? Sarah was suddenly going all in, and part of him was annoyed that she was making these changes to the inn, but damn, if she wasn't uber-appealing when she was getting her own way. The smug look on her face when she'd called his bluff had made him want to kiss it right off. The gleam of challenge in her eye and the pretty pursed lips... He had no idea what was going on there with this unexpected attraction to her.

He'd hoped the physical labor would help set him right again, but he couldn't help catching a glimpse of her as she directed the delivery guys. She was definitely more confident and self-assured than the girl he remembered. And despite his personal feelings about these changes to the inn, her new take-charge attitude was sexy.

"Dad, are you listening?" Marissa asked from below on the wraparound deck.

Unfortunately. No amount of hammering could deter Marissa from continuing to tell him all about the different course offerings from Camp STEM. And it was the latter that was making his brain hurt.

When he'd brought her to work with him that day, he'd hoped she'd ride her bike around the property or head down to the beach and build a sandcastle… Instead, she'd brought along her backpack full of books and the brochure for Camp STEM that she'd read cover to cover a million times and was now reading to him.

"It says advanced students can skip the beginner courses and take the more advanced ones…we just need to take an online submission test once we register," she was saying from her cross-legged position on the deck below him. She twirled a piece of strawberry-blond hair around one finger absentmindedly as she talked. "Do you think I'm good enough to pass that test?"

Wes hit the next nail harder than he intended, sending it straight through the wood. "I'm sure you are," he mumbled, Carmen's warning echoing in his mind.

"So do you think we can do that soon? Register, I mean. Spaces are starting to fill up," she said, looking hopeful.

He had to be honest with her. He couldn't put it off any longer. He set the hammer on the roof and climbed down the ladder. "Hey, Rissa, can we talk for a second?"

"Sure. What's up?" She didn't look up from the

brochure, and he bent in a crouched position and gently took it from her. "What's wrong?" she asked, seeing his expression.

"Camp STEM isn't happening this year," he said. Like pulling off a Band-Aid. It was going to hurt, but better to do it quickly.

She frowned. "Dad, I promise you, just let me go for the two weeks, and then I'll do whatever activity you want me to for the rest of summer vacation. And I'll still go to Girl Guides camp."

Of course she thought he wasn't on board with it because it wasn't something physical. "No, it's—"

"Fine, I'll join the fall soccer league, too, and I won't complain about going to the games. Anything. Dad, please!" She folded her tiny hands in front of her body, and Wes's heart shattered into a million pieces.

Saying no to her sucked the life out of him, but he wasn't comfortable with letting her go. He ran a hand through his hair. "I'm sorry, Rissa." He had to tell her the real reason—otherwise she'd think he was punishing her for something. "The camp is just a little too far away."

Her face fell, but she hid her disappointment quickly, seeing his. "Oh. Okay. That's totally fine."

It wasn't fine. But he'd promised Kelly that he'd take care of their daughter, and she was only nine. She hadn't been away from home like that before. Two weeks was a really long time. What if she was homesick or scared? What if she got sick? And the age group of the camp went all the way to eighteen. He didn't like the idea of her at a sleepaway camp with older kids. Older boys in particular.

"There's always next year." She took the brochure from him, folded it, and put it into her backpack. Then she stood. "I'll get out of your hair."

Damn. "Hey, I'll break for lunch soon, and we can have a picnic on the beach. The ice cream cart should be setting up down there soon." Ice cream hardly made up for disappointing her, but there was nothing else he could do. He had to think about her well-being and safety…that didn't always include the things she wanted.

"Sounds great," she said with a smile that was definitely forced.

Wes sighed as he watched her head off toward the backyard of the B&B. Was he doing the right thing? How on earth was he supposed to know? It was major decisions like this that always had him feeling at a disadvantage being a single parent. At least when Kelly was alive, they made decisions together; he had someone to discuss things with, bounce ideas off. Somedays he felt completely alone navigating this whole parenting thing.

"She okay?" Sarah asked, joining him at the side of the house. She nodded toward Marissa as his daughter sat on the swing inside the gazebo.

Wes nodded. Sarah had no doubt heard their conversation, with all the windows being open. "She's just disappointed that she can't go to STEM camp this summer." He started to reclimb the ladder, needing to put some distance between himself and the two women causing him varying degrees of conflict. "She'll be okay," he said, hoping it was true.

"Is it the one in Long Beach?" Sarah asked.

It didn't surprise him that she knew about it. He nodded. "Yep."

"That's not that far away," she said.

His spine stiffened. "She's only nine." Not that he needed to explain this to her. She didn't have kids, so he didn't expect her to get it.

"You were only seven or eight when you started going away to football camp, weren't you? And those camps were in Arizona," she said.

How on earth did she remember that? He shook his head. "That was different," he said as he started hammering again.

"How?"

Was she seriously still standing there, challenging him on his decision-making regarding his daughter? "She's not ready to be that far away from home on her own yet."

"She sounded ready..."

"Sarah!" The hammer hit the roof a little too hard, and his voice was a little too loud, but damn, the woman was driving him wild. "It's a family issue," he said, quieter but firmly.

She nodded, taking the hint. "Right. Absolutely."

Wes sighed as he watched her disappear back inside the inn. He felt bad enough. Now he also felt like a hypocrite. Sarah wasn't wrong. He'd started to go away for camp for a lot longer at a younger age. But his parents hadn't had the same fears he did as a single dad. His parents had barely had time to even realize whether he was around or not. They'd shown their love with money. He was trying to be the caring, protective father he never had.

Unfortunately, even his voice of reason was starting to sound unfair.

• • •

She'd overstepped and hadn't even realized she was doing it. Raising a child wasn't something she knew anything about, but it couldn't be easy.

Especially not alone.

Standing in the kitchen, Sarah stared out the window, across the yard at Marissa, reading a book on the swing, and her chest ached for her. Her parents had never agreed to send Sarah to camps like STEM as a child, either. They hadn't wanted to encourage her passion for all things nerdy. They weren't bad parents; they simply didn't get her. Instead, they'd always tried to change her, forcing her to get outside with the other kids, put down the book, get away from the computer screen. They never understood her. While she didn't think that was the case with Wes, she got Marissa's disappointment.

Grabbing two Popsicles from the freezer, she went outside and crossed the yard to the gazebo. "Hey, Marissa…can I join you?"

The little girl shrugged. "It's your swing."

With her strawberry-blond hair and emerald-green eyes, Marissa looked exactly like Kelly. She had Wes's height, though, and looked older than her nine years. This was the first time Sarah had met her. She'd been polite and sweet when Wes had made the introductions that morning, but Sarah could sense she wasn't thrilled about being at work with her father that day.

Sarah handed her a Popsicle and sat on the old, faded cushions. Using her foot, she pushed off, swinging the chair gently.

"Thanks," Marissa said.

"So your dad mentioned that you're into science and technology?" Wes hadn't said much at all, but the book on advanced coding the little girl was reading gave it away.

Marissa nodded, peeling the frozen treat.

"That's kinda what I do for a living. The technology part anyway."

Marissa glanced at her, her interest piqued. "Really?"

"I work for a digital marketing company in L.A. creating apps for different businesses." Which she should be working on right now. Unfortunately, she couldn't blame the inn for the distraction. She was stuck. She had no idea how to revise the proposal to something Gail wanted or the client wanted. The inn was an excuse to avoid it.

Marissa put the book down and turned to face her. "I made an app," she said, excitement in her voice.

"You did?"

"Yeah, it's a sports app for my dad to help him

organize the Little League teams better—it takes attendance and keeps a schedule of all the weekly games, player positions, that kind of thing."

"Impressive. I bet it saves him a lot of time," Sarah said.

"It would if he used it," she said with a frustrated sigh. "He's old-school and prefers his clipboard."

Come on, Wes! His daughter creates a program to make his life easier and he refuses to use it? Sounded like poor time management and also a way to create a gap between father and daughter, but who was she to judge? She had no idea what their lives were like. "Well, maybe I can help you make it available to other coaches," she said, ignoring the voice in her mind that warned her about getting involved in Wes's business or too close to a little girl she could easily adore. She sensed that Marissa could use a friend—someone who understood her.

"You'd help me with that?" Her eyes widened, and Sarah was happy that maybe she'd helped to ease the disappointment about camp just a little.

Maybe she could ease it a lot. And maybe the little girl might be able to help her with her own dilemma. She was a kid, after all. Who better to advise Sarah on technology that kids would want to use?

She hesitated briefly, then decided to go for it before she could overthink. "Hey, how would you like to be my intern this summer? Help me with my app programming and I can help you get yours to market?"

Marissa's eyes lit up as though Sarah had just given

her a new puppy. "Really? You'd help me sell my app?"

Sarah nodded. "If you want to…"

"I do!" Her head bobbed up and down so fast, it looked like it might pop off.

Sarah laughed. "Great…so start tomorrow?"

"Not right now?" The little girl's pout immediately reminded Sarah of Wes, and she felt an inexplicable tug at her heart. A terrifying, unsafe tug…

"We should probably talk to your dad about it first." That realization came a few minutes too late. Hopefully Wes wouldn't have an issue with this. It would be tough if she'd offered a consolation to Marissa only to have him shoot it down. And her own job might be dependent on this collaboration. If she didn't get something impressive to Gail soon, she could kiss the pending promotion goodbye.

"That's probably a good idea," Marissa said. "I'll ask him at lunchtime after he has his ice cream. Sugar always makes him more agreeable."

Sarah laughed as she got up from the swing but paused as Marissa reached out to touch her hand.

"Hey, Sarah, thank you," she said.

And that little tug at her heart wasn't so little anymore.

CHAPTER SEVEN

Wes climbed the stairs to the living quarters of the B&B after lunch. From the hallway outside the master bedroom, he saw Sarah sitting at her laptop at the desk. She'd changed into jean shorts and a tank top, and her long, tanned legs stretched out under the desk, her pale-seafoam-green-painted toes stealing his focus. Had those legs always been that shapely? His mouth was slightly dry and his palms were clammy.

He hesitated. Maybe he should come back. She looked busy.

Nope, he had to do this now.

He knocked on her open door, and she looked nervous when she turned to see him standing in the entrance. "Hi…"

"Hi." *Just say thank you and go back to work.* He cleared his throat. "So, good news, there's no sign of termites, just wood rot." So he was postponing his gratitude. Truth was, he was still feeling conflicted about Sarah's offer to let Marissa work with her that summer. Not about letting Marissa do it. Hell, he hoped to avoid having to say no to Marissa again for quite some time to make up for the camp disappointment. But he was torn between his gratitude toward Sarah and a reluctance to start letting his guard down around her.

He was already attracted to her, and this situation could become…dangerous. He had no intentions of opening himself up to a woman who hadn't exactly been

warm and fuzzy toward him since he'd rescued her from
a staircase. Or one hell-bent on getting back to her life
in the city as quickly as possible.

"Oh, great," she said. "I was seriously freaked out
thinking those little creatures were eating through the
place."

"Yeah. Well, they're not. So that's a relief." He stared
at his work boots and licked his upper lip. Should he say
something about his reaction to her prodding into his
life earlier? He hadn't meant to lose his cool. "Hey,
sorry about earlier."

"No, it wasn't my place to say anything."

"Still, I shouldn't have gotten so upset." He paused.
"Marissa told me what you did…offering her an intern-
ship."

Her expression was one of regret. "Did I overstep
again? The offer just came out, but I'm sorry, I should
have asked you first," she said quickly.

"No! No, it's fine." He cleared his throat again. "It's
actually really amazing of you to do that for her." His
gaze locked on hers, and the heat radiating through him
had nothing to do with the un-air-conditioned room.
How had he never noticed how dark brown her eyes
were? Or the bright starburst pattern around the
center? It was all he could see now.

Sarah's chest rose and fell in relief, and she looked
away first. "It was nothing. I could actually use the help
with some of my coding…a few things I'm working on.
A different perspective of sorts."

"Well, thank you. Again." He didn't know what else to

say other than that. She couldn't possibly understand the impact her offer to help Marissa had on him. He couldn't quite understand it himself. Marissa hadn't had a female role model in quite some time, especially not someone as smart and amazing as Sarah, and Wes sensed his daughter might be needing exactly this.

"Sure," she said. "And thanks for the good news… about the termites."

He nodded and turned to leave.

Just go. You apologized and said thank you.

He turned back. "It's not that I don't think it's amazing what she can do." For some reason, he felt the need to explain that. "She's super smart and I'm really proud. I just…" He ran a hand through his hair and released a slow, deep breath. "I just can't relate to it, and I'm not sure how to connect with her. I know sports. I know the outdoors. I know working with my hands." He shrugged. "Computers and technology aren't my thing."

Sarah looked surprised by his openness. "You don't have to share her interests or know anything about it… Just maybe support her and ask her about it? I'm sure she'd love to show you the things she's working on sometime," she said carefully.

"I can do that." He entered the room. "Maybe you can show me something first…you know, just so I don't seem completely dense. Maybe teach me some buzz words I could use to at least sound like I know what she's talking about?"

"Sure." Sarah laughed, and the sound hit him square in the chest. Her smile was mesmerizing. It wasn't the grin she wore when she knew she was getting the better of him or the grimace she wore when she seemed to be struggling to tolerate being around him when they had differing opinions about the inn, but a genuine smile. One that brought him back to when they used to be friends.

If he was a smarter man, it would have sent him running out of the room.

Instead, he pulled the armchair toward the desk and sat next to her. His shoulder brushed against hers as he moved the chair closer to look at her computer screen. He swallowed hard; the feel of his solid shoulder muscle against her soft bare skin had him experiencing a buzz of electricity through his entire body. He didn't move away.

If she was as affected by the contact, she hid it well as she turned her laptop toward him and clicked an icon on the screen. "So, this is called coding. It's the back-end programming on all the apps."

He nodded. "I know what apps are."

"That's a start." She shot him a smile, then clicked over the design, demonstrating how she created different elements of the program she was working in.

He wouldn't lie and say he was following it exactly, but it was interesting. "Wow, that's actually pretty cool."

She smiled. "It really is, and if Marissa is already designing her own at such a young age, with the right training and guidance, she could create something great."

He nodded, his gaze locking on hers and holding. She was gorgeous and smart and all the things he knew someday he'd be looking for in a new partner. A role model Marissa could look up to. His heart pounded and his mouth was dry. Was he ready to find that person now? He hadn't really given it much thought...

Sarah continued to stare at him, and the mood around them seemed to shift as he found himself unable to tear his gaze away. Those damn dark eyes were captivating, and the high cheekbones and soft contours of her face had him leaning slightly closer. Those full, pink lips seemed to be luring him in...

A buzzing sound on the desk made her jump, and he immediately backed away. The spellbinding moment shattered as the vibrating cell phone continued.

"My phone," she said, reaching for it, her cheeks blushing. "My boss. I have to get this."

"Right," he said as he stood and moved the armchair to the corner. "I should get back to work." He paused at the doorframe. "Thanks again for showing me and for the advice."

"No problem. Anytime," she said, her voice sounding slightly hoarse.

Wes escaped the room and took the stairs two at a time as he descended, needing fresh air to clear the fog surrounding him.

Not falling for the woman who was not only creating a stir in his own healing heart but who was also making his daughter happy wouldn't be a problem at all.

CHAPTER EIGHT

The next morning at 8:55, Marissa was eager to get started. She'd brought along her dinosaur of a laptop and at least a dozen workbooks she'd made notes in regarding her app.

Detailed and organized—Sarah didn't think she could like the kid any more than she did.

"Oh my God! Are these all yours?" Marissa's eyes lit up like it was Christmas morning, eyeing Sarah's two laptops, her iPad, and her phone on the desk.

"You should see my setup in my home office," she said, feeling a tinge of guilt for not being in said office. But it wasn't the location causing her distraction the past few days. It was Wes Sharrun. The day before, she'd been 99 percent sure that he was about to kiss her. The way his gaze had lingered on her face, the way he'd started to lean in closer, the way his breathing had changed…

She wasn't an expert on men or dating, but they had definitely shared a moment.

Of course the moment had been interrupted. But what if it hadn't? Would he have kissed her? Would she have kissed him back? And what the hell would it have meant? She'd caught his stare a few times the day before, but she'd assumed it was simply gratitude about her offer to help Marissa that had his expression softening and his grumbling over her upgrades to subside.

Was there more to it than that?

All night, she'd driven herself to distraction

wondering. Unfortunately, that morning, he'd been back to his old self, focused on the job.

"Okay, show me what you've been working on," she said as Marissa set her own stuff down.

Marissa opened her account on Android Studio and typed in her access code and password. Immediately, her app in Kotlin language appeared on the screen.

Impressive. She'd thought the little girl would be using some kid-friendly coding program, not the highest-level-technology app-building system on the market. She moved her chair closer to examine Marissa's work. "This is really good," she said.

Marissa beamed. "Really?"

"Yeah. Like almost ready to go to market good," Sarah said. She turned to look at Marissa. "Where did you learn to do this?"

"I took a few courses at school...but mostly I taught myself. A lot of reading and playing around with the program."

"Well, you must be a fast learner. What are you, ten?"

"Almost," she said.

"Honestly, I think other than a few bugs we might have to work out, this looks ready to test..." She hesitated. She'd wrongfully assumed that she'd need to coach and direct the kid. She had made a list of things to teach her the night before, but Marissa was far more advanced than Sarah had thought.

"So what should we work on?" Marissa asked.

Good question. She wanted to offer Marissa some value to this experience, not just pick her brain for the

SmartTech app. "Um, what about updating your dad's website?" She didn't even need to visit it to know it could probably use some work. Wes didn't strike her as someone who updated and maintained an online presence.

"What website?" Marissa asked, her tone conveying her own disdain.

"He doesn't have a site?" Sarah needed to sit down. She pulled up a chair at her desk. "How is he getting business?" Was he taking out ads in the *Blue Moon Bay Gazette* or advertising on the bowling alley display screens?

"Word of mouth around town and a Facebook page," Marissa said with a shrug of her tiny shoulder. "He stays busy, but I know we're not doing so great…money-wise. He had to close his office on Main Street after Mom died. Aunt Carmen is his assistant, and she works out of our kitchen." She seemed reluctant to admit all of this to Sarah, as though she sensed she was betraying her dad's confidences.

"Okay, well, I think it's time he had one, don't you?" she asked Marissa.

Marissa smiled. "I think it's way overdue."

"Great. I have a fantastic hosting site we can use for free. I'll set it up, and then I'll leave you to your first official intern assignment," Sarah said.

Marissa's smile was full of eagerness when she looked at her but also something else—gratitude, respect, and friendship…and Sarah felt herself being drawn in to the family even more.

If she wasn't careful, leaving Blue Moon Bay might be harder than she thought.

. . .

From his perch on his ladder two days later, Wes could hear Marissa's laughter coming from inside the B&B as he worked, and the sound warmed him to his core. All week she'd been so excited to get to the inn to work with Sarah that she'd been up early enough that he hadn't needed to wake her. Plus, all her chores were done before breakfast. He wasn't sure what magic carrot Sarah was dangling in front of her, but he'd never seen his daughter so hyped about something before.

Which made his affection for Sarah grow to an unhealthy level.

So much so that he'd purposely avoided her as much as possible the last few days. He had to get a grip and see things for what they were—she was a friend from his past doing what she felt was the right thing out of obligation…she had no plans to stay in Blue Moon Bay. And while she was the hero of the moment for his daughter, it only meant Marissa would get hurt again once she left.

Sarah might be bonding with his daughter, but she'd definitely been prickly toward him since being back in town, and that was good. Knowing she was not struggling with the same sudden attraction to him helped keep his in check.

Except a few days before, that prickly exterior had

vanished. He'd been seconds away from kissing her. Thank God her phone had interrupted them before he could do something foolish.

The sun dipped low in the sky, signaling quitting time, and he climbed down the ladder and gathered his tools. He paused outside the den window. Inside, Marissa and Sarah were sitting at the old-fashioned mahogany desk, their laptops opened in front of them, both typing furiously...but obviously chatting and making jokes as they burst out laughing every few seconds.

The knot in Wes's stomach tightened. Marissa was getting attached to Sarah really quickly. Every evening, all he heard was Sarah this, Sarah that... Hell, he was starting to like having her around. Her easy, unassuming confidence; her determination in this venture; and the way she was the complete opposite of his usual type, he already knew he would miss seeing her every day once the renovations were done.

And he had no idea what to do. He certainly didn't want to get in the way of the connection his daughter was making. The first real one in a long time, but he also didn't want to see her get hurt...

He didn't want to get hurt, but he suspected there would already be a void in both their lives once Sarah left town.

. . .

A week later, Sarah stood staring at the refinished staircase leading to the upstairs guest rooms. They'd preserved as much of the original structure as possible, and with the treated wood finish, it was hard to tell the original planks from the new.

Her grandmother would be proud.

"Don't worry, we've reinforced all the stairs from beneath, so no one…else…will be falling through," Wes said, wiping his hands on his jeans as he came up behind her in the foyer.

"It looks so great. Thank you, Wes," Sarah said, wanting to hug him.

And not just because his white T-shirt hugged his muscular chest and biceps. Or because seeing him every day, while he worked relentlessly to help her get the place in decent enough shape to sell, had turned her formerly innocent crush on her friend into something fierce.

Not *just* for those reasons.

Wes checked his watch. "We should get going. We have dinner plans with my in-laws…former in-laws…" He shrugged. "I'm still figuring out the terminology." His smile looked pained.

"Marissa's grandparents," Sarah said.

"That's definitely an easier way to put it. Thank you," Wes said, removing his tool belt and closing his toolbox.

"I really can't thank you enough for all of this. It means a lot."

At one time, *he'd* meant a lot. Sarah hadn't realized the extent of her teenage feelings for him until those long-repressed emotions had returned with a new maturity. When she'd moved away and he'd married Kelly after high school, she'd firmly closed the door on thoughts of a relationship with him, ignoring the dull ache she'd felt seeing family photos on social media. They'd been so happy together that she hadn't felt any jealousy or longing. She'd respected their relationship enough not to allow herself to pine for a man she couldn't have.

Wes had been filed in the off-limits drawer for so long, she couldn't take him out now. Could she?

At first she thought she was imagining the sexual tension between them, but after the near-kiss, she was certain of it lingering on the air whenever they were near each other. She was painfully aware of his presence all around the B&B as he worked…and she definitely hadn't been imagining the looks she'd caught him sending her way when he thought she wasn't looking.

But in the last few days, he'd also seemed to be trying harder not to be around her…avoiding her, even.

"My guys will finish the kitchen renovations this week, and then we will start on the guest room balconies."

"Sounds great."

"Ready to go?" he asked Marissa as she joined them in the foyer, her laptop under her arm and backpack on her back.

"Yep," she said, then glanced at Sarah. "Hey, you should come to dinner with us tonight."

This wasn't the first invite, and Sarah was running out of excuses. She sensed a slight matchmaking attempt on Marissa's part that she wouldn't be completely averse to if Wes seemed at all interested in exploring the attraction between them, but as usual, he interjected.

"We're having dinner with Grandma and Grandpa, re-member?"

Marissa looked disappointed that they kept putting her off. "Oh, right. Well, maybe another night?"

Sarah looked at Wes, then nodded slowly. "Yeah, maybe."

Wes shifted from one foot to the other and cleared his throat. "Um…Marissa's spending the night at her grandparents' house, so a few of us were going to Trent's Tavern. If you're not busy, you should come," he said.

Okay, that was different.

She hadn't been out since she'd been back. A night out sounded great, and she wouldn't lie to herself—seeing Wes in a different setting, enjoying a few drinks and laughs, didn't sound terrible at all.

Which was why it was a bad idea.

Marissa's hopeful expression confirmed how much of a bad idea it would be. They probably shouldn't encourage the matchmaking going on in that genius little mind.

"That would be fun; thank you for the invite…but I thought I'd get started on the guest rooms." She'd bought the paint the day before, and there was no time like the present to get started. She may not be great with a hammer and nails, but painting wasn't that hard, and the faster she could get the renovations done and the place listed, the better.

"Are you sure?" Marissa asked as Wes led the way outside. "You deserve a night out."

Sarah laughed at the persistence as she stepped out

onto the deck and wrapped her cardigan around herself while the ocean breeze blew the flaps open. "Yeah. I should probably start pulling my weight around here."

And stop giving in to any ridiculous notions that things could be more than what they were with Wes. Once the renovations were done, she'd be putting the B&B on the market and she'd be leaving. Their relationship would go back to consisting of her stalking his rare Facebook posts.

That was good. Out of sight, out of mind.

Though that hadn't been the case before.

"Okay. Well, if you change your mind, you're welcome to join us," he said, opening the back door of his truck for Marissa. He climbed into the driver seat, and his gaze met hers through the windshield, but she couldn't read the expression behind those ocean-blue eyes, so she waved as they drove off, knowing she wouldn't be going out that night.

If Marissa's gentle coaxing that the two of them spend time together wasn't enough of a red flag, her own desire to take him up on the invite certainly was. She couldn't start a relationship with him when she wasn't planning on staying. It wouldn't be fair to any of them.

And when had Wes Sharrun ever given her a second look? Obviously any affection he felt for her was wrapped up in her giving Marissa an alternative to camp.

She headed back inside and into the den for her laptop. Noticing her grandmother's journal still in the open desk drawer, she picked it up and carried it to her room. She'd forgotten all about it. But now, as she changed into painting clothes, her gaze continued to wander to it.

So odd that the journal had been sitting on the bookshelf. Wasn't her grandmother worried that a guest might find it and read it? Or had she left it there precisely for that reason?

Sarah went to her dresser and, taking a bobby pin, she picked up the journal and wiggled the pin into the lock hole, moving it around until she heard a *click*.

That was easy.

Opening the cover, Sarah removed several old and yellowed newspaper clippings, then carefully scanned the headlines.

U.S.A officially enters the Second World War after attack on Pearl Harbor.

Under the articles were two pictures. The first she recognized as her grandfather; the other was a man she didn't know. Both men were dressed in Air Force uniforms. Her grandfather had served in the Second World War for three years before returning home to marry her grandmother within six months, and Sarah's uncle was born months later. Her grandmother had always talked about Martin Lewis's bravery and how he'd won medals for his courage, but Sarah had never met her grandfather, as he'd died two years before she was born. Dove had never remarried, and as far as Sarah knew, she hadn't even dated after that. She always thought it was sad that her grandma had spent the rest of her life alone, but the older woman had always insisted that you only find true love once.

She laid the photos aside and squinted to read the first entry in the journal.

Dec 5, 1941

Dear Jack,

Jack? The other man in the photos?

We said our goodbyes last night, and I've yet found a reason to smile. The United States joining this war has already caused my heart to break. I admire your courage and strength, my dear Jack, but I am angry and scared. Angry that you have left and scared that you won't return. I have no way to contact you. I have no idea where in this world you are, so I will write to you in this journal, until someday I can give it to you.

This violence overtaking the world is cruel and senseless and I wish no part in it. But I have no choice—the biggest part of me, my heart, is with you. Fly safe, my love. Be safe. And come home to me.

Dove

Sarah sat blinking, staring at her grandmother's script handwriting on the yellowed page. Then her gaze moved to the picture of the unknown man.

Jack? Her grandmother had called him *my love*.

Holy shit.

She picked up the pictures, along with the news clippings, and closed the book quickly, a shiver dancing down her spine. Dove had never mentioned a Jack. Ever. She'd been right about her grandmother having secrets, and this journal obviously held her grandmother's confessions.

Sarah opened the bedside drawer and put the journal inside, unsure if she'd read anymore. What she already had had shaken her.

You only find true love once.

Sarah had always assumed her grandma had been talking about her grandfather.

CHAPTER NINE

His in-laws' house was like taking a step back in time. And not entirely in a good way. Their older bungalow near the highway stretching along the coast was a museum of the past. His past. And Kelly's.

The McKenna home hadn't changed at all since he'd practically lived there in high school. The same comfy, dated furniture. The same curtains in the windows. The same appliances that Mr. McKenna miraculously kept running, fixing them whenever they broke and refusing to buy new ones. As a self-employed business owner himself, Wes could appreciate his former in-laws' frugal ways.

It was the memorabilia from their past that always unsettled him.

His own parents hadn't cared much about his football career and aspirations. They hadn't really shown much interest in anything he did. An only child, he was clearly one they hadn't exactly planned for. He wasn't neglected; they just showed their love through financial support, paying for his gear and equipment and football camps but never really involved.

That was probably why he'd been so drawn to Kelly's family. They were supportive of their children, the kind of parents who were at every game, every recital, every school event. They all sat around the table for breakfast in the morning and dinner every evening. They had board game nights and movie marathons.

And they'd always treated Wes as part of the family. They'd been over the moon when he'd gotten drafted after college, and their home was still a shrine to his past accomplishments.

He cringed as he entered the home, hearing the game on the television—his game. One he'd played ten years ago, his best game ever. His father-in-law watched it every time he visited, and Wes didn't have the heart to tell the old man that seeing the game, seeing the future he could no longer have, ate away at his soul.

He loved his life in Blue Moon Bay. He liked his job. He loved being a dad. But there was definitely a part of him that longed for the dream that was cut too short.

"Hey, there he is!" John said from his old, worn leather recliner as Wes and Marissa entered the living room. A perfect spiral of an old football came toward Wes, and as per their routine, Wes caught it and tossed it back. "And he brought my favorite granddaughter."

Marissa laughed warily and played along with the overplayed joke. "Pop, I'm your only granddaughter." She accepted a hug from him as Wes sat on the sofa. The springs creaked under his weight, and the cushions molded to his shape.

"Your grandma could use some help setting the table," John whispered to Marissa, sneaking her a five-dollar bill.

"I asked *you* to set the table," Carolyn said, joining them in the living room and swatting her husband's head playfully.

"I don't mind," Marissa said, winking at her

grandfather. She hurried out of the room, and Wes stood again for a hug from Carolyn. Her four-foot-eleven frame came to his chest, and the scent of her lavender shampoo was the same as always. She was an older version of Kelly—same red hair, green eyes, thin nose, and heart-shaped face, and his breath always caught at the sight of her.

"Hi, darlin'. Hope you're hungry."

The familiar smell of her baked tuna casserole had his stomach twisting, but not from hunger. It had been the Friday night meal at the McKennas' before every high school football game. It was tradition. The family was superstitious and believed in not breaking the school's winning streak by making something else. Carolyn still made it every time they came for dinner.

Wes could appreciate their need to hold on to the past as a way of remembering their daughter, of holding on to a part of her and a better time, but these visits were only getting harder and harder as time passed and he tried to move on.

And he worried about the impact they had on Marissa. Discussions never seemed to stay in the present for long. Always returning to memories of the "good old days." Reminiscing was okay, but Wes wanted to focus on the future and how that looked for all of them.

"Starving," he said with a forced smile.

"Hey, here comes the play," John said, nodding his balding head toward the television.

Wes turned and watched as his younger self caught

the ball and ran like lightning down the field in the Rams' stadium, making the game-winning play, then fought the what-if thoughts that were never too far away whenever he was in this house.

Five minutes later, they bowed their heads in prayer around the dining room table and started to eat.

"Drove past the inn the other day," his brother-in-law, Dustin, said as he passed the casserole to Wes. He was still dressed in a suit, having come straight from the bank where he worked as a mortgage broker. "Almost didn't recognize the place."

"Sarah's making it so much cooler," Marissa said before he could answer. Her expression lit up at the mention of her mentor.

"Sarah?" Carolyn asked with a frown. "As in, Sarah Lewis?"

Wes nodded. "She inherited the place. Plans to sell it." He scooped the casserole onto his plate.

"Wasn't she that young girl who tutored you all throughout high school?"

Carolyn's memory was incredible.

"Yeah," he said, forking the food into his mouth and ignoring her look that said she wasn't completely thrilled about some aspects of this situation. Years ago, Carolyn had suspected that Sarah had a crush on him...

What would she think if she knew he'd almost given in to the urge to kiss Sarah? Or that he found himself attracted to the woman? He'd never been serious about another woman since Kelly, so how his in-laws would feel about him dating someone had never really been a factor. But what would they think, how would they feel if he eventually found someone and settled down again?

"Sarah used to tutor you and now she's mentoring me? You never told me that," Marissa said. "That's so cool!"

Carolyn glanced at Marissa. "Mentoring you?"

Wes heard the concern in Carolyn's voice, but obviously Marissa didn't catch it.

"Yes! She's helping me with my app and with a secret project," she said with a grin his way.

Wes did his best to send her a smile, but the food stuck in his throat.

"That's interesting," Carolyn said, moving her food around her plate.

His father-in-law didn't look like he was even listening to the conversation, but Dustin was sending him a look. One he couldn't quite decipher, but his head nod toward his mother meant Wes needed to say something about the situation.

Wes cleared his throat. "The renos are almost done. Sarah will be leaving soon."

Carolyn nodded, looking slightly relieved. "Of course. I remember she was always so eager to leave town. I can't imagine anything would make her want to stay now, not even that old inn," she said as she resumed eating.

Not even the old inn.

Wes glanced at Marissa, and his daughter's disappointment had his uneasiness growing. His mother-in-law might be eager to see Sarah leaving town again, but his daughter sure wasn't.

Unfortunately, Wes couldn't determine where exactly he fell on the spectrum.

• • •

Themed rooms were cliché and, thank God, her grandmother had thought so, too. It made repainting the B&B guest rooms a lot easier when Sarah didn't have to worry about painting over Western or Hollywood Night themes, like other inns along the coast boasted.

Every room in Dove's Nest was decorated in the same nautical colors and accents. Seafoam-blue walls with white baseboards and trim, black-and-white pictures of local surfers tearing up the waves, a uniquely handcrafted surfboard in the corner that duplicated as a full-length mirror, and seashell-decorated dispensers in the bathrooms.

Simple and old-school elegance. Or at least they used to be and would be again.

The walls were chipped and some of them stained from years of allowing smoking inside, but the decorations still held up, and the cosmetic work wouldn't take more than a few nights to finish.

Sarah stood in the middle of the first room, already prepped. Painting tarps covered the floor, and blankets were draped over the furniture. Even the edges along the door and window frames and along the ceiling and baseboards were taped, thanks to Wes's work crew.

She shuffled through her iPad for appropriate

painting music. The problem was, she couldn't define her mood. Since being back in Blue Moon Bay, her world had been an emotional roller-coaster ride—the death of her grandma, deciding to renovate the inn, and her growing attraction to Wes had her turned completely upside down, as though the ride had stopped mid-rotation on a loop.

Would she fall to her death? Or survive the cyclone of indecision and uncertainty?

And despite her best attempts at resisting, she was being drawn back to that journal. She was desperate for more answers about who this Jack guy was and just how much he'd meant to her grandmother, but she was also terrified to read any further. How many journal entries were written to him? Had her grandfather known about this man from her grandmother's past?

She tried to remember as many details as she could, but all she knew was that her grandfather had returned from serving in the war and the two had fallen in love while her grandmother was working in a factory in San Francisco. During wartime, women had stepped up to fill in jobs that the men had vacated. They'd gotten married quickly, her grandmother had returned to running the B&B, and that was it.

But that wasn't it. Not even close.

One true love…

Was her grandmother right? Was there just one person out there destined for someone else? Sarah had never felt the same pull of attraction for anyone the way she always had for Wes…but he'd been happy with someone else. If soul mates were a thing, how was that possible?

She sighed. She was being ridiculous. Letting the nostalgia of being at the inn and the secrets she'd discovered in the journal get to her.

She'd definitely be opening it again, but fear of what else she might discover that she wasn't ready to learn gave her pause. For now.

Hitting shuffle on the iPad, she tucked it into the pocket of her faded, ripped jeans. Her favorite pair that she'd been clinging to far past their life span. They were like her comfort blanket—the ones she turned to when she just needed to relax. She tied her hair back into a high ponytail and got to work.

Opening the seafoam-colored paint, she stirred it until the consistency was just right and poured it into the rolling tray. She'd painted her bedroom in her family home countless times as a teenager, new inspiration demanding new vibrant colors as frequently as her changing hormonal mood swings.

So she had a little experience with a rolling brush.

She dipped it into the paint and started on the far wall, covering the patches of white where Wes's crew had repaired dents and holes.

Humming along to a hip-hop track, she swayed her hips as she worked, feeling better with the completion of the first wall. Things had come together a lot faster than she'd expected. Dove's Nest would soon look like a brand-new inn.

But what secrets were these walls hiding?

"Not bad."

She shrieked and jumped as she spun around to the sound of the voice. Her hand flew to her chest, where her heart threatened to break through, and she yanked the earbuds from her ears. "Jesus, Wes. Trying to kill me?"

He laughed. "Sorry. I knocked and rang the doorbell for, like, ten minutes; then I started to worry about you…"

Her cheeks warmed. "How did you get in?" She'd locked all the doors downstairs.

"Yeah, we may need to put a new lock on the front door," he said, clearing his throat.

"You broke in?"

"I was coming to your rescue," he said, entering the room.

She cocked her head to the side. "And what were you going to protect me from? Spiders? Dust mites? Hard work?"

"Asks the woman who was stuck in a staircase weeks ago," he said, shooting her a pointed look.

"Touché," she said. "But why are you here anyway? I thought you were enjoying a free night out while Marissa was with her grandparents?"

He was wearing old jeans, ripped at the knees and already speckled with multicolored paint, and his black T-shirt had a hole in the collar—obviously old working clothes. But his hair was gelled in a spiky mess, he'd shaved his usual five-o'clock stubble, and a faint smell of cologne lingered on the air, competing with the scent of wet paint. Obviously, he'd been intending to go to Trent's Tavern that night.

Why the change of heart?

He entered the room and handed her a coffee. "I did go out, but then I felt guilty that you were here working alone, so I went home and changed, and here I am."

Needing to hide her overly pleased expression, Sarah took a sip of the coffee and nearly choked on the taste of a strong liqueur.

"Wait, that one's mine. Spiked."

"You think?" She handed the cup back to him and accepted a new one.

"So you gave up a night out to work?" She struggled to hide her pleasure as she studied him. He looked even hotter than usual, and her pulse raced. She'd refused the offer to join him at the bar, so as not to complicate things or risk encouraging the growing sexual tension between them further, and yet here he was.

"Yeah… Though it looks like you have things under control." He looked around the room. "What were you rocking out to a few minutes ago?"

A few minutes? "How long were you standing there, creeping on me?" And God, what dance moves had she busted out? She didn't claim to be the most graceful person on the planet, and there had definitely been some ill-timed hip thrusts. Oh jeez, would she ever not come across as awkward and goofy in front of him?

"Long enough." Wes picked up an earbud and put it in his ear.

A twangy country song about broken hearts now

played from the other one dangling at Sarah's chest. Great. Of all songs, a swoony country ballad?

But Wes closed his eyes and started singing along, off-key…and not exactly the right words.

Sarah looked at him with amusement. "You know this song?"

"It's my anthem these days. Girl left me, truck keeps breaking down, and dog ran away."

Her eyes widened. "Your dog ran away?"

He laughed. "Okay, two out of three."

She held out a hand, and he gave her back the earbud. She hit Pause on the music. "Really, what are you doing here?"

"Told you, I'm here to work." He set his spiked coffee on the dresser, moved to the middle of the room, and opened a new roller and tray.

"You didn't have to…" She was glad he did, but having him there, having him choose helping her over a night out, had her feeling all kinds of emotions she had no business feeling.

"Sarah, I'm here. I want to be here," he said, his gaze burning into hers until she could barely breathe on the thick air surrounding them. He cleared his throat. "Any plan of attack I should know about?" he asked, pouring more paint into the tray.

"Yes. Get it done," she said in as bossy of a tone as she could muster. He'd come back to help her. He'd given up a rare night out. She wouldn't read anything into it. She'd practically guilted him into it. And he probably just wanted more billable hours…

"I like it," he said, getting to work on the opposite wall.

A long beat of silence fell between them before she asked, "So is running your own construction company everything you'd hoped it would be?" She dipped the roller in paint and started on the wall adjacent to him.

"My dream was football," he said, the longing in his voice after all this time surprising her.

Guess dreams didn't just evaporate when reality shat all over them. Sarah remembered Wes's desire to go pro. In fact, one of her best memories of Blue Moon Bay was watching their high school team, the Panthers, play on Friday nights. Wes was a wide receiver, and seeing him out there on the field in his gear had set her teenage hormones ablaze. "At least you got to do what you loved for a little while," she said.

"Yeah, I mean, a lot of athletes don't even make it that far. And this career works," he said quickly. "I make my own hours, which is great for raising Marissa. I'm the volunteer dad at school." He laughed as though he'd never have believed it if he weren't living it.

"I'm sure the volunteer moms love that," Sarah said before she could stop herself. "I...just mean, having a dad in the class."

I will not flirt with him.

Marissa may have been trying to set up the two of them, but they'd both resisted...which had to mean something, right?

But when he grinned, the gorgeous dimples in his cheeks made her vow that much harder to keep. Why did he have to be so good-looking? Teenage crushes should at least have the decency to age poorly. What she wouldn't give for the ability to say, *Phew, dodged a bullet there.* Instead, she'd launch herself in front of this particular sexy bullet given the opportunity.

"So, is there anyone special you've left behind in L.A.?" he asked, his tone casual, but she detected a definite curiosity.

"Nope. Not even a friend with benefits," she said honestly. Maybe a little too honestly, but truth was, her sex life was practically nonexistent. She worked far too much for a real relationship, and hookups might be the cool thing these days with dating apps on everyone's phones, but she wasn't interested in swiping right unless it had the potential to be more than a one-night stand. As much as she put her faith in technology for all other aspects of her life, she wasn't sure it was the way she wanted to find someone. Whenever she did decide to make time for it.

"Hell, if I'd known you were sexually frustrated, I'd have let you take the sledgehammer to that kitchen wall last week."

She swiped at him with her paint roller, narrowly missing his arm. Then cautiously she asked, "Do you think you will ever be ready...for another relationship?"

Asking for a friend.

"Somedays I think so. Other days, I'm not sure. Marissa and I have a good life together. We've figured out how to make things work just the two of us. I'm not sure I'm still actively grieving Kelly, but a part of me definitely died with her, and unless I can give someone else the full love she deserves…" He shrugged.

Sarah had let the roller drop to her side as she'd listened to his rare moment of open vulnerability, and now seafoam paint covered her thigh.

What was she supposed to say to that?

"Sorry, that got deep. Fast," Wes said with a laugh.

"No, I get it." She did. And despite the pull she'd always felt toward him, it was enough to ground her in the reality of their situation. He wasn't sure if he was ready to move on, and she had no idea how she felt. Her life was far too complicated at the moment to think about a relationship, but she was starting to think she wanted one. Finding love had always taken a back seat to her career, but she'd hoped as she neared thirty, her career would be established and she could turn her attention to other aspects of life.

Maybe once she got this promotion…

"I worry about Marissa," he said, and he sounded reluctant to confide in her, but also like he was sensing she might be the perfect person.

"About what?" she asked carefully.

"We used to be so close." He shook his head. "Now I feel like I don't even really know her sometimes."

Sarah bit her lip, unsure what to say. She didn't want to overstep again or cross any boundaries. The family's dynamic was none of her business, but he was opening up to her, so she had to say something, right? "I think you're both just very different people, and maybe it might help if you tried to understand her world a little," she said gently.

He nodded. "I'm not sure I'm smart enough for her world. All that coding stuff you told me went in one ear and out the other, but I have been trying lately," he said, attacking the wall with the roller. "I just don't get why she doesn't want to play sports and hang out with friends...actual friends, like she used to."

Sarah had dealt with the same issue. Her parents never fully understanding her... She could never get them to understand. Could she help Wes for Marissa's sake? "Maybe don't try so hard to put her into a box she doesn't want to fit in."

He stopped and turned to face her. "You think that's what I'm doing?"

"I don't know, but I think your relationship would be easier if you gave her some space to be her own person."

He frowned, and Sarah tensed. Too far. She should have minded her own business.

But then he nodded. "You're absolutely right," he said with a heavy sigh. "I'm messing this up, aren't I?"

He looked wrecked, and Sarah reached out and touched his shoulder. It was meant as a comforting gesture, but the intense, immediate shock that radiated through her core at the contact had her body reacting. She could see her pulse vibrating in her wrist and her mouth was dry.

Wes's gaze met hers, and he looked as conflicted as she felt.

Nope. Nope, nope. This was definitely not the time... The guy just admitted he wasn't sure he was ready for another relationship. Things between them were complicated, and there was Marissa to think about...

But his gaze fell to her lips, and she could see his breath pick up with the heaving of his chest. So she hadn't imagined things the week before. Wes Sharrun did want to kiss her.

As if on autopilot, she dropped the roller and moved toward him, her body not listening to any of her mind's warnings. Standing on tiptoes, Sarah wrapped her arms around his neck and pressed her lips to his.

Wes hesitated only a second before his arms went around her body, pulling her against him. She closed her eyes and sank into him, enveloped in the manly scent of his aftershave and savoring the taste of sweetened, spiked coffee on his lips.

Her fingers tangled into the back of his hair and she deepened the kiss, slipping her tongue into his mouth.

His grip tightened at her waist, and then his hands slid higher around her ribs as he held her close to his body. Eager, hungry lips and hands—his *and* hers— frantic, unthinking, they explored and caressed until she could barely breathe.

She didn't want air; she just wanted him—his kiss, his touch...

She was kissing her high school crush and he was returning it with as much passion as she was giving. No kiss had ever felt this intoxicating. No touch had left her craving more the way his did in that moment. Nothing else mattered right now. Just years of unrequited feelings mixed with weeks of chemistry and sexual tension came out of her in a whirlwind of pure emotion...zero logic.

Her hands cupped his face when she sensed he might pull away, and he groaned as he rotated them and pushed her up against the wet wall. His entire body connected with hers as he continued to steal her breath away.

Far too soon, he broke the connection between their mouths, gasping slightly for air as he rested his forehead against hers. Wes opened his eyes, and a look of guilt mixed with panic at the realization of what he'd just done. "Shit. Sorry, Sarah." He released her and ran a hand over his face.

She had no idea what to say, so she remained silent as she peeled herself away from the sticky paint, leaving an imprint of her ass on the wall.

"That should not have happened," he said as he took a step toward her. "Sarah..."

She shook her head. "It's fine." *Totally wasn't fine*. "That was a silly thing to do. I'm not even sure why I thought..." Mumbling incoherently was all she could muster at the moment. Her cheeks were flushed, and she could still taste him on her lips.

He sighed. "No, it wasn't your fault. I was definitely into it."

That helped to ease the sting...slightly, at least.

"I mean, you had to be able to tell."

She nodded. So her instincts weren't completely off-base; they were just ill-timed?

"I've felt things shifting...between us. You too, right?"

he asked, suddenly looking unsure.

Would she have attacked him otherwise? She nodded.

"The kiss was amazing. It's just…"

He looked pained and confused, and Sarah couldn't deal with the tension simmering in the air around him. "You're not ready for a relationship."

"And you're too busy for one. You don't want one, either. You're just here to fix up the inn, and then you have a life to get back to. That's what you said, right?"

That one kiss had just shattered her entire perception of what she thought she wanted. But she nodded. "Yeah. Absolutely. One hundred percent," she said, turning her attention back to the painting to hide the bitter sting of disappointment.

Yes, that's what she'd said. Turns out she was a liar.

CHAPTER TEN

The next morning, a group of eight- to ten-year-olds waited not so patiently on the sandy beach to learn how to surf. But as he prepped his surfboard, Wes's mind was anywhere but on the mid-morning waves. The night before had been catastrophic. There was no other way to describe it. He applied the wax roughly to the bottom of his board, desperate to stop the scene from replaying in his mind.

He'd kissed Sarah Lewis. Then he'd backpedaled his way out of acknowledging that the kiss had had an impact on him.

His emotions were a mess. The impulsive kiss itself had been fantastic, and that judgement wasn't coming from a place of not having kissed a woman in years. Sarah Lewis was an amazing kisser.

Her lips had been soft and delicious. They'd instantly fallen into a rhythm so in sync, it was as though they'd been kissing each other forever, the heat between them off the charts. All the sexual tension that had been building had exploded as soon as their mouths and bodies had connected. He'd enjoyed the kiss far too much.

But was he really ready to kiss someone else? Move on with someone? Just seconds before the kiss, he'd claimed he wasn't sure, and the passion that had ignited between them hadn't helped clarify things.

He should never have gone back to the inn in the

first place. Canceling on his night out with the guys had been foolish. His intentions had been muddled, falling somewhere between wanting to help Sarah finish the renos as soon as possible to get her out of town again and simply wanting to see her after the tense, strained dinner with his in-laws.

He ran the wax over his surfboard a final time and sighed. What the hell was he supposed to do now? They still had renovations to finish at the B&B. He couldn't avoid her.

Most troublesome was the fact that he didn't want to. He did somehow have to make up for the blunder, but how did he do that without addressing the kiss and whether or not it would be happening again?

Did she want to talk about it? Did she want to kiss him again?

He doubted it. What woman would after that aftermath of excuses and regret?

He stood and forced a smile as he addressed that morning's group. Mostly beginners. Should be an easy class. Focus on balancing on the board.

Balance. Not an easy thing to do when his world felt like it had been upended the night before.

"Okay, everyone ready to get out there in those waves?" he asked the group.

"I am!" the camp counselor, a young girl about eighteen who was eyeing a group of male surfers with obvious interest, said.

Wes forced a smile. Obviously he'd be in charge of making sure these kids didn't drown that morning.

"Wonderful," he said. "Today, we're going to learn to stand on the board. It sounds easy, but believe me, it can be tricky," he told the kids. "Head on down to the water's edge, and I'll be right there."

He picked up his and Marissa's surfboards and glanced across the beach to where she sat reading a book on the edge of the boardwalk. "Hey!" he called out.

She glanced up, and Wes hesitated.

Don't try so hard to put her into a box she doesn't want to fit in.

Sarah's advice the night before had impacted him as much as the kiss. She was right. He was trying to encourage Marissa to be someone she wasn't. That stopped now.

"Make sure to put on sunscreen, okay?" he said, putting her surfboard back on the sand and joining the others out in the water.

He may not have a clue how to fix things with Sarah, but at least he could start making a better effort with his daughter.

• • •

Sarah rolled the painting tarps in the last room and pushed the furniture back into place. That day, she'd attacked the walls with a new urgency. These renovations couldn't be done a moment too soon. Her desperation level to get back to the city was higher than ever. This inn was now the site of a second rejection from Wes Sharrun.

Unbelievable.

The guy wasn't interested in her years ago and he wasn't interested in her now. The impulsive kiss had been silly. She hadn't been thinking. She'd been wrapped up in the moment.

Why couldn't it have been a bad kiss at least? If her high school crush had turned out to be a horrible kisser, knowing she'd never get a chance to kiss him again would be easier to swallow. Instead, his kiss had been everything Sarah had always thought it would be. Emotional, passionate, and delicious. His desire had shocked the hell out of her in the best possible way.

Until the aftermath had her feeling even worse than before.

"Hello?" Whitney's voice drifted up the staircase from the foyer.

"Up here!" Sarah called, hearing her friend's heels on the staircase. Normally, she'd be excited to see Whitney that day to gush about the long-awaited, pined-after kiss, but now, she'd keep it to herself. Damn Wes for stealing her opportunity for a hot gossip sesh with her bestie.

"Wow! I cannot believe this is the same place," her friend said, admiring the room, as she handed Sarah one of the coffee cups she carried. "Everything looks amazing, Sarah."

The smell of dark roast hazelnut reaching her nose was like a lifeline. She hadn't slept at all the night before, and the coffee was definitely needed. "Thanks so much. So it should be easy to sell, right?" she asked, taking a sip.

Whitney nodded, but she avoided Sarah's gaze as she continued to scan the bedroom. "I don't know if you need to be in such a rush. I mean, you do want to get the best price."

Sarah's stomach knotted. "Why do you look so guilty? What are you up to?" They'd been friends for a long time, and whenever Whitney bit her lip, she was hiding something.

"Nothing."

"You're not a good liar."

"I'll wait until you take a few more sips of that first," Whitney said, nodding toward the coffee.

Sarah eyed her friend over the rim of the cup as she savored more liquid courage for whatever bomb her friend was about to drop on her. "Okay, spill it," she said.

"It's not a bad thing. In fact, it's an incredible opportunity…"

"Don't spin me with your sales tactics, Whit." She took another gulp of her drink, grateful it was the perfect temperature.

"I've booked a reopening event. For the inn," Whitney said as her phone chimed.

Sarah frowned. "I don't remember that being part of the plan." The details were fuzzy because of the wine, but she remembered all of them agreeing that as long as Sarah could have the B&B finished by the fall, it would be great timing to list it for sale. Offers would come in, and a sale could be completed before the holidays and still give the new owners time to prepare for the following year's tourist season.

"I know, but this event came across my desk today, and I thought maybe it would be a good idea to host it here so that the community could actually see the place after its makeover." Whitney typed furiously and then tucked the phone into a pocket in her white-and-tan-striped dress.

"What it is?" she asked carefully. Whitney was a go-getter. She shot for the moon with everything she did and had never failed enough to learn how to lower her standards. Sarah was a little bit more cautious in her goals. Which was why she was still working for Gail and not going out on her own, which had been her original plan after graduation. Get the experience and an established client base, then get out. Instead, she was climbing the ladder and making someone else rich.

But that was fine, right?

"A family reunion," Whitney said. "The client was insistent that she needed a place for guests to stay, and she'd originally committed to the Seaview Inn, but they overbooked that weekend, and she was left scrambling to find another suitable venue. This was the perfect choice. She's really excited."

"But an event really isn't necessary. I mean, we can just hold open houses for potential buyers."

"Right…but this way, so many people who love this place will get to see it and experience it in its new splendor before someone else buys it. You've done so much work. Show it off before you ditch town again."

Sarah sighed. It would be nice to at least soak up some of the credit of restoring the inn before she handed it off. "When is the event?"

"Labor Day weekend," Whitney said.

"That's two weeks away." She'd been planning on leaving sooner than that. Extending her stay in Blue Moon Bay didn't exactly appeal to her after the night before. Sarah took a deep breath and drank more coffee. "I'm not sure, Whitney. I really should get back to the city."

"You've been working remotely all this time anyway. What's another two weeks?"

She hesitated. Could she really last that long in town? Should she tell Whitney about the kiss with Wes and his rejection? Both of her friends were so successful and happy; she hated that she seemed to be the only one still trying to establish herself in her career and her love life. "It's just getting complicated," she said noncommittally.

"Come on, Sarah. Trust me. It's the mayor's niece hosting the reunion, so the mayor will be there. It's the perfect time to show off the place to some impressive influencers who will help block any attempt at a big chain succeeding in buying it and tearing it down to put up some flashy resort."

Whitney made a good point. Having the mayor's support would go a long way toward preserving Dove's Nest as the community landmark it was. She didn't want to have done all of this in vain.

"Okay," she said reluctantly. Gail was going to shit, but their pitch to the client wasn't until after Labor Day. "Mayor's niece? Do we know her?"

"Yes, we do know her," Whitney said casually, but

Sarah detected a note of apprehension in her voice. She paused before continuing. "You remember Lia Jameson from high school, right?"

Lia Jameson? As in her high school *frenemy* Lia Jameson? She shook her head quickly. "Oh no…"

Whitney forced a smile that said, *Please don't kill me.* "I kinda already told her yes."

"Whitney!"

"Sorry, Sarah. She needed an answer, and you have to admit, this is a good idea."

"But Lia? Really?" The former gossip queen had always been just one step ahead. When Sarah placed second in the science fair, Lia placed first. When Sarah got an A on a math test, Lia got an A-plus. And according to Facebook, Lia was now happily married with a successful law career in New York City with a penthouse apartment overlooking Central Park. Once again, she'd beaten Sarah at life. Seeing her old high school rival right now when her own career was on the line and her heart was a mess wasn't exactly appealing.

"Look, the rivalry you two had years ago was a teenage girl thing. You are both mature, successful women now. The past is in the past, right?" Whitney said.

Unfortunately, Sarah wasn't so sure. That certainly wasn't the case with Wes.

• • •

As Wes packed up his surfing gear an hour later, Marissa approached on the beach. The summer sun had her freckles darkening on her pale skin, and the sight always made him smile. She had Kelly's coloring and was prone to burns, hence the thick white glob of sunblock on her nose. "Hey, all done?" she asked.

"Yeah, how was the book?"

"It was good. I finished it, but now I have to wait a whole month until the next one comes out," she said with a sigh.

Wes laughed. "A whole month, huh?" He couldn't remember the last time he'd finished one full book, let alone this never-ending sci-fi series Marissa was obsessed with.

"Thanks for not forcing me to surf," she said, eyeing him suspiciously behind blue-rimmed sunglasses.

"I was too tired to save you from pretending to drown multiple times today," he said teasingly. "Ready to go?"

"Actually, I was wondering if we could maybe take a walk along the boardwalk, since we're down here anyway?" she asked.

Wes hesitated, checking his watch. He really should get to the B&B, but maybe his guys could handle it that day without him, allow him to avoid coming face-to-face with Sarah just yet.

And he hadn't really spent a whole lot of time alone with Marissa so far that summer vacation, and she was leaving for Girl Guides camp soon. If she wasn't in a hurry to get back in front of her computer, Wes would take advantage of it.

"Sure, that sounds fun," he said, collecting his gear and heading toward the parking lot, where he put everything in the bed of the truck. Then they headed down the path to the boardwalk on the south beach. It was rockier here than the north beach near the B&B and the waves were bigger—a hot spot for expert surfers, but not kid-friendly for swimming. But it was the hipper, trendier part of Blue Moon Bay with great shops and expensive restaurants with outdoor patios.

Nothing had the same calming effect as the sights, sounds, and smells of the coast. Here in Blue Moon Bay, the pace was slower. No one was in a hurry, no one was demanding anything or expecting anything, and walking along the boardwalk, Wes tried to let all the stress he was under fall away as well. At least temporarily. "What do you want to do first?" he asked Marissa.

"Ice cream, and then how about a sandcastle-building competition on the beach like we used to?" she said.

When Kelly was still alive, family sandcastle competitions were a weekly event in the summer months. Marissa and Kelly would team up and beat him every time. His builds were always structurally sound, but they won on points for creativity with their unique additions like moats and gargoyle statues. "Deal, but I'll warn you—I've been brushing up on my castle-building skills."

She smiled, but then she was quiet as they headed toward the ice cream shop.

"Hey, you okay?" he asked.

"Yeah, I'm good." She paused. "I know it sounds weird, but I can feel Mom here. More so than anywhere else. This was her favorite place to go during the summer." She hesitated. "Do you believe in ghosts?"

Wes thought before responding. "I believe that people have a unique energy that ties them to everything around them and that it exists even once a person is gone. Does that make sense?"

Marissa nodded. "Energy, yeah, I like that. I feel Mom's energy here."

"Well, she had a lot of it." Kelly had been one of the most vibrant, magnetic people Wes had ever known. He'd been drawn to her like everyone else who met her. She was kind and compassionate and had a way of making others feel good just being around her.

Life with Kelly had been nice, easy, and relaxed. They worked well together. He'd loved her and he'd loved the life they'd been building together. Letting her go had been difficult, but he hadn't had a choice, and time had a way of helping him realize the necessity of moving on. Having Marissa in his life certainly made that easier. Striving to be the best version of himself was easy when someone was looking up to him, depending on him.

The chill of air-conditioning and the smell of chocolate syrup hit him as they entered the ice cream shop. The place was packed...mostly teenagers on summer break loitering to talk to their unlucky friends forced to get a job, working behind the counter that summer. Wes had done his own fair share of ice cream scooping as a teen.

"What flavor are you craving today?" he asked, peering into the glass case. The store boasted thirty-two different flavors, and this month's featured one was a tiger tail twist. Orange mango with a black licorice swirl. "That looks interesting."

The fifteen-year-old ice cream scooper sighed. "That's one way to describe it."

Obviously not a best seller.

Marissa wrinkled her nose. "I don't like black licorice. I think I'll stick to my vanilla, chocolate, strawberry triple scoop."

"Triple scoop, huh?"

"Yeah, I'm a kid; I don't have to watch my diet like you do," Marissa teased.

Wes laughed. "I just burned a ton of calories out there riding those waves." Mostly, he stood in the shallow area and made sure the summer camp kids could stand on the board for a few seconds, but he'd skipped breakfast, not having much of an appetite after the crash-and-burn situation of the night before. "I'll have the same," he told the guy behind the counter.

Marissa's eyes widened as the guy handed her the overflowing ice cream cone. Wes accepted his, paid, and they headed back outside. The hardest part would be eating it before the sun turned it into a big melting mess.

Spotting a free picnic table on the sand, Wes nodded toward it as he licked around the base of his cone. "Let's sit for a few minutes," he said. "I can't walk and eat at the same time." The top chocolate scoop looked dangerously, haphazardly placed, and any sudden wrong moves could ruin a good thing.

Kinda like his sudden wrong moves with Sarah the night before. Shit, he'd really messed things up and had no idea what to do next. Would she want to talk about it or pretend it hadn't happened? What did *he* want?

"So what's going on with you and Sarah?"

Wes choked on the ice cream, the creamy vanilla flavor sticking to his throat. He coughed. "Nothing." He coughed again. "What gives you the idea that something's going on?" Marissa had no idea that he'd returned to the B&B the night before...or about the untimely kiss.

She shrugged casually, but her perceptive little nine-year-old gaze was daring him to bullshit her. "Just a vibe, I guess."

Kids obviously noticed and saw more than adults gave them credit for. He wasn't a great liar, and she was the last person on earth he'd want to deceive, but he actually didn't know what was happening between him and Sarah.

"Well, we go way back," he said carefully. "And I do like her..." More than he realized, maybe. The kiss suggested he more than liked her, but he couldn't quite define his feelings. Suddenly he found her hot as hell. She was amazing with his daughter...

"I've always loved Dove's Nest and felt sad when it closed, so I'm glad she's making it better and reopening it. Do you think she might consider staying?" Marissa asked.

Obviously that's what *Marissa* wanted. Wes didn't hate the idea of Sarah staying in Blue Moon Bay, either, but she had her own life goals and a career she was working hard to advance in. Wes knew firsthand what it was like to have dreams derailed, so he didn't think for a second that Sarah should stay. "I'm not sure," he said honestly. "Hey, I know you really like her and like hanging out with her…"

"We have a lot in common," she said.

He turned to face her, his own ice cream forgotten and dripping down his forearm. "Yeah, and that's wonderful. I just don't want you to be too disappointed when she goes back to L.A."

Marissa licked her own dripping ice cream. "She said we'll keep in touch."

Would she want to keep in touch with him as well? Probably not after last night. And did he want to stay in touch? That part was still frustratingly unclear. He'd had the first kiss—best possible kiss—since Kelly, and it had definitely spurred something in him, but a long-distance relationship wouldn't work when he had Marissa to consider.

"Hey, I have an idea—why don't we bring something back for her?" Marissa said. "You know, as a thank-you for letting me work with her."

"Sure," he said. It was actually a good idea. It would also serve as an apology from him about the night before. "What were you thinking?"

"What about one of those?" Marissa said, pointing to the hut behind them. Harrison's Blown Glass. Hanging outside were hand-blown glass ornaments in different shapes and colors, capturing the sun's light and reflecting against the sidewalk and surrounding buildings. "She could hang it in her house in L.A. and it will remind her of home. Of us."

Wes smiled, inhaling the entire melting mess in one big bite and standing as brain freeze threatened to numb his mind. "I think it's perfect. She'll love it."

He may not know how to fix the tension between himself and Sarah, but this apology present was a great first step.

CHAPTER ELEVEN

The next day, a light tap on her bedroom door had Sarah getting up from her laptop and opening it. No one was there, but on the floor sat a pretty box with a tag on it. She picked it up and read: *To Sarah…From Wes and Marissa.*

Wes was here?

Her heart raced a little at the thought of seeing him. The day before, he hadn't shown up and neither had Marissa, and she'd hoped he wouldn't prevent the little girl from continuing to work with her, just because of the obvious tension that would be between them now. So far, she'd helped Marissa with the website and her sports app, but she'd yet to pick the little girl's brain for ideas for her SmartTech proposal, and time was running out.

Opening the box, she took out a beautiful blown-glass ornament and gasped. It was breathtakingly beautiful with various shades of blue mixed in an intoxicating way inside the dome. Her heart warmed as she carried it inside the room and hung it near the window. The colors reflected the sun, and the kaleidoscope effect across the bedroom floor would have had a calming effect if her pulse wasn't frantic.

Hearing their voices downstairs, she took a deep breath before leaving the room. She couldn't avoid him now. Following the sound, she found them in the den. "Hey, did someone leave a gift outside my door?" she asked, trying desperately to sound casual. Normal. But her voice sounded slightly too high-pitched to pull it off.

Marissa didn't seem to notice any tension as she grinned. "Did you like it? We bought it yesterday on the boardwalk."

"It was beautiful and very thoughtful," she said, avoiding Wes's gaze. Her heart was pounding so loud, he had to hear it across the room. "Thank you."

"It was Marissa's idea," he said.

Of course it was.

"I thought it was a nice gesture as well," he said awkwardly.

"What Dad means is, you're welcome," Marissa said with an exasperated look at her father. "We thought it might be a nice reminder to visit us when you go back to the city."

Us? Sarah swallowed hard. "Um, well, actually. I may be staying a little longer than planned."

Wes's head shot up. "You are?"

Was he happy about it or pissed? Impossible to tell by the surprised expression on his slightly sunburned face, but the awkward tension filling the air when his gaze met hers made the room suddenly feel suffocatingly small.

"That's awesome!" Marissa's reaction was better, so Sarah turned her focus to the little girl.

"Yeah. Whitney thought hosting an event here might be nice to show the community the new and improved inn before I put it on the market," she said.

Wes nodded. "That makes sense."

Again, difficult to know how he felt about it. She wasn't great at trusting her gut instincts these days.

"What's the event?" Marissa asked.

"A family reunion. An old high school friend of ours," she said, glancing at Wes. He'd definitely remember Lia. She'd been part of the popular crowd he hung out with. "Lia Jameson."

Marissa shrieked in delight. "Aunt Lia's coming home?"

"Aunt?" Sarah frowned, looking at Wes. Neither Kelly nor Wes was related to Lia as far as she could remember.

"Lia is her godmother," Wes explained.

"Oh." Sarah hadn't realized Wes and Lia were that close. Maybe Lia had been friends with Kelly.

He checked his watch. "We should get going," he told Marissa. "We just wanted to drop off the gift."

"Oh, we're not working today?" Sarah asked Marissa, genuinely disappointed. Again, she hoped the untimely kiss didn't have Wes rethinking letting Marissa hang out with her.

"Dad's going fishing," Marissa said, rolling her eyes.

"Yes, and I've got to be on the road in an hour, so I need to get you home to pack your things. I know you didn't do it this morning when I asked," he said, shooting his daughter a look.

Marissa glanced at Sarah. *Guilty*, she mouthed.

Despite the awkward situation with Wes, Sarah had to suck in her lips to avoid laughing out loud. The kid was really funny as well as smart. She had Sarah cracking up all week with her nerd jokes that only the two of them would get.

"Then I need to drop you off at your grandparents' place," Wes said.

Marissa groaned. "Do I have to stay there all weekend?"

"Yeah. We've talked about this. Aunt Carmen can't be with you at the house all weekend and you can't be alone. And there's a winning rockfish with my name on it," he said.

Ah, the annual fishing trip. Sarah had seen photos posted online every year. It looked more like relaxing, eating, and drinking than actually fishing, but there was always the customary photo of the biggest catch of the weekend.

"But Grandma and Grandpa don't even have Wi-Fi," Marissa said.

Sarah did a double take. "How is that even possible?" The McKennas weren't that old.

Wes sighed. "They have a playset in the backyard and a basketball net in the driveway…"

Marissa looked at Sarah, and she could only offer a sympathetic look back at the child. She'd rather die than be stuck someplace without Wi-Fi, too. She understood Wes's desire for Marissa to get outside more and play with kids her own age in real life, not online, but she could also relate to Marissa's desires. Sarah had always preferred her books and inside, too.

There had to be some sort of balance or compromise they could reach. But she kept her thoughts and opinions to herself. She'd already inserted herself in the middle of their family dynamics enough.

"Wait, I have an idea." Marissa's eyes lit up. "Why don't I stay here at the B&B with Sarah?"

What? Had the air in the room suddenly evaporated? "Oh...um..."

Wes shook his head quickly. "No...that's probably not the best idea. Sarah has a lot to do."

"Exactly! She could use my help. And it will give me time to finish the...surprise I'm working on for you," Marissa said.

The new website was coming along really well. The little girl had used Sarah's camera to secretly capture some photos of the renovations to use, and her write-up on Wes and his company was truly touching. Sarah was eager for Wes to see the end product as well.

Right now, he was staring at her. They both were.

Was he actually leaving this up to her? She didn't know anything about babysitting. An only child, she hadn't even had to take care of a younger sibling before. But it wasn't like the little girl was in diapers or anything, and she could feed herself... Plus, it would be kinda fun having her around the B&B that weekend. Jessica had a wedding out of town, and Whitney was working around the clock as usual. And she desperately needed the child's perspective on the SmartTech Kids app.

Still, she hesitated. They'd been spending a lot of time together already, and Wes didn't look entirely thrilled by the idea.

"Please, Sarah. Save me from a weekend in the

eighties," Marissa said.

Sarah laughed, any resolve weakening at the little girl's plea. How did Wes ever say no to her? "Okay, well, it's fine with me if your dad's okay with it."

They both looked at Wes, and he didn't look completely convinced, but he nodded slowly. "I guess it's okay." He checked his watch. "Well, let's get your things and I'll drop her back here in an hour?" he asked Sarah. The questioning look in his expression reflected her own uncertainty about where they stood, and she had no more answers than he did. But she could save Marissa from boredom that weekend and maybe find some inspiration to try to save her promotion that was slipping away with each failed attempt to wow Gail.

Sarah nodded. "Sounds great."

• • •

He was going to be late for check-in if he didn't leave now. Still, Wes lingered on the front porch of the B&B almost an hour later. "Did you pack enough clothes?" he asked Marissa, eyeing her Minnie Mouse suitcase in her hand. The one they'd bought for her first trip to Disneyland when she was four and the one she always took on sleepovers.

"Yes."

"Toothbrush?"

She nodded.

"Toothpaste?"

"I assumed Sarah had some," she said, looking at

Sarah for confirmation.

Sarah nodded.

"Your nighttime retainer? The dentist said the grinding was causing cavities."

"Yes, Dad. I have it. I packed everything just like if I was going to Grandma and Grandpa's," Marissa said, her small hands against his stomach, pushing him off the deck and down the steps. "Go. If traffic is bad, you'll be late."

Wow, she was eager to get rid of him. Guilt washed over him. Years without a female role model in her life might be taking their toll. Or maybe it was just having someone in her life with shared interests, someone she could bounce ideas off and have them understand, someone she could learn a lot from.

Maybe this time with Sarah would be a good thing… but then what?

Could he, should he try to protect Marissa from potential disappointment and heartache by cautioning her not to get too attached, or would that be teaching her to be guarded, closed off in relationships?

Where was the parenting book on how to deal with situations like this?

"Dad. Go," Marissa said when he continued to stand there like a statue.

"Okay…I'm going." But he paused at the base of the steps. "You sure?" he asked Marissa. Sure, she liked Sarah, but the woman was still virtually a stranger. They'd only really met a week ago. Would Marissa be comfortable with her for two full days? What about at night?

"Yes, I'm sure," Marissa said confidently. Confidently annoyed.

He glanced at Sarah next. "*You* sure?" She seemed less so, but she nodded.

"Absolutely. Go. We're going to have a great weekend," she said with what might have been forced enthusiasm—he couldn't be sure. He really couldn't read her at all. Seeing her for the first time after the kiss had been as awkward as he'd thought it would be. He was torn between wanting to talk about it and wanting to pretend it hadn't happened. Torn between wanting to avoid her at all costs and grabbing her and getting another taste of those lips.

Luckily, he'd been saved from having to make any decisions because Marissa was around, listening and watching. Closely.

"Okay…" He didn't move. His gaze shifted from his daughter to Sarah and back again.

"Go!" they both said in unison.

Right. He was worrying for nothing.

The two of them would probably be glued to computer monitors all weekend and not even notice the time passing. It wasn't the ideal way he'd like Marissa to spend her weekend, but she'd have a much better time there than she would at her grandparents' place.

Unfortunately, his in-laws hadn't been thrilled about this change of events. Carolyn's "Well, if you think that's a wise decision…" response had him questioning it even more. Especially when he couldn't exactly dismiss the woman's concerns about Sarah's potential feelings for him, since his own feelings for Sarah were confusing the hell out of him. That kiss had been anything but friendly. But this was about Marissa, and how he was raising his daughter was his call to make.

"Why are you still here?" Marissa asked.

"Okay, I'm gone," he said, actually walking toward his truck this time. "I'll have my cell. Reception is usually pretty good at the lodge, a little dicey out on the water, but call Bridget at the desk of Blue Moon Bay Sportfishing if there's an emergency; they can radio out to the boat."

Both of them looked bored as he rambled on.

"Okay...bye," he said. "Love you...Marissa," he said quickly, as though he needed to clarify, then feeling like a fool, he climbed into the truck and gave a quick wave as he backed out of the driveway.

He sighed as he rested his arm outside the window and honked the horn twice as he drove away.

Marissa would be fine. Sarah was the one he should be worried about. Nine-year-olds had a lot of energy, and Sarah had never been around a lot of kids. But so far, she'd been a pro at keeping Marissa both occupied and content while he'd worked, and he knew he could trust her.

What was actually bothering him was that he'd almost wanted to stay and hang out with them that weekend instead of going fishing. Which was a new feeling. He looked forward to this weekend's fishing trip every year: getting together with his best friends from high school for the once-a-year boys' weekend.

They rented out the private charter, and there was more fooling around and drinking beer than fishing, but their annual competition for the biggest rockfish added a competitiveness to the weekend and kept them all coming back year after year.

He cranked the music as he drove along the coast toward Blue Moon Bay Sportfishing. It was about forty minutes outside of town, but the owners were originally from Blue Moon Bay and had kept the name when they'd relocated down the coast years before. The sun reflecting off the ocean and the mild breeze blowing through the cabin of the truck made him feel good. Better than he had in a while.

Pulling up into the lot of the dockside sportfishing outfitter almost an hour later, he grabbed his tackle box, rod, and reel and headed down to the pier where the other men were waiting.

"Hey, man...thought we were going to have to leave without you," Phil Parker, his best friend from high school, said as he approached. The man was dressed in a pair of fishing coveralls, rubber boots, and a Boonie hat, looking the part of a fisherman, at least, even though he held the record for no rockfish caught six years straight. The guy had as much interest in fishing as Wes had in crunching numbers, but his accountant-desk-job friend came to hang out with the old gang every year.

Wes returned his fist bump and waved to several of the others still inside the shop, buying new gear and bait. "Ran a little late dropping off Marissa."

"How is she?"

"Nine going on thirty," Wes said as he climbed on board the charter.

"I hear that," Phil said. Phil was on his second marriage with seven children in their new blended family. All girls, ranging in age from eleven to six months old. If Wes enjoyed this free-from-obligations weekend, Phil needed it to survive.

"How's the family?" he asked.

"Good. The oldest ones are doing a spa weekend with their mom, and the baby is with the grandparents." He reached into the cooler and handed Wes a beer.

"Thanks." He cracked the seal and took a gulp as he stared out at the water. "Perfect day for this." The conditions looked pristine out on the water. Soft waves crashed against the boat as they baited their hooks with squid, attached the appropriate amount of weight, and prepared to drop their lines to the bottom of the ocean floor once the rest of the group boarded and the captain set sail.

"Hey, man, any day away from work is the perfect day," Phil said, sitting on top of the cooler.

"How's business?"

"Same old thing." He shrugged. "Steady work, so I can't really complain. I hear you're renovating Dove's Nest."

"Yep. Luckily I was able to talk Sarah Lewis into not immediately demolishing it."

"Sarah Lewis?" Phil asked with a note of interest in his voice. His buddy had once had a crush on Sarah in junior high. Unfortunately, Sarah hadn't returned the interest. Or she'd been oblivious to it. Or she'd had a crush on *him*, the way Carolyn had suspected. Did she still? "She's back in town?" Phil asked.

Back in town and unexpectedly messing with *his* emotions this time around. "She inherited the place from Dove."

Phil's eyebrows rose above his sunglasses. "Odd choice."

Wes shrugged. "I don't know. I had originally thought so, too, but I'm starting to think Dove knew exactly what she was doing leaving it to Sarah. She's upgrading it to be competitive in the tourism market, and now she's planning to stick around a few more weeks to host a reopening event."

A development he hadn't at all expected. Her announcement that day was one he didn't exactly hate. Marissa was ecstatic, but he'd almost been hoping she'd be leaving soon so he could shake off this unexpected attraction to her and get on with life.

Yet, some part of him was happy she was sticking around a bit longer, even if he was determined not to act on his attraction. "For someone outside her comfort zone, she's kinda killing it," he said.

"Uh-oh," Phil said, studying him, one hand shielding the sunlight from his eyes.

"What?"

"Something going on there?"

His buddy had always been perceptive. "Nah...she's just an old friend." One with delicious lips and a rocking body. He took a swig of beer. "And Marissa's really taken to her...the whole computer technology thing has bonded them, I guess." He paused. "She's actually spending the weekend there with Sarah," he said as casually as possible.

But Phil's warning, knowing look had him even more uneasy. "Be careful, buddy."

Be careful...Why did it feel like that warning was coming a little too late?

CHAPTER TWELVE

Empty ice cream bowls, pop cans, and bags of Doritos littered the desk in the den between their laptops, and they hadn't changed out of their pajamas all day. If she was being completely honest, it had been one of the best days Sarah had had in a long time.

"This app is incredible. I can't believe your dad won't use it," Sarah said, her mouth full of Doritos as Marissa displayed the features and functionality of the coaches' app she'd developed. Sarah had helped her fine-tune a few things that day, and they'd uploaded it to the app store under a new account Sarah created for her a few hours ago. It was linked to her bank account for now, but she'd talk to Wes about transferring it to Marissa's once he got back.

"He says his paper and pen are more reliable," Marissa said, dipping her finger in her empty ice cream bowl and then licking the melted chocolate sauce.

"Well, they can't be hacked, I guess," Sarah said.

Over her career, she'd met a lot of technology resisters. People like Wes who were reluctant to get on board with online trends or systems that could make their life easier. For most it was fear of change, and for others it was the inability to learn something new. Sarah suspected that with Wes, it was the former. He liked consistency and routines. He trusted things he could rely on. But if he gave this app a chance, she knew he'd quickly appreciate the efficiency.

"He doesn't like technology because he says no amount of science and technology was able to save my mom," Marissa said quietly.

Sarah's stomach lurched. This was the first time Marissa had mentioned Kelly or her illness, and she wasn't exactly sure what to say. She'd let Marissa lead. If she wanted to talk about it, Sarah would listen. "I can see how he could feel that way," she said gently.

Wes and Marissa had been through the unimaginable, losing a wife and a mother. Sarah wouldn't even pretend to know how hard that must have been. And it could be easy to lose faith in medical advances and technology when they hadn't worked to save the most important person in their lives.

Marissa sighed. "I was little, so I don't remember a lot about it, but I remember how sad Dad was all the time."

Sarah nodded. "I was very sorry to hear about it."

Marissa crunched on a chip and looked pensive for a moment before asking, "Did you know my mom?"

Sarah nodded as she curled her legs under her on the chair. "We had different friends in school, but we had some classes together, and she was on the debate team with me. I remember her personality the most. She was as vibrant as her red hair." Kelly was fiery and bold and brave. Everyone liked her. It was impossible not to—she had a magnetic personality. Her presence lit up a room, and she was kindhearted and nice to everyone.

"People say I look like her," Marissa said.

"You do. So much," Sarah said, reaching out to brush

a strand of the little girl's hair out of her face. "But I see a lot of your dad in you, too."

"Really?"

"Yeah. Mainly your facial expressions, and of course your smart-assery," she said with a grin.

It made Sarah feel good that Marissa trusted her, but it also made her slightly uneasy. They were getting close, and she'd miss her when she left town and went back to L.A. Leaving after high school had been easy, and she'd been so busy in college and then working to prove herself in a male-dominated industry that she hadn't paused long enough to acknowledge any void of personal connections she had in her life. She maintained her friendships with Whitney and Jessica as best she could, but even those had started to slide. Being back here was making her realize that maybe she was missing out on some things. Important things.

"So you said you needed my help with your work. What's up?" Marissa asked, suddenly all business.

Sarah grinned. "Well, I'm kinda stuck and I'm hoping your perspective as a nine-year-old can help. You use apps all the time, so if you could have an app that did anything, what would it be?"

Marissa frowned, tapping her finger against her lips. "Message friends? Upload videos to YouTube?"

Sarah nodded. "Got those features already."

"Play games."

"Yep…" Maybe those things really were the main focus for kids. "Anything else?"

She thought for a long moment; then she nodded

slowly. "Yeah, what about something that organized toy collections digitally?"

Sarah's ears perked up, and she pulled her laptop closer. "I'm listening."

"Well, there's a Funko app that allows people to add their Funkos to their collection, and it gives the value of the toys and allows people to add new ones to the wish list, that kind of thing."

Sarah nodded. It was good, but that app already existed. How could she make it different? Relevant to SmartTech Kids. "It's good, but unfortunately it already exists."

Marissa pointed a finger at her, her left eyebrow raised as though she were on to something. "But only for Funkos. I collect Beanie Babies and I know some of them are worth big cash. I'd love to scan the barcodes and get an idea of the overall value... And my dad has old football cards. Some are even signed." The more she talked, the more excited she sounded, and Sarah caught the enthusiasm as well.

"That's actually really great." She typed several notes into her proposal file as she listened. "I'm sure there are a million things kids collect. SmartTech could apply that technology to a lot of different things." As a kid, she'd collected Barbie dolls. Expensive, special-edition ones. Never played with them, kept them in their boxes. They were stored at her parents' house in Phoenix, but it would have been great to have an app like that as a kid to organize her collection and determine its value. "Marissa, I knew you were a genius," she said.

Marissa beamed at the praise. "And you could also add a feature that lets kids send their wish list to adults for Christmas and birthday gift ideas."

"Like an online registry of sorts." Sarah typed frantically, ideas finally starting to take shape. She sat back, and her shoulders sagged in relief. "Thank you so much. I think you might have just saved my ass."

Marissa laughed. "Think I could apply at that company you work for?"

Sarah wasn't sure she'd want Marissa stuck working for a company the way she was. Corporations had a way of limiting their employees' creativity. "I'm sure you could do anything you set your mind and heart to."

The app store open on Marissa's laptop screen chimed, and they both turned to look at it.

"Oh my God—someone downloaded my app," Marissa said, awe in her voice. "It worked. It actually worked."

Sarah turned the laptop toward her and scanned the screen. Someone had definitely downloaded it. "That's awesome! I told you this thing was great."

Marissa jumped up out of her chair, and her tiny arms went around Sarah's neck. "Thank you, Sarah. You're the best."

Sarah's entire world seemed to shift as emotions strangled her and made it impossible to respond. Damn. She could deny her feelings for Wes all day long, but there was no denying that she was falling for his little girl.

How inconvenient.

...

Wes knocked on the door of the B&B early Sunday evening, then opened it and went inside. He hadn't been home to shower and change yet, coming straight from fishing, and he was painfully aware that he probably smelled of bait and fish guts, but he didn't want to impose on Sarah longer than necessary.

Phil's warning wasn't far from his mind. He did need to be careful. His own feelings aside, he didn't want his daughter getting hurt when Sarah went back to the city. He appreciated what she was doing for Marissa—maybe a little too much—but maybe he needed to put some distance there.

His little girl had been through enough loss for one lifetime, and she'd feel the sting when Sarah left. Sarah had the best of intentions saying they'd keep in touch, but once she got back to her life in the city, he wasn't sure she'd really be able to follow through.

"Hello?" he called out as he entered the foyer.

No answer.

He made his way through the rooms and the kitchen, but they weren't there. Taking his cell phone out of his pocket, he texted Sarah.

Hey, I'm here. Where you guys at?

Backyard came her reply.

Outside. That was good. He'd almost expected to find them still in their pajamas from Friday night, buried under takeout containers and bleary-eyed from staring at a computer screen.

Wes made his way to the backyard and stopped short.

Was his daughter actually playing soccer? Without his coaching and urging and begging?

Marissa ran around the gazebo in the middle of the yard with obviously a new soccer ball and Sarah was using her cell phone to record her.

What were they doing?

He walked across the grass toward them, and Sarah turned to face him. She wasn't in pajamas, but the yoga pants and tank top...sans bra was a close second. The thin, body-hugging fabric accentuated her hourglass shape, and the spaghetti straps of the tank top made her collarbone and sexy shoulders that much more pronounced. The nipples visible through the material had his mouth feeling like a desert.

So much for two days out on the ocean to clear his head. One sighting of her had his heart and mind a complete mess again.

She folded her arms across her chest, and he lifted his gaze quickly, embarrassed to be busted checking her out. But then, her messy ponytail and face free of makeup actually took his breath away. She was naturally pretty, and her lack of vanity was attractive as hell.

He was in trouble. "Hey," he said, his voice slightly hoarse. "What are you two doing?"

"Testing out a new element to add to my app," Marissa said as she kicked the ball toward him.

Wes stopped it with his foot and glanced at her. "The coaching app?"

Marissa beamed proudly as she said, "Yep. Sarah uploaded it to the app store yesterday, and there've been twenty-six downloads so far."

Twenty-six downloads in a day. Wow... "That's awesome, sweetheart." He really had no idea, but she seemed happy about it, and that's what mattered.

"We're only selling it for a dollar, so I'm not rich yet, but soon, right, Sarah?"

Sarah laughed. "Absolutely. Especially if we can figure out this new feature the reviewers mentioned."

"Reviewers?"

Sarah turned to face him, looking just as hyped about it as his daughter, and his pulse raced even faster. Her passion for this technology stuff was surprisingly turning him on even more. "Yeah, users are providing feedback, and Marissa is listening. We're trying to upload an imaging tool that will track a player's speed with the ball, kicking strength, that kind of thing."

"An app can do that?"

Marissa rolled her eyes at him. "Have you been listening to me at all?"

Apparently not. Maybe he needed to start.

That feature alone could help determine player position quickly within a team. But he wasn't quite ready to jump on board yet. "Hey, do I get a hug?"

Marissa moved closer but then crinkled her nose. "Oh my God, Dad, you stink."

He cleared his throat, embarrassed as he glanced at Sarah, who took several steps away from him as well and covered her own nose. "I haven't been home yet...I thought maybe you were ready to go."

"We actually still have work to do. Right, Sarah?" Marissa asked.

Sarah nodded. "I'm happy to keep going on this."

She was incredible. As much as the grandparents adored Marissa, after two days, they were usually exhausted and happy to hand her back. Sarah seemed to be enjoying the time as much as his daughter was.

"Okay, I'll head home and shower and then come back... If it's okay she stays a little longer?" His question was directed at Sarah, but Marissa answered.

"It's fine."

He shot her a look. "I was asking Sarah."

Sarah nodded. "It's fine. No rush."

Marissa ran off with the ball again, and Wes shook his head. "Two years of trying and failing to get her to show any interest in sports, and you were able to do it in a weekend."

She shrugged. "Just needed the right motivation, I guess."

"Yeah, I guess." Or maybe Sarah was an even better role model for his daughter than he'd already thought.

• • •

Wes still wasn't sure how he felt about that hours later as he put Marissa to bed. He was happy that she was being more active, so did it matter the motivation? He was more disappointed in himself that he hadn't figured it out. And he owed Marissa an apology.

"Hey, I'm sorry I was reluctant to use your app," he said, pulling the bedsheets up over her as she fluffed her pillows behind her head.

"It's okay. But before it was free; now you'll have to buy it," she said with a smirk.

"Do I at least get a family discount?"

"I'm a small business owner, Dad, with a new start-up. I can't be giving my product away."

He laughed. "Good answer." He needed to adopt his daughter's business sense.

"So did you catch anything this weekend?" Marissa asked.

Other than feelings for Sarah Lewis that he'd been trying hard to write off as just attraction to a beautiful woman? "A few small ones. Nothing noteworthy," he said. He sat in the chair beside her bed and turned on the lamp. "You had fun…with Sarah?"

"It was so much fun. We finished the app, then we got a lot of work done on our secret project." Her grin was full of secrecy. "And I was able to help Sarah with one of her work projects, too."

"That was nice of you, and I can't wait to hear more about this secret project whenever you're ready to tell me." He paused. "Just remember that Sarah has a life in L.A. She's only here in Blue Moon Bay for a little while, and then she's planning to go back." He'd do well to remember that, too.

"She might decide to stay," she said.

Wes frowned. "Did she say that?" Was Sarah changing her mind about selling? She couldn't actually be contemplating keeping Dove's Nest and running it herself.

"No. I just thought she might be enjoying being back home."

"I'm sure she is, but I think her plan is to go back," he said gently.

"But anything can happen, so who knows, right?"

Wes sighed. "Who knows," he said reluctantly. "Get some sleep, okay?"

He stood and turned off the lamp. After a good-night hug, he headed toward the bedroom door.

"Hey, Dad, I was thinking—if I'm going to ever have a stepmom someday, it'd be cool if it was Sarah."

He nearly wiped out on the pile of books on the bedroom floor. Stepmom? Where was that coming from?

"Sarah and I are just…friends." Friends who'd shared an amazing kiss a few nights ago. A friend he couldn't stop thinking about. And a friend whose braless state earlier that day had had him almost drooling with lust.

Yeah, sure, they were just friends.

"I'm just saying that I'm throwing Sarah's name into the hat of possible options," she said with a sly smile.

Damn, his daughter had noticed the connection and chemistry between him and Sarah. Had Sarah said anything about him that weekend? "There's not even a hat," he said gently. "Let alone options."

"Then it should be an easy win for her," Marissa said.

"Rissa…" How did he explain to her where he was emotionally on the whole "moving on and dating" thing when he didn't quite know where he was on that himself?

"I know you like her, Dad. You can admit it."

She'd suddenly become a little matchmaker. She'd never shown any interest in him dating or finding someone before now. Maybe it was her age and the length of time since losing her mom that had her feeling a void. Or was it because it was Sarah? "I do like Sarah. Night, sweetheart," he said, turning off the light and leaving the room.

In the kitchen, he opened the fridge and took out a beer. He twisted off the cap and leaned against the counter as he took a swig.

Maybe letting Marissa spend the weekend was a bad decision if his goal was to protect her from disappointment in the long run. Especially since she was envisioning the two of them getting together.

He ran a hand through his hair and sighed.

And unfortunately, his daughter was right. Winning his heart could be an easy victory for Sarah if he let it happen.

CHAPTER THIRTEEN

Sarah's fingers flew over her keyboard that evening as she revised her proposal for SmartTech Kids. Marissa was a genius. A collectibles feature was the perfect addition. Kids loved to collect things—sports cards, mini-figurines, dolls—and this new generation also loved the idea of making money.

She'd only hit Send on the email to her boss when her cell phone rang three minutes later. Gail's number lighting up the call display had her heart pounding.

Did her boss love it or hate it?

"Hi, Gail," she said as she answered.

"Finally!"

Sarah breathed a sigh of relief.

"This collectibles thing is unique and cool," she said. "How did you come up with it?"

Sarah ignored the implied suspicion in her boss's voice. "A friend's daughter actually suggested it. She collects Beanie Babies…"

"Well, it works," Gail said. "I hate to admit it, but maybe this time away was good for you. Helped you expand your limited creative side a bit more."

Even a compliment contained an insult. "Thank you," she mumbled. "Hey, Gail…I was wondering whether or not you'd had time to review those other app ideas I submitted last month?" If her boss was in a good mood, now might be the time to ask for the freedom to work on some of her own ideas.

"I did."

Sarah waited.

"Honestly, Sarah, I was underwhelmed. Let's focus on this SmartTech account. Don't divide your focus."

Sarah resisted the urge to argue that she could do both, and while the SmartTech Kids account might not be her strong suit, she could really come up with something great for the telecommunications side of the company, given the opportunity. Arguing with Gail was futile. Her boss's open-door policy simply meant she was always working and expected everyone else to be as well. "Okay."

"I'll see a complete revised proposal tonight?"

Sarah checked the time on her phone. It was already ten o'clock. "Absolutely," she said, disconnecting the call.

Sitting back, she sighed. Would she ever get the chance to work on projects she was passionate about while employed by Gail? Would she get to demonstrate what she could do? Or would she constantly be striving to prove herself without the end rewards she really wanted?

The downstairs doorbell ringing made her frown. Who was here this late?

Grabbing her cardigan, she slid her arms into the sleeves and pulled it around her body as she left the bedroom and descended the stairs.

The doorbell echoed throughout the inn again.

"I'm coming," she said as she hurried to the door. She peered out through the window in the side of the door and saw a vehicle parked in the circular driveway, but she couldn't see anyone. She cautiously unlocked the door and opened it.

Lia Jameson stood on the step, two large suitcases behind her. What the hell was she doing here? The reunion wasn't for another two weeks.

"Surprise!" Lia said, opening her arms wide for a hug.

It was indeed a surprise. And not entirely a good one.

• • •

His beer untouched on the table in front of him, Wes shifted his weight on the wobbly barstool near the back of Trent's Tavern later that evening. Carmen had stopped by to work on some accounting for the business and had offered to babysit, so he could accept his brother-in-law's last-minute, late-night invite for drinks.

The local hot spot on Main Street was quiet for a Sunday evening, and Wes appreciated the low-key vibe as his thoughts continued to return to his conversation with Marissa.

A stepmom. Wow.

"You okay, man?" Dustin asked, sliding his gaze away from the SportsNet game recap playing on the flatscreen above the bar.

"Yeah," he said, then turned his cell phone toward Dustin now. "Check out this app."

Dustin's eyes widened over the rim of his own beer bottle, and he coughed as he choked on a mouthful. "I'm sorry, did you just say app? I would have bet big money that you didn't even know the term."

His brother-in-law might have won that bet a few weeks ago, but lately he was really making an effort to get on board with the whole technology thing that Marissa was so caught up in. He was starting to understand more of the appeal.

"It's the one Marissa designed for coaches," he said. He'd bought it and downloaded it that evening and was still trying to figure out exactly how to use it, but so far he'd entered in all the names of his Little League players and the dates of their upcoming fall games.

Dustin took the phone, and his smile was wide as he scrolled his finger over the screen. "That little girl of yours is a genius. She must have gotten it from my sister," he said.

"Obviously," Wes said. "But it really is useful, right? I mean, no more clipboards or having to look up player positions…it's all there next to each player's name. Emergency contacts are listed, and I can call them by clicking the phone number on the screen…" He was in awe, and he'd barely scratched the surface of what the app could do.

"Damn right it's useful. This thing can even track players' speed and ball-handling techniques. Where did she learn to upload it for sale?" Dustin asked, playing around with the app's features.

"Sarah helped her. Apparently, I have to stop by the bank tomorrow to open a bank account for her." He chuckled at the thought. Marissa was growing up so fast, and so far that summer, she'd learned a lot from Sarah, but more importantly, her own confidence had grown.

Sarah was supportive, offering advice but letting Marissa experiment with her own ways of doing things.

Sarah acted like a sounding board for his daughter's ideas and helped to enhance them. She encouraged and celebrated the wins with Marissa and helped her come up with solutions to the challenges. That meant more to Wes than he could ever verbalize.

"The owner of the B&B? The one Rissa couldn't stop talking about at dinner?"

"That's her. She works in technology and offered Marissa an opportunity to work with her the last few weeks." He peeled the label on his beer bottle.

"That was nice of her," Dustin said, eyeing him. "Smart and caring—makes sense that Marissa would get attached."

Wes could hear the implication in Dustin's voice, so he cleared his throat and nodded toward the phone. "Anyway, that thing is great, huh?"

"This is really impressive for a nine-year-old. Pretty soon she'll be making more coin than you." He handed the phone back with a grin.

Wes stared at the app. In just a few days, it had been downloaded almost a hundred times. Marissa was over the moon about it, and he'd seen her drawing of her L.A. mansion that she planned to buy once she was a millionaire from her technological creation.

It wasn't about the fact that she was making money off something she'd created that had him feeling so freaking proud. It was the fact that despite resistance— mostly from him in the form of lack of understanding— she'd persevered and continued to work toward something she was passionate about.

As much as he worried about her, he knew she would be just fine.

His own life, he was less certain about. Once the inn renovations were done, he didn't have any big projects scheduled for the fall. Carmen's visit that evening had definitely been to remind him of that fact.

"Have you reached out to that real estate agent regarding the office space on Main Street yet?" Dustin asked, as though reading the direction of Wes's thoughts.

Wes shook his head as he took a gulp of his beer. "Not yet."

"Look, man, you need to start taking risks. Come into the bank and let's look at some options," Dustin said.

Borrowing from the bank to secure the space didn't appeal to him. What if business continued to be slow and he defaulted on the loan? Every opportunity he'd ever taken had been calculated on low risk. Starting the company had been using his savings from his football career. That money was gone, and he needed to make sure Marissa's future was taken care of. "I don't know…"

Dustin nodded but gave him a look. "So you're going to let your daughter put herself out there and take risks, but you're not willing to?"

Dustin had a point. He wouldn't be a great role model for Marissa if he was too afraid to take the necessary chances for a better future. In business and with his heart, too, for that matter…

He swallowed another gulp of the warm beer. "Buy the app, support your niece, wise guy." He paused. "And schedule me in for an appointment next week."

CHAPTER FOURTEEN

This was how she was going to die. Which, given her current situation, might be a welcome respite.

Sarah's lungs hurt as she gasped for air the next morning, following far behind Lia down Main Street in what the other woman had called a "leisurely" jogging pace. The last time Sarah had jogged was…so long ago, it had been blocked from memory.

Lia stopped in front of Delicious Delicacies and waved at her to hurry up.

Sarah resisted the urge to offer her own less friendly hand gesture as she came up next to her. Lia's surprise arrival would have been annoying at any time, but last night's timing wasn't ideal. After the call with her boss, Sarah hadn't exactly been in a great mood to catch up and start planning the reunion with her former high school frenemy. She'd had the proposal to submit to Gail and in truth, she hadn't really thought she'd have to help Lia plan the event. Just offer the venue. But apparently, the other woman was expecting her to be involved.

Sarah placed her hands on her knees and bent at the waist, wincing at the pain radiating through her rib cage.

"I take it you're not a jogger?" Lia said, not even the slightest bit out of breath.

"I prefer…being able to…breathe," Sarah said. Her legs were jelly and her mouth was a desert. She needed water. Lots of water.

Lia's fake look of concern only irritated her more. "You really shouldn't neglect your health, Sarah. You're not getting any younger, you know."

"We're...the same age," she said through clenched teeth.

"My FitTrack scale would have a hard time knowing it," she said, opening the bakery door and heading inside.

This time, Sarah didn't resist the hand gesture as Lia allowed the door to swing back toward her.

"Oh my God, it smells like heaven in here."

From the kitchen, the sound of a tray being dropped revealed Jessica had heard the familiar soprano voice. A second later, her friend pushed through the swinging door of the kitchen, nearly colliding with a panting Sarah.

"Water. Lots of water," Sarah said, reaching into the fridge for a bottle and twisting off the plastic cap.

"Why are you sweating?" Jessica asked, removing her cat-patterned oven mitts.

Sarah held up a finger as she guzzled half the bottle. "Lia thought it would be fun to jog here," she said through clenched teeth as they headed into the front of the bakery. After pulling an all-nighter on the SmartTech proposal, Lia banging on her bedroom door at eight a.m. to rise and shine only two hours after Sarah had crawled into bed had been met with many protests. Only Lia's persistence that they needed to secure the event's desserts ASAP and the promise of baked goods had finally gotten Sarah out of bed.

"All four miles?" Jessica looked as though the idea was ridiculous as well, and it justified Sarah's own lack of motivation to exercise.

"I usually start my day with five," Lia said, hurrying forward to hug Jessica. "So great to see you."

Over Lia's shoulder, Sarah's wide eyes silently pleaded with Jessica to take over occupying the woman. Since the night before, she'd been glued to Sarah's hip. Reminiscing about the old days was a lot less fun when two people remembered those days in two completely different ways. Lia's memory had seemed to block out the competitiveness between the two of them... Then again, being the one who won all the time might have rewired Lia's brain to see things differently in hindsight.

"I thought the event wasn't for another two weeks," Jessica was saying to Lia, her eyes watering slightly as she looked to be repressing a sneeze.

Must be by the slightly too strong perfume Lia wore. Sarah had been sneezing all morning. She was tempted to put up a SCENT-FREE ZONE sign in the B&B. "She got here early...to plan. Isn't that great?" she said, still struggling to catch her breath.

Lia glanced at her. "You look like you ran the Boston marathon—sweat is dripping down your forehead, and your legs are barely supporting your weight. This is not a good sign, Sarah."

In contrast, Lia looked like she'd just come from the salon, her high ponytail swinging back and forth and her makeup still perfectly in place.

Lia stretched a hamstring, and it was impossible not

to marvel at how tiny she was. Her thighs were the size of Sarah's calves. Her expensive matching running outfit hugged her size zero body, as if it had been painted on. And Sarah hadn't even realized women could have such defined abs.

"I really want everything to be perfect. The desserts will need to include some vegan and sugar-free options. Mal and I are climbing Mount Kenya in January and we're in training." She reached behind her to stretch one hamstring, then the other one.

Sarah was still trying to get air into her lungs.

"Wow. Mount Kenya. That's ambitious," Jessica said.

"No. They have a full...very detailed training schedule. Lia explained it all to me last night," Sarah said, giving up pretenses and slumping onto a stool in front of the counter. Otherwise, she thought her legs might give out from beneath her anyway.

"Preparation and planning are the keys to success when taking on challenges," Lia said as though repeating something she'd read on a Facebook meme. "We climbed Everest on our honeymoon."

Didn't most couples lounge on a beach somewhere sipping cocktails and making love in the afternoon? That was the way Sarah planned on spending hers if she ever got married. An image of Wes's bare torso flashed in her mind, and she forced it away.

"Seriously? You went rock climbing on your honeymoon?" Jessica asked as a timer sounded in the kitchen and the smell of cinnamon rolls made Sarah's mouth water.

"Yeah. Didn't you see the pictures I posted on Facebook?" Lia finished stretching and yanked her dark hair free of her ponytail, shaking it loose around her thin, muscular shoulders. Not even so much as a ripple appeared in the dark locks from the elastic band.

If Sarah took her hair out of her ponytail holder right now, she'd have a huge lump in the back of her head all day.

"No, sorry, no Facebook account," Jessica said.

Jessica preferred face-to-face connections. She always insisted on FaceTime phone calls and said texting couldn't replace an actual conversation with a friend, while social media seemed to be an addiction for most. She'd survived this long without having an online presence besides her bakery website, and Sarah had given up trying to convert her friend.

Obviously Lia thought Jessica was a bit too out there. "How is that possible?"

"Jess is one of those weirdos who doesn't need constant validation," Sarah said, shrugging. "I know, bizarre, right?"

"I see you caught your breath finally. Good, because we're jogging back," Lia told her. "Anyway, Jess, I have pics on my phone I'll show you." She pulled her phone out of who knew where, and Sarah frowned as she examined her own stretchy workout pants but couldn't find a pocket anywhere. Maybe splurging on a big name brand was worth the price… They probably made Lia's ass look better than it actually was as well.

That's what she'd tell herself.

Jessica moved around to the other side of the counter to get a better look at Lia's photos.

"Ugh," Lia said, unlocking her phone screen with her thumbprint.

"What's wrong?"

"Nothing, just a text from my brother, Mitch…" she read quickly. "He's not going to make it to the reunion after all. He has to be in Cambodia until December." Her beaming smile made Jessica frown.

"Isn't that a bad thing—that he'll miss it?" Jessica asked, shooting a look at Sarah above Lia's head.

She hates him, Sarah mouthed.

"Oh, of course," Lia said quickly, but her smile didn't completely disappear. "He'll be missed."

Not by her, by the sound of it.

"I would just feel bad for those sick kids if he abandoned them early, that's all," she said tightly.

It didn't escape Sarah's notice that she could have planned the reunion for a time that Mitch could actually attend. Leaving him out on purpose, maybe? Not to have the spotlight stolen from her for a change? Everyone loved Mitch. He was almost ten years older than they were, so they were never close friends, but having an older brother who looked out for her was just another thing Lia had that Sarah had envied. Lia didn't count herself quite so lucky, having to fight for her parents' attention and approval.

"He's working over there?" Jessica asked.

Lia nodded. "Doctors Without Borders. He gave up his practice in L.A. two years ago to travel with them."

"Wow, that's incredibly noble..." Jessica stopped. Lia's glare was absolutely paralyzing. "You were going to show me pics of Everest," she said.

"Yes, I was," Lia said, scrolling through thousands of photos—a lot of selfies—to find them.

The phone on the wall rang, and Lia squinted as though not recognizing it. "Is that a landline?"

Jessica laughed. Everyone gave her heck for it, but her friend didn't care. She refused to put her cell phone number on her website or business card, claiming work-life balance was important. She said customers could place their orders online or leave a message. Sarah had mad respect for her friend's ability to run a successful business without becoming a workaholic. She'd love to know the secret.

Maybe if she didn't work for someone else, she could set her own boundaries, make her own hours, take on the clients and projects *she* wanted...

But Jessica had put years into building up her business and reputation in town. Could Sarah really take that leap of faith?

. . .

Wes fixed his tie as he waited in the lobby of the bank on Main Street. Dustin hadn't wasted any time getting him in to see the loan manager, and while he appreciated his brother-in-law's help, he couldn't shake the nagging uncertainty in the pit of his stomach.

He'd already lost the office space once before. He'd

hate to get in there and have to close up again if things didn't go as planned, if his goal to expand his business failed. He had a good reputation in town, and people in the community would support him, but would that be enough without actual construction accounts?

Maybe he shouldn't have gotten there so early; waiting was torture. He wasn't concerned about the loan. Despite his financial setbacks, he still maintained good credit, and he had a small retirement savings account he could use to secure the loan, but that would be a risk he wasn't sure he was prepared to take.

"Wes?" The loan officer appeared in the lobby. Shawn Loder had worked at the Blue Moon Bay branch since Wes had applied for his mortgage years before. The man wasn't originally from town, having grown up in L.A. but he'd been in town so long, no one held that against him.

"Hey, Shawn, thanks for seeing me," he said as he stood and, after wiping his palm on the leg of his pants, extended a hand to the other man.

Shawn nodded enthusiastically as he pumped Wes's hand somewhat longer than necessary. "Yes, yes! Come on into my office."

Wes entered, and Shawn closed the door behind him.

"Have a seat," he said.

Wes sat in the soft, plush leather chair and immediately noticed all the items on Shawn's desk with the Rams logo. His mug, the picture frame holding a photo of Shawn at a Rams game wearing a team jersey and holding a foam finger, a plush toy, and a water bottle.

"Fan of the Rams?"

Shawn laughed as he sat behind the desk. "Guilty." Lifting his foot into the air, he pulled up the leg of his dress pants to reveal Rams logo socks; then he leaned forward. "Gotta say, I'm kinda fangirling a little on the inside right now."

Wes forced a smile. "Well, I only played a few seasons…" While it was nice and to be expected that everyone still associated him with football, he really wanted to move on and be known within the community for his new endeavor. He may not be able to be a source of local sports pride anymore, but he could help families in the community have their dream homes with new affordable developments.

Shawn nodded, his light-brown hair falling into his eyes. "That must have been incredible. Being in the action, tasting the blood and sweat out on the field, the rush of adrenaline and the roar of the crowd."

Obviously they weren't done talking about football. "Yeah, it was amazing." While it lasted. "Do you play?" The man was six foot and about 110 pounds, but Wes had definitely asked the right question.

"Only beer leagues, but I'm pretty good. Fast," he said with a look of pride. "Hey, you should come out and play sometime."

"Yeah, sure, yeah…" He cleared his throat. "So, about the loan application, I was wondering how soon I'd know." If he was going ahead with this, he didn't want to lose out on the space to someone else. And the faster he could get the ball rolling, the less time he had to chicken out.

Shawn sat straighter and turned to his computer. "Usually takes about a week or ten days." He reached for several documents on the printer behind him and slid them across the desk toward Wes. "Just fill these out, and we can get the process started."

"Great," Wes said, reaching for a pen and hesitating only briefly before starting to answer the questions. He was painfully aware of Shawn's starstruck gaze on him. He paused and glanced up at the man. "Okay, hand it over," he said.

Shawn reached into his desk and produced Wes's football collectible card. "Can you personalize it?"

Wes sighed. "Sure thing."

CHAPTER FIFTEEN

Why had she tried to keep up with Lia on that ridiculous run the day before? Already the muscles in Sarah's legs ached, and the hot shower hadn't helped.

She'd barely had any time alone since the woman's arrival, and she'd had to sneak away while Lia was on a call. Sarah was convinced she didn't sleep—up well past midnight the night before planning the catering menu and then knocking on Sarah's bedroom door before seven a.m. that morning to go over the table and chair rentals.

They still had twelve days before the reunion, but Lia was hell-bent on finalizing all the details right away. Sarah was creative when it came to figuring out solutions to technological issues or designing new ways for people to communicate across distances, but coming up with pretty party decorations or knowing how to communicate with large groups of people face-to-face were skills that eluded her.

Wrapping one of the new, oversize terry-cloth bath towels around herself, she heard her cell chime with a new text message from Whitney.

"Ow…ow…ow," Sarah said, practically sliding her slippers across the hardwood floor of the bedroom. She wouldn't even think about tackling the stairs. Maybe she could slide the rail like she did as a child. Either way, the bending of the knees was not happening today. And maybe not tomorrow.

She picked up her phone and opened the message.

Check your email—I just sent over the reopening/sale brochure design for your approval.

Sarah sighed. Reopening/sale brochure. Seemed almost like an oxymoron. She was going through all this trouble to turn the B&B into something amazing...then she was giving it up. But that was the plan, and that's what she'd told Whitney she wanted.

Whitney never let up once she was committed to something, and while Sarah appreciated her friend taking time out of her busy schedule to get the ball rolling on selling the place after the reunion, it meant leaving Blue Moon Bay, and her heart was suddenly conflicted. Which was strange. It was the right thing to do. Hell, the *only* thing to do. Letting teenage fantasies and one amazing kiss throw her off course would be ridiculous. She wasn't cut out for running a B&B.

Did you check yet?

Wow, her friend had friendly harassment down to a science. No wonder she was so successful.

Going to her laptop on the desk, Sarah opened her email and clicked on the link from Whitney. Vibrant, high-quality brochures featuring the photos Sarah sent her the day before of the B&B with its new exterior and solar panels lit up the screen.

A newly renovated B&B in a picturesque location that maintains its charm while providing modern-day conveniences with a breathtaking view of the ocean is the perfect choice for your next investment. Submit your offer on this property today and get updates once the sale auction begins!

Sale auction. Wow. It sounded impressive as hell. Would there be more than one buyer interested in the place? That would be amazing if she could really get a great price for it. So why didn't she feel more excited about that possibility?

Scrolling through the three-page design that would become a trifold flyer, Sarah almost couldn't believe it was the same place she'd walked into weeks before. She might actually believe this was *the* place to stay on the California coast, like the description claimed.

All thanks to Wes.

He hadn't been there the day before, but his crew had arrived and were still working hard to finish the balconies. It was hard to think that his absence was because of anything else other than the kiss, and it was weird not seeing him there, even if it would be awkward. Either way, he hadn't been far from her thoughts.

If she could go back in time and rethink her actions, would she have held back? As embarrassing as the aftermath had been, she didn't entirely regret the kiss. It had been mind-blowing and knee-weakening and everything else she'd heard a good kiss should be, and after all these years keeping her feelings to herself, she'd put herself out there.

And it wasn't as though Wes hadn't been into the kiss. She still had a pair of jeans with the ass covered in paint to prove it.

At least she'd have a new memory now besides an almost chance she didn't take.

A loud knock on the door made her jump. "Sarah! You in there?"

Sarah held her breath and froze, watching the door handle wiggle.

Seriously? Where was Lia's sense of privacy? Thank God she'd locked the door before showering.

"Sarah!"

There was no way she was opening it. She needed some time to herself. If she had to endure another story about Malcolm and their fantastic, perfect little life, she was going to explode.

She was happy for Lia—mostly—she just didn't like to be reminded of her own shortcomings ten times in the same day. Lia had the successful career and the loving husband. Sarah was still single and contemplating the career she'd thought she wanted.

She waited until she heard Lia's footsteps descend the stairs before picking up her phone and texting Whitney. *Amazing. As usual.*

Whitney's reply was immediate. *Fill in the info I left blank regarding your preferred contact and I'll get these sent to promotions for printing.*

Did her friend ever just pause for a second? Sarah wished she could move ahead with things as fast as Whitney. There shouldn't be any reason to hesitate, but she still had reservations. Over the last few weeks, the idea of selling had grown increasingly murkier. As the place slowly came back to life, so did the feeling of being somewhere that felt like home, a place she'd always been safe... L.A. with its constant hustle and ever-changing mood for what was "in" and "now" meant always adjusting.

Dove's Nest offered consistency and the opportunity to slow the roll a little. But was it just the inn making her contemplate her future or a certain father/daughter duo who'd lodged themselves in her heart?

Seeing her grandmother's journal, she picked it up and sat out on the new deck off the room. Wes had instructed the crew to finish hers first so she'd have an opportunity to enjoy it, and the view of the bay and ocean from there was spectacular. The mid-morning waves crashing on the sand, getting bigger and louder as each new one rolled in was one of the best sounds for a frazzled mind and conflicted heart.

If she sat there long enough, maybe they'd whisper the answers she was looking for.

Sitting on the rocking chair she'd moved out there, she opened the journal to the next entry. She hadn't read any more since the first one, but that day, she was looking for inspiration any way she could get it.

As before, the next entry started as a letter to her grandmother's mystery man.

Dear Jack,

The world looks so different these days. The changes are scary, but some of them are also exciting. Factories all over the country are hiring women to fill the positions vacated by the men. The San Francisco Bay Area is in desperate need of workers to weld ships and rivet bombers. I know you would hate to think of me working to further this war, but I'm considering it.

The war is happening all around us, and peace is just a dream. No one is vacationing these days. Young families are either struggling to pay the bills or the mothers are leaving their homes to fill these vacant factory positions, so the coast has been quiet. I had one guest here last month, and I fear I won't be able to keep the inn open much longer.

The idea of closing the doors and selling it makes me tear up. This is my home. This was the place we first fell in love. You being away is hard on my heart, but at least I feel you here. You're everywhere — in the ocean air, whispering through the leaves, in the rain falling from dark clouds.

If I leave here, I'm afraid I'll lose you even more.

But going to work in the factories would mean being able to afford to keep the inn and just maybe, I'd feel even closer to you through our mutual efforts in this fight for peace.

No matter what I decide, you will be in my thoughts and in my heart.

Stay safe. Come home to me.

Yours in love,

Dove

Tucked inside the journal behind the entry was a tattered, faded propaganda ad for Rosie the Riveter. A shiver ran through her simply holding the first real feminist empowerment movement. The strong, powerful message resonated with her now more than ever in this turbulent social and cultural climate. She knew from her grandmother's stories that she had closed the inn and gone to San Francisco for a year, working on the dock factories, welding ships.

She'd done it to save the inn and to feel closer to the man she loved.

Sarah closed the journal and sighed. An eerie sense of history repeating itself washed over her like the waves on the sand in the distance.

What would have happened if her grandmother had sold the inn when times were tough and played it safer with an office job, which was customary, instead of rolling up her sleeves in a factory position?

How different would life have been for them all?

As much as Sarah loved the city, she adored her hometown. She couldn't imagine having grown up anywhere else.

And now, she was facing a similar dilemma that her grandmother had so many years ago. Her grandmother had chosen to stick to her dream and do whatever was necessary to protect it.

But what did that mean for her? Which path *would* be following her dream? Staying and pouring her heart into this new business—and launching her own side hustle doing what she loved—or working for an established company, doing what was expected of her until someday she had the confidence to break out on her own?

She continued to read several other entries, detailing her grandmother's journey to San Francisco and the early days on the job, marveling over her strength and commitment. She'd always known her grandmother was an amazing woman, but this inside glimpse into her heart and mind had Sarah wishing she'd had just a little more time with her.

Seeing Jessica's car pull into the driveway an hour later, she put the journal aside and headed downstairs, her legs screaming in pain with each step.

"Hey, were you up there the whole time?"

Lia's voice on the landing behind her would have made her jump if her legs were capable. "Jesus! Don't sneak up on me like that."

"Is that Jess and Whitney?" Lia asked, hot on her heels. As usual.

"Yes," she said, wincing in pain on the last step. So much for hoping maybe Lia would go visit her parents that evening so she could have her girls' night with her friends without her.

Lia frowned as she glanced at her legs. "What's wrong? Why are you walking weird?"

"Oh jeez, I don't know. Could be the ten-mile run you forced me to do," she mumbled as she opened the front door. "Hey, guys," she said, never more grateful to see her friends. Maybe Lia would leave them to visit alone? Nope, instead she invited herself to girls' night.

"Yay, this is going to be so much fun. I can't wait to hear all the latest gossip."

Lia loved gossip. In high school, she knew everything about everyone and had no problem sharing her knowledge. She'd even started a gossip rag in junior high and used the printer in the school library to circulate copies of her newsworthy headlines like *Who Wore the Same*

Dress to the Fall Dance and *Who is Crushing on Whom*...
until the school shut her down, thanks to Sarah's anony-
mous tip. She'd caught a glimpse of the upcoming issue
while Lia was working on it in the school computer lab,
and Sarah refused to have her secret crush on Wes revealed to the entire school.

Of course, she hadn't been able to shut down Lia's
loud mouth.

"Didn't I promise you the place would look amazing?"
Whitney asked Lia, standing back to take in all the renovations herself. She nodded her approval. "The pictures
you sent don't even do it justice," she told Sarah.

The praise from her friend lifted Sarah's spirits.
Whitney wasn't one to dole it out at random.

"There's still some work to finish up," Lia said, because
of course she had to throw in her two cents. She moved
past Sarah to take a bottle of wine from Jessica. "Oh...
this isn't chilled to the right temperature for a Shiraz."

"I thought red wine was supposed to be room temperature," Sarah said.

"No, Sarah... Red needs to be chilled to exactly sixty-
two degrees to bring out the best variations in flavor...
Do you have a wine chiller?"

Thank God her grandmother did have one. "In the
dining room," Sarah said, then waited until Lia
disappeared before turning to Jessica and Whitney.
"Let's go out. Hurry, before she comes back."

Jessica laughed. "We can't do that."

"She's your client, remember?" Whitney said.

"It's the only thing keeping me from killing her. At

least until after she pays the invoice," Sarah muttered as Lia reappeared.

"Deck?" Jessica asked.

"Definitely. I need to enjoy the ocean sunsets as much as possible. We don't get these in New York," Lia said. "Though the views of Central Park and the city skyline from the penthouse are pretty spectacular."

She had to throw that penthouse part in.

"So, Lia, when will your husband be flying in?" Jessica asked, taking a seat on the new large porch swing as Whitney opted for the large, comfy plush chair.

Sarah sat on the other side of the swing...and Lia wedged her ass right in the middle of her and Jessica, instead of taking the other available chair.

Oh my God! The woman had no sense of personal space. Sarah shifted as far to the edge as possible.

"Oh, he has back-to-back cases right up until next week, and then he's flying to Napa to see his parents. I'm actually planning to meet him there for a few days, and then we'll be back for the reunion."

The news was music to Sarah's ears. At least she wouldn't be there driving her batty the week leading up to the event.

"Aren't his parents coming to the reunion?" Jessica asked.

"Yeah, but he wanted some extra time with them, since he was flying all this way. He's so busy, he rarely gets time off for vacations."

"Well, except to climb mountains with you," Sarah mumbled.

"Right, of course," Lia said quickly.

A little too quickly.

Sarah had picked up an odd vibe several times that week whenever Malcolm came up. Something was definitely off. It almost seemed like Lia was singing her husband's praises to convince or remind herself of them.

"Have you seen your parents yet?" Jessica asked.

"Not yet," Lia said dismissively.

Obviously the subject of her family was still a touchy one. So why was she holding this reunion in the first place? If she disliked her family, why bring them all together like this?

"Enough about me. I want to hear about you two. Sarah and I have already caught up on her life…" Lia's look suggested there wasn't much news there, and she was hopeful Jessica's and Whitney's lives were more exciting.

Jessica looked at Whitney to go first, but her cell phone rang and she stood. "Sorry. Work. I have to get this." She turned to Lia, shaking the cell phone. "This is my life in a nutshell. Excuse me."

She stepped down off the deck to answer the call, and Lia looked at Jessica expectantly.

"Well…nothing too interesting to tell," Jessica said. "Life around here is pretty quiet."

"Oh, come on! There has to be some juicy gossip somewhere in this sleepy little place." Lia looked unconvinced that things could be simple and uneventful. "Are you seeing anyone?"

Jessica shook her head, her dark curls falling across

her tanned shoulders. "No one special. I think I've exhausted all dating potentials here."

Lia shrugged. "That's one of the reasons I love the city. Lots of new faces. It's where I met Malcolm. Our law firms were actually on opposite sides of a case. The battles in the courtroom led to another kind of fire."

Sarah had heard this story twice now.

"Funny how we both grew up in California but had to cross the country to find each other," Lia said, a dreamy look appearing in her dark-brown eyes. "It was fate."

Sarah rolled her eyes. Though a month ago, that concept of the universe intercepting a person's plans would have been met with an eye roll *and* a scoff...

"That does sound exciting." Of course Jessica would think so.

A note of wistfulness in her friend's tone made Sarah frown. Her friend always loved living here. Unlike herself and Whitney, Jessica had never talked about moving away. She had everything she needed—wanted— right here with her own company and all her family still living in town. But suddenly Sarah wasn't as convinced of her friend's happiness.

"Well, why don't you do it? Move to a bigger city, I mean. Fresh blood," Lia said with a malicious-looking grin.

"Jess is perfectly happy here," Sarah said, earning her a look from her friend. "I mean, I think she is... Aren't you?"

Jessica nodded. "Of course. Yes. I just sometimes doubt that I'll find someone to spend my life with here."

Sarah sucked in her bottom lip. Jessica was obsessed with connecting with her true love; Sarah just never thought her friend would consider leaving their hometown to find him.

The idea that she didn't seem to know her friends as well as she thought she did anymore was unsettling. Maybe friends did grow apart over time. Even being in L.A. she hadn't felt that—hadn't experienced the sensation of her best friends slipping away like grains of sand under her feet.

But maybe she just hadn't realized it until being there to see things in a different light. Jessica and Whitney were much more connected, and she longed for that again. Staying in Blue Moon Bay would fulfill that missing element in her life as well.

"You know, I bet that wine is chilled to perfection by now," Lia said, smiling as she used Sarah's sore thigh to push herself up off the rocking chair.

The pain was nothing compared to the tightness in her chest.

"You know what, sit tight—catch up some more. I'll get it," Sarah said, standing. She needed a second. She hoped once she returned with the wine, the dark cloud that had appeared out of nowhere out on the bay would have passed.

• • •

The next morning, she found Lia doing what looked like an extreme form of yoga in the front room. The woman's tiny body was twisted in some sort of pretzel shape that she looked stuck in. "Need some help?"

Lia glanced over her shoulder at her, a peaceful expression on her face, then gracefully maneuvered her body back into a cross-legged position on her yoga mat...that apparently she traveled with.

Because who didn't travel with a yoga mat?

"Morning yoga is a great way to start the day," she said, tapping the floor next to her for Sarah to join in the practice.

"Yeah, that's a no." She was still hurting from the last workout the woman had forced her to do.

"Aunt Lia!"

Sarah turned and dodged out of the way as the front door to the B&B closed and Marissa ran straight for Lia.

"Hi... Oh my God, you look like a teenager," Lia said, getting up from the impossible pose with ease and hugging the little girl tight. "How old are you now? Fourteen?"

"Nine and three-quarters."

"Nine and a half," Wes corrected. "Hey, Sarah," he said, sounding slightly awkward as he walked past her for his own hug with Lia.

Looking at him that morning in his jeans and paint-splattered old T-shirt, she wished she could wrap her arms around him. Was it her imagination or did he look even better that day? His hair was gelled and he was definitely wearing cologne.

Great, so he'd decided to torture her even more by looking and smelling amazing.

"You guys are here early," Lia said.

Wes nodded. "This one woke up at six a.m. demanding to come see you. I was barely able to hold her off until a decent time."

The little girl still had her arms around Lia. "It was actually five thirty."

Lia laughed, and Sarah looked around. That genuine sound must have come from someone else. She hadn't seen a relaxed, un-put-on version of the other woman until now.

"Well, I was up that early for a morning run and some follow-up emails with clients in New York, so next time, come as early as you want," Lia said.

"You're on vacation. You're supposed to sleep in, take a break," Wes said.

"Sleep in? Wouldn't that be a treat?"

Watching the interaction, Sarah blinked. Where was the obnoxious Lia who was driving her wild? Holding Marissa's hand and smiling at Wes, she was almost unrecognizable. The square of her shoulders had disappeared, and her face looked relaxed. Happy. Real happy.

"Well, Sarah's been working hard, too," Wes said. "She's breathing new life into this place." His gaze met Sarah's, and the tension in the air had to be obvious to everyone. It was impossible to look at him and not remember the kiss. The way he'd tasted, the scent of his cologne, the way he'd backed her up against the wet wall...

Her breath caught in her chest and she just mumbled

something *she* didn't even understand.

Yeah, things were totally going to go back to normal between them.

Lia glanced back and forth between them as though she caught a vibe of her own, then turned her attention to Marissa. "Hey, what do you say we head down to the beach while your dad works?"

"Yes...I mean, can I, Dad?"

"Of course. Thanks, Lia." He glanced at her. "Hey, why not invite Sarah to join you?"

Was he trying to get rid of her? She wasn't going to intrude on Lia and Marissa's time together, but she would grant him time to work alone. She needed an escape as well.

"Actually, I'm about to head out," she said. She was now, anyway.

Lia tapped his shoulder as she passed, following the little girl outside. "I'll bring her to your place later and we'll catch up tonight, Wes."

As they left, Wes turned to Sarah and cleared his throat. "So, other than the remaining decks...the last thing we need to finish is the staircase leading to the cellar. I want to refinish the concrete to prevent chipping. My crew is busy and I don't want to forget about it, so I thought I'd just do it myself."

"Great—thank you."

His gaze locked with hers, lasting a few seconds too long. The silence echoed around them a little too loud, and there was an odd energy circling her that she'd be a fool to read too much into. But her pulse raced, and when his gaze lowered to her mouth, she knew he had to be thinking about their kiss, too.

He glanced out the window toward Lia and Marissa, breaking the moment, and she remembered to breathe.

"Anyway, I should get going," she said quickly.

"Yeah, I should get to work."

Heading outside, she took a deep breath of fresh air as she headed toward her rental. There was one place in Blue Moon Bay that always cheered her up, and if no one needed her at the inn that day, that's where she was headed.

• • •

Using a chisel and wire brush, Wes removed the loose concrete on the winding stairs leading down into the wine cellar. Sweat pooled on his lower back in the heat of the dimly lit stairwell. It was actually kinda creepy being there alone, so he picked up his pace as he applied the concrete re-surfacer to the top of each stair.

Seeing Sarah that morning hadn't provided any of the clarity he'd been hoping for. Over the last few days, he'd had time to digest and process what had happened, and he'd thought things would be fine. It was just one impulsive kiss. It didn't have to mean anything. People had casual hookups all the time...

Unfortunately, the moment he'd seen her that morning, there was no way he could write off the kiss or the attraction between them as casual. It was anything but.

She'd looked so beautiful in a long, flowy sundress that hugged her waist and displayed the swell of her breasts so perfectly. Her dark hair in a high ponytail, no makeup on, it had taken all his strength not to take a chance on a do-over on that kiss.

And the look of jealousy on her face when she'd watched their interaction with Lia had made him want to reassure her that she was just as important to them. It had also told him how deep his feelings were. It was more than just physical attraction for both of them.

But where did they go from here? If she did want to explore things, was he ready for that?

CHAPTER SIXTEEN

It had been years since Sarah walked the beach on this side of the bay. The scenic drive along the coast of town was breathtaking, and it was exhilarating to cruise along the twisty coastal road, feeling the warm breeze through the open windows, the sun breaking through the disappearing clouds. Pulling into a lot a block away from the beach, she parked the car, grabbed her purse, and headed down the boarded walkway.

Along the busy boardwalk, clothing and jewelry stores had tables of merchandise set up outside, sale signs broadcasting amazing deals for the beautiful handcrafted pieces. Long, flowy bohemian skirts caught her attention, and she stopped to admire them. Soft fabrics of various shades for deals she'd only find here in Blue Moon Bay. In L.A., the prices would be double.

Life here was wonderful. The ocean, the weather, the slower pace, all these amazing local shops and restaurants…

A street musician played a beat on bongo drums in the distance and up ahead, a local artist drew a family caricature sketch for a group of tourists. Sarah stopped to watch, then reluctantly moved on.

Seeing Harrison's Blown Glass hut, she entered through the already open door. Lack of air-conditioning in the space made it stifling with the variety of heating machinery generating warmth throughout the store. Just a light breeze from a floor fan in the corner blew her

sundress around her ankles and offered any form of relief from the heat. Sarah removed her light sweater and
wrapped it around her waist.

It was definitely one of the oldest and smallest shops
along the boardwalk. Wooden exposed beams in the
ceiling and unfinished shelves along the walls gave the
place a rustic, beachside appeal. The smell of paint
mixed with a slight wood-burning scent left no question
that the art was created on-site.

She slid her sunglasses to the top of her head as she
scanned the dozens of differently shaped bulbs hanging
from the ceiling, like the one Wes and Marissa had given
her. Round, teardrop, oval…some with a delicate point
at the bottom. All shapes and variety of color blends,
picking up the sunlight through the window and casting
a warm glow across the wooden floor.

"Hello?" she called out.

She didn't see anyone inside, and she couldn't hear
anyone working in the back. Maybe they'd gone on
break. Vendors rarely worried about theft on the
boardwalk. They all looked out for one another in the
community. She may not see anyone around, but no
doubt, there were eyes on her.

She continued to look through the various shapes
and sizes of the multicolored bulbs. Fiery red and
orange combinations in the essence of flames adorned
one shelf and she moved closer, not trusting her eyes.
The vibrant mix of colors tricked the mind into
believing the flames were actually moving.

"Amazing," she breathed out. Whitney would love

one of those for her birthday in March—a fiery Aries, it would suit her personality perfectly.

Along the next row of shelves, there was an assortment of red and green and gold combinations. A Holiday Sale sign announced 50 percent off the seasonal collection.

Immediately, Sarah envisioned a twenty-foot Christmas tree in the B&B foyer that year, decorated in these blown-glass bulbs. Classy, modern, elegant.

Christmas. Would she still own the inn by then? Whitney was being optimistic that Dove's Nest would sell quickly once it was on the market, but maybe it would take a while to find the right buyer.

She reluctantly moved away from the holiday selection. She could always come back for them if she was in town for the holidays. Right now, she was on the hunt for green and blue mixes. She'd buy them to hang in the guest rooms at the B&B. A parting gift of sorts. Something she could leave behind.

She found what she was looking for along the far end of the tiny shop. A Seashore collection sat on the top shelf.

"Hello, miss," a man said as she reached to pick up one that was perfectly round and a little bigger than her palm.

"Oh, hi…" she said, turning. "Do you work here?" The man had to be in his nineties, dressed in a pair of board shorts and a bright orange T-shirt, his skin dark, wrinkled from years in the sun. He wore an old baseball hat and an apron covered in multicolored paint around his waist.

"This is my place." He stared at her as he wiped orange paint from his hands onto an old rag.

Sarah's gaze drifted to a curtain behind the cash counter. "You make these back there?" she asked. His hands shook slightly, and it was hard to imagine them being capable of such delicate artistry.

He nodded. "Yes, ma'am. I've been making them for more than forty years. Right here in this tiny shop." His old eyes studied her, and she shifted from one foot to the other.

He looked vaguely familiar, but she couldn't pinpoint where she'd seen him before. "I'm Sarah Lewis...I own Dove's Nest B&B... Well, I just inherited it, anyway. I may be selling it, but right now, it's mine."

Why had she mentioned that last part? This man was a stranger; he didn't care if she stayed or left. Yet she felt the need to make the people in Blue Moon Bay aware of her intentions of restoring the B&B to its original landmark status in town.

He looked down. "I was sad to hear of Dove's passing."

"You knew her?" Though it shouldn't be too surprising—they looked close in age, and Dove's Nest had a great reputation in town.

Or at least had at one time. A reputation she hoped she could restore. Hopefully new owners wouldn't change the name. She hadn't really considered that until now.

"Yes, I knew her for a long time," he said, his gaze

rising to meet hers.

She squinted. "Hey, were you the man who came by to do the landscaping out back about a month ago?"

He hesitated, then nodded. "I used to help Dove sometimes with the maintenance of the place and such."

"That was nice of you," Sarah said, but the hair on the back of her neck peaked and she shivered slightly.

"I'm sorry to have trespassed on the beach the day of her funeral, but I just wanted to say goodbye," he said, looking embarrassed.

The picture. *He* was the man in the background of their family picture. She opened her mouth to say something, but he spoke first.

"What brings you in, dear?"

Right. The reason she was here. It suddenly wasn't so clear. "I wanted to buy about a dozen of these," she said, picking up the one she'd been eyeing. "In this shape but various sizes ranging from this being the smallest to maybe twice this size, if you have them."

He took it and scanned it, glancing at a few other shelves. "I think this is the last of this color scheme…in this shape anyway."

"Darn. It was perfect." She looked around, but the rest in the seafoam blue and aqua designs were a little too small.

"How many did you say you needed?"

"A dozen in total."

He nodded. "When do you need them?"

Her plan was to go back to L.A. right after Labor Day. "A week from now?"

"Okay," he said, carrying the bulb around to the back of the counter, where he reached for a pad of paper.

"Okay?"

"I'll custom make them for you. Exactly like this one?"

"You'd do that? I mean, yes—exactly. Of course, the coloring swirls can be different, but similar colors and sizes." Still in awe, she reached for her wallet. "I'll pay in advance."

He held out a hand. "No need, dear. When you come back to get them is fine."

She put her wallet back slowly, glancing around the shop. Other than a few beach photos and a few decorative surfboards hanging on the walls, there was nothing inside but the shelves of blown-glass items. There had to be five hundred different pieces—all unique in some way. "These are really incredible."

"It's my life. It gives me joy. I don't even worry about selling them…it just passes the time, you know?"

She nodded. "Well, they are beautiful."

"Thank you."

She cleared her throat. "I didn't receive your in-voice…for the yardwork."

"There's no invoice. I did it for Dove."

Her chest tightened. "Well, I could use the help if you're interested in continuing…but I'd insist on paying you."

He smiled, and his eyes looked ten years younger. "I think I'm getting a little old for the work now. Besides, it was just for her."

Sarah nodded. "Okay, I understand."

Unfortunately, she understood too much and not enough at the same time. Her stomach knotted as she tried to picture him as a young man... It could be the man in her grandmother's journal, but she couldn't know for sure without his name.

"I'll have these ready for you next week." He tore the slip of paper off the notepad and folded it, then tucked it under the glass bulb on the counter.

"Great. Thank you." She hesitated.

Just ask. Ask him his name.

Maybe she could find the information online. Chickening out, she put on her sunglasses and headed toward the door.

"Sarah."

She stopped.

"Your grandmother would be proud to see the place and what you've done with it. It looks just like it once did," he said.

The words warmed her. "I hope so." She paused. She had to know what her gut already did. "I'm sorry...what was your name?"

"Jack Harrison."

"Nice to have met you, Jack," she said, hurrying out of the shop and away from any other answers she wasn't sure she was ready for.

• • •

Wes kissed Marissa's forehead as he tucked her into bed

that evening. "Okay, time to sleep."

"I don't know why I can't stay up later tonight. Aunt Lia's here," she said.

"You spent all day with her, and now you need rest. She probably needs a rest, too," he said with a laugh, glancing at Lia in the bedroom doorway.

Nine-year-olds were exhausting, especially for people who didn't have kids of their own, and four hours at the beach that day, followed by board games and a full rundown of her Fortnite progress must have Lia ready to call it a night as well. She stifled a yawn behind her hand.

"See?" Wes told Marissa.

"Fine. Will I see you tomorrow?" Marissa asked her.

"Lia might have to visit her parents tomorrow," Wes answered for her.

"Lia doesn't like her parents. She'd rather spend time with me," Marissa argued.

"True that," Lia said with a laugh. "Don't worry, I'll see you at the B&B. You'll be there working with Sarah, right?"

"Yes," she said excitedly. "And I can show you the secret project Sarah and I are working on."

"Can't wait," Lia said.

"Wait, Lia gets to see this amazing secret project, but I don't?" Wes faked a look of hurt.

Marissa grinned. "You'll see it eventually. Have some patience."

"I'll try... Now sleep," Wes said, pulling the pink covers up over her and cocooning her in tight.

"I forgot to kiss Mom," Marissa said, struggling to un-tuck an arm. She picked up the picture frame with the photo of Kelly in it on her bedside table. It was taken just months before she'd been diagnosed. After that, Kelly had refused pictures, saying she only wanted to leave behind good memories, snapshots of the good times for her daughter to recall whenever she remembered her.

Wes looked away. Time might dull the ache they all felt, but Kelly's absence was still strongly mourned. Time couldn't erase just how much better the world had seemed with her in it.

"Good night," Wes said as she put the picture back. He turned off the bedroom light and followed Lia back out into the living room.

"Think she has enough toys?" Lia scanned the room that looked like a toy tornado had passed through. They'd played every board game the family had, built a Lego Friends Treehouse kit, played hours of video games, and made a mess experimenting with Marissa's new chemistry set that had finally arrived in the mail. Marissa was definitely making up for Lia's lack of visiting, cramming everything she could into the day.

"You're the one spoiling her with all of this. You have to stop sending presents all the time." Wes had fought against the gaming console, but somehow Marissa had conveyed her desire for one to Lia months before and one had arrived shortly after. Unfortunately, he was almost as addicted to it now as his daughter was, and he'd needed to put screen time restrictions on both of them.

"It's guilt," Lia said, kneeling to put away the game controllers as Wes packed the board games away onto a shelf.

"Are you hungry? Did you want anything else to eat?"

She laughed. "Not after all that meat you fed me." Hot dogs, hamburgers, and steak had been barbecued that evening, and they'd consumed them all. He'd made veggie burgers as well, but Lia had opted for the real stuff.

"Yeah, I thought you'd gone vegan?" Wes said.

"I'm on vacation. You said yourself I'm supposed to be vacating my life."

"But I don't want to be a bad influence on you. Aren't you and Malcolm training for another climb? I thought I saw a post about it on Facebook a few months ago."

Lia turned off the game console and stood, shoving her hands into the pockets of her shorts. "Actually, it's just me."

"You're climbing Mount Kenya alone?"

She shook her head. "With a guide. Malcolm decided not to join me this time."

"Things still rocky between you two? Pun intended," he said, his concern evident despite his attempt at lightening the question. Lia and Malcolm had only been married a few years, but the year before, things had started to go downhill. Wes didn't know all the details and he respected her privacy not to ask, but he suspected their busy careers might have something to do with it.

"Everything's fine. Or it will be eventually," she said,

refusing to meet his gaze.

He suspected things weren't fine, but he really hoped they could work it out. Malcolm wasn't his favorite person—the guy was a little high on himself for Wes's taste, but he seemed to suit Lia's high-strung personality well. It took a special kind of partner to keep up with his friend. Malcolm had the energy and stamina and had seemed up for the challenge...at least initially.

"Is that what this reunion is about?" he asked gently.

Lia studied her perfectly manicured fingers. "Maybe a little. I guess I'm hoping that bringing our families together might reignite a spark or something." She paused. "So...Marissa tells me you get a lot of attention from the single moms in town."

He groaned at the change of subject. He'd rather be talking about *her* love life. His was basically nonexistent...or it had been until Sarah had planted that kiss on him. "She's noticed, huh?"

"FYI—she notices everything. Seriously, though, anyone caught your eye?" She sat on the sofa, curling her legs under her.

Should he tell her about his connection to Sarah, the kiss? He wasn't eager to know her opinion on that yet or confess his embarrassing retreat, so he shrugged as he sat next to her. "Not really...I don't know. Besides, this place isn't exactly a bachelor pad."

There were signs of Marissa and Kelly everywhere in the house, including all the family photos still hanging on the walls.

What was the right way to deal with those things?

When Wes finally decided he was ready to move on, what did they do with all of Kelly's memories? Just one of many reasons to stay single and keep any developing feelings for Sarah repressed.

"So, how are things going at the B&B with Sarah?" she asked. Was she asking out of simple curiosity or was she fishing for information? He couldn't detect if she sensed anything between them or not, but someone would have to be completely out of tune to not have picked up a vibe between him and Sarah that morning. He'd tried to keep things casual, light…but there'd been unresolved tension.

"Fine. Why?"

She studied him. "Were you two close in high school? Before she moved away?"

"We were…friends, and she tutored me in math all through my junior and senior year. She's probably the only reason I graduated." He leaned back against the cushions and stretched his legs out in front of him.

At the time, he hadn't realized just how much he owed Sarah, but looking back, he would have failed miserably without her. She not only helped him understand the math concepts, she kept him on track and focused whenever he wanted to quit.

"Have you guys kept in touch over the years?" Lia asked.

"Nah, not really. Just online, but those connections never feel real, you know?" He wasn't a fan of Facebook or Instagram… But when she went back to L.A., maybe he would use those online programs more to stay in touch. "I think she might actually pull off this reopening. Dove's Nest is important to the people around here." He shot her a look.

"What about Sarah? Is she important to the people around here?" Lia asked pointedly.

Wes sighed. "I don't know yet." He paused and relented under Lia's look. "I mean, I do know, I'm just not ready to admit it. Did you ever think adult life would be this complicated?"

"If by 'complicated,' you mean 'shitty,' then nope," she said. "I did not."

CHAPTER SEVENTEEN

Sitting on the edge of the bed the following morning, Sarah reached inside the bedside table drawer and took out her grandmother's journal. She'd met her grandmother's mystery man, but she was still no closer to knowing what had happened between them. And the next entry in Dove's journal only made things even more complicated.

Dear Jack,

I saw you today. On the docks.

I don't think the pieces of my shattered heart will ever be glued back together. It was you. On the street. And you walked by me as though I were a stranger.

I called to you as you passed, but you kept walking.

I ran after you and grabbed your arm, but you pretended to be someone else.

You must have recognized me, yet your face held no trace of love or familiarity.

My world has never been so lonely. You didn't tell me you were coming home. I had no idea you were so close. You are here now, but you are further away than ever.

You slipped into the crowd gathered on Main Street to welcome the soldiers home, and it was Martin who comforted me and told me what had happened.

The reason you weren't yourself any longer.

He said you acted like someone I didn't know because you weren't that man anymore. War changes men, and that has never been truer than for you.

I'm not giving up, though.

In my soul, I know somewhere inside is the man I've loved. And somehow, I know you'll come back to me.

Heartbreakingly,

Dove

Sarah closed the book and sighed.

These snippets were driving her to distraction. Each one revealed another layer to the story, but not enough for her to put the whole thing together. Her grandmother had loved him, he went away to war...but he'd come back and they'd never reunited because he'd ignored her?

That didn't make sense. If they'd been in love, if Jack's love for her grandmother was even a fraction as strong as Dove's love for him, how could anything—even war—have come between that?

She really was starting to sound like Jessica. Real life probably got in the way, the same way it always did. Her own conflicted heart was evidence of that.

But she'd met the man, and he'd obviously kept in touch with her grandmother over the years. He'd done the landscaping, and he'd been on the beach the day they'd spread her ashes.

She was desperate to hear the full story, but she couldn't exactly ask Jack—the only other person still alive who knew the truth.

Was he the only one?

She'd assumed she was the first one reading her grandmother's journal, but maybe she wasn't.

She closed the journal and picked up the landline on

the bedside table to dial her mother's long-distance number in Phoenix. Three rings later, she heard her mother's voice on the other end.

"Hey, darling, you still on the coast? That looks like Dove's Nest's number on call display."

"Yeah, Mom, I'm still here."

"Have you decided what you're going to do with the B&B? I assume you've met with an appraiser?"

That would probably have been the best course of action. "Um…no. Actually, I had an inspection done and…" She paused, shutting her eyes. "Just about finished renovating it."

"Really? Is the market strong enough to make back what you spent on fixing it up?"

Her mother didn't even entertain the thought that Sarah might be keeping the inn. And why would she? Sarah had never expressed any interest in owning or running it. The family assumed that Dove's Nest would disappear along with her grandmother's ashes and become just a memory. Sarah had thought that letting it go would be easy as well, until she'd spent time there.

"I'm planning to keep it for a while to host an event, kinda a reopening thing to show the community how great it is again."

"You're running the B&B?"

Shocked or disappointed, Sarah couldn't decide. "No. I'm holding an event here, then putting it on the market." There it was—that gut wrench that kept happening whenever she said that. As if her grandmother's ghost was kicking her in the stomach. "Whitney says that Blue

Moon Bay's tourism is going up, and part of that is due to visitors planning retreats and events here, so I thought it would be a good idea to show potential buyers that the inn was perfect for those things."

"You're planning an event? Like a real one? Not an online virtual reality thingy?"

Her stomach fell. Why should her mother have confidence in her that she could pull this off? She'd never been outgoing or sociable. She liked her privacy and the anonymity that the internet world provided. Her parents had always called her shy, reserved... withdrawn. They'd never gotten her, so this had to come as a shock.

"What's she doing?" Sarah heard her father ask in the background.

"Is that Dad?"

"Just a sec, darling. She renovated the B&B and she's hosting an event," Sarah heard her mother whisper to her father.

"What the hell would she do that for? That place is a lawsuit waiting to happen."

So much for family support. Though she couldn't blame them. Her father was right—before the renovations, the B&B had been just that.

But if they could see it now...

"Shhhh," her mother said. "Okay, I'm back, sweetheart. Your dad says hello."

Sarah rolled her eyes.

"Though we are both worried about this decision. I thought once the will was read, you'd made up your mind to sell for whatever you could get for it. The place really was dangerous."

She couldn't exactly argue when she'd fallen through the staircase, but that was before. "It will be fine, Mom," she said, turning the journal over in her hands. "Wes and his crew have really made the place feel like new, and tell Dad not to worry; I have insurance."

"Oh, you heard him."

"Yeah."

"He just wants what's best for you. We both do."

"I know." She did know, but sometimes she wished her practical, down-to-earth parents would encourage her to take risks. She'd always played it safe, going into a career that was in her wheelhouse, doing what she was good at.

But maybe getting out of her comfort zone and trying something new was a good thing. Being back there hadn't been the headache she'd assumed it would be…at least not completely.

"Well, just be sensible about this, and when it doesn't work, let it go, move on. Don't hold on to it too long just because you don't want to admit failure."

Zero confidence in her abilities to pull this off.

"Okay, Mom. I should go." She wanted so badly to ask her mom about the journal and Jack, but something made her pause.

"Oh, okay… Was there another reason you called?"

She stared at the embossed cover, running a finger along the design. "Um…did Grandma ever mention a friend of hers—a Jack Harrison?" Just the simple question made her feel odd, like she was somehow betraying her grandmother's trust.

"Jack Harrison... No, I've never heard that name before. Why do you ask?"

"No reason. He just passed along his condolences, that's all." Such an understatement. "Anyway, I should go. Just wanted to let you know my plans...for now."

"All right, darling. We trust you know what you're doing."

"Bye, Mom." Disconnecting the call, Sarah lay back on her bed, clutching the journal to her chest.

If her grandmother had kept this secret so long, maybe it was better it stay that way. After all, it wasn't Sarah's secret to tell.

• • •

The renovations were done.

Wes toured the B&B, a sense of pride and accomplishment washing over him. They'd pulled off a ridiculous amount of work in a short time, and the place looked better than ever. Dove's Nest was once again a place tourists would be happy to visit.

Unfortunately, the construction project being done meant he didn't need to be at the B&B every day anymore, and it brought them one step closer to Sarah leaving town again.

Maybe his team should have worked a little slower.

Or maybe it was time to man up and ask Sarah out. Spend time with her in a different setting, with a different purpose. A sole purpose of exploring the connection between them and letting things sort themselves out whatever way they were meant to. He'd fought his attraction long enough, and he couldn't keep fooling himself into believing the kiss had meant nothing.

He scanned the dining room and kitchen for Sarah, then heard her voice coming from the den. He checked his reflection in the mirror in the hallway above the antique table, running a hand through his hair and wiping a speck of dirt from his forehead. Maybe he should wait until after he'd showered and changed…

Nope. If he didn't do this now, he might not ever.

Before he could talk himself out of it, he headed into the den. "Hey…"

"Wait! Don't look!" Marissa said, turning her laptop away from him as he entered.

Sarah quickly shut down her screen as well.

His surprise. Marissa still hadn't told him what it was. "Sorry to interrupt—I just wanted to let Sarah know that we're done."

"Already?" she asked. "Like…everything?"

Her surprised look held a tiny tinge of regret, which made his own hope rise. Was she as disappointed at the prospect of not seeing him around there every day as well? Or maybe she was disappointed that she wouldn't have Marissa around anymore?

"Yeah. The waste management bin just arrived, so my guys are cleaning up the debris outside, and then that's it."

"We're actually done with what we were working on as well," Sarah said with a smile at Marissa.

The little girl looked less pleased. "I guess that means I won't need to come here every day anymore," she said, her tone echoing how they all felt.

Sarah's gaze met his, and his palms started to sweat and his mouth ran dry. Now was his opportunity. Invite her to hang out with both of them…easier than asking her out on a date in front of his nine-year-old.

This was perfect. Marissa had teed him up for the invite.

But the words refused to surface as he continued to stare at her, drowning in his inability to vocalize how he was feeling. Damn, the silent pleading in those eyes was killing him…

Sarah cleared her throat and looked at Marissa. "You can come visit anytime you want, and Lia invited you both to the reunion…so there's that," she said.

Wes nodded his agreement.

Come on, man, just ask her to dinner or something!

Marissa's eyes widened. "Hey, tonight is the annual firework competition on the boardwalk pier," she said. "The fair is in town, too… We should all go."

Yes, they should. Thank God for his nine-year-old. Wes had zero game.

Sarah looked at him again, and he nodded. "Yeah…I mean, that sounds like a good idea to me, if you're not busy."

Marissa rolled her eyes. "What Dad is trying to say is that we'd really like you to come with us."

Sarah laughed. "Okay, yeah." Her gaze met his again. "I'd like that."

She would? So it wasn't just him struggling with these new feelings. Wes smiled like a child as he nodded again. "Great... We'll pick you up around seven?"

"Sure," Sarah said as Lia entered the den with Popsicles for the three of them.

"Where are we going at seven?" she asked.

Wes's heart raced, and Sarah's eyes widened.

Marissa smiled as she accepted a Popsicle. "The fair and the fireworks competition. We're all going," she said.

"Awesome, I'm free," Lia said, her lips turning purple from the grape-flavored ice treat.

And just like that, his first "date" in five years turned into a group thing.

CHAPTER EIGHTEEN

She'd forgotten how magical the pier fairgrounds could be at night. Bright fluorescent lights lit up the night, reflecting on the ocean below. The Ferris wheel's silhouette against the cloudless sky and the loud music playing through the speakers brought Sarah back to summer nights spent at the pier with Jessica and Whitney when they were teenagers. Too much Cotton Candy and corn dogs and allowances spent on games of chance. Hours in line for their favorite rides.

"I love this place," Marissa said as the four of them climbed out of Wes's truck later that evening and headed toward the entrance gate.

"Definitely one way to get her outside," Wes said, the three adults following the excited little girl as she skipped on ahead.

"I remember coming here all the time as teens..." Lia said. "This place definitely evokes some pretty great memories."

Lia had always had some guy falling all over himself to try to win her a big plush toy.

"Hey, didn't you come here with Ryan Fieldman in junior year?" Wes asked Sarah.

How on earth did he remember that? She barely remembered that.

Ryan had been her science lab partner. He'd clearly wanted more than just dissecting the same frog, but Sarah had never felt the connection to him. She'd agreed to the date because it was his birthday, but when he'd tried to kiss her with breath that smelled like chili cheese dog, she'd called it a night.

"That was just as friends," she said.

"You didn't date much in high school," he said.

Since when had he been paying so much attention? She hadn't thought he'd known she'd existed beyond their tutoring sessions…like a teacher when you saw them in the outside world at the grocery store or at the movies and it felt surreal. "I was focused on my studies, that's all."

And she'd only had eyes for him. She kept that to herself.

They arrived at the ticket kiosk, and he bought a twenty pack and refused Sarah's and Lia's money when they offered to pay for theirs. "Please. Marissa dragged everyone here. It's the least I can do," he said.

They'd barely dragged her. She'd wanted to go. Now that the renovations were done and Marissa was heading to Girl Guides camp in a few days, Sarah wasn't sure how often she'd see them before she headed back to L.A.

"I want to ride the Fireball first," Marissa said once they had their hands stamped and were inside the gate. She ran off toward the terrifying-looking ride that raised carts into the air, then twisted them in all directions, including upside down.

Oh, hell no.

"One of my favorites," Lia said, looking as excited as the nine-year-old.

At least someone was.

Wes looked apprehensive as well. He turned pale watching the riders being tossed around at lightning speed. "I might sit this one out," he said.

"Come on, Dad. Don't be a wimp in front of Sarah," Marissa said with a grin.

Lia shot an intrigued look between them as though wondering what Marissa was implying. Sarah's cheeks flushed slightly, and she avoided Lia's questioning gaze and pretended not to read absolutely everything into Marissa's comment.

Wes sighed as he glanced at Sarah. "Apparently, I can't be a wimp, but if you want to get us out of this..."

She desperately did, but she didn't want to look like a wimp, either, so she shook her head. "We're here, right? May as well go for it."

Wes's gaze lingered on hers a fraction too long, and her heart raced.

What else should they go for?

Right now, she'd like to go all in. There had been a moment in the den earlier that day when it felt like he was going to ask her out...before Marissa suggested the fairgrounds and Lia showed up, inviting herself along.

Staring at him now, she knew she would have said yes. Give in and put herself out there one last time for him.

Might be a risky move that would once again lead to heartache, but she'd never been successful repressing her feelings for him. And that night, he looked amazing in a pair of board shorts, sandals, and a shirt unbuttoned down his chest. His dirty jeans, bare chest, and work boots was still her favorite look, but this casual, relaxed air around him that evening reminded her of the guy she used to know in high school, and that familiarity combined with the new sexual attraction she was fighting made him impossibly tempting.

"Okay, I guess we're doing it," Wes said, and they fell into step behind Lia and Marissa as they joined the long line waiting for the ride.

Sarah stared up at it. From a distance, it hadn't looked so bad. Up close, she could see how scary it was. The mechanics holding it together looked slightly rusted with peeling paint, and those grinding noises couldn't be good. The riders' reactions were a combination of screams and laughter. She knew which one she'd be.

But there was a small kid on the ride, so it couldn't be that bad, right? Though the little boy did look kinda green and petrified—the open-mouth, soundless expression plastered on his face each time his car passed them didn't instill much confidence.

"This is going to be so awesome," Marissa said, dancing from one foot to the other excitedly as they waited, her strawberry-blond braid swinging back and forth.

"Awesome" seemed like an overstatement, but Sarah refused to chicken out now. Being with Wes and Marissa was good for her soul. She liked spending time with them. The little girl was smart and funny and sweet, and Wes was an amazing dad. He obviously put Marissa's needs first and was doing his best raising her on his own.

Sure, they had their differences, which made it difficult to connect sometimes, but Wes clearly adored his daughter, and that made him even more irresistible.

The ride stopped, and Sarah scanned the row of people in front of them. A quick math calculation had her pulse racing. Shit, they were on next. The exit gate opened, and she watched the slightly dizzy group of people leave the ride, swaying left and right as though trying to get their sea legs.

"Well, they survived," Wes said.

"That's debatable," she said, nodding at the man running toward the nearest trash can.

The line shuffled forward, and Wes tore four tickets off the set and handed them to the young kid operating the ride.

"How many?" the kid asked.

"Four!" Marissa said, jumping up and down.

"Three adults? You'll need two cars—two in each. Make sure the lightest is on the inside," he said, reaching past them for the next riders.

"I'm with Aunt Lia," Marissa said, and Lia nodded.

Wes looked slightly panicked. "You don't want to ride with me?"

"I can do that later. Have fun, you two!" she said, shooting them a grin as she and Lia ran off to get the light-blue car she'd been eyeing in line.

"We'll meet you at the ride exit…" Wes called after them before turning to Sarah. "So, it's you and me?"

Her heart was pounding out of her chest, and she hadn't even gotten on the ride yet. "Or we could sneak out the exit. They'd never know."

The gate clicked, locking them in, and Wes looked terrified. "I don't think that's an option. That one is still empty," he said, nodding to a green car behind her.

Sarah followed him to the car, and he opened the small metal door for her to climb in first. "Lightest on the inside," he said.

She was very aware of his gaze on her ass as she climbed into the seat, and her pulse was racing as he climbed in next to her and his large thigh touched hers in the cramped space. He closed the door, secured the latch, and pulled the safety bar down over their laps. It clicked in place, and Sarah gripped it tight, her mouth going dry as she forced a calming breath.

Across the way, Marissa leaned out of her car with Lia to wave at them. The smug little smile on her face suggested she'd planned this.

Next to her, Wes cleared his throat. "Um…is it just me or do you get the feeling we were set up?"

Oh, that little shit was totally playing matchmaker again.

Sarah wasn't exactly opposed to the idea of time alone with Wes, but since their kiss…she wasn't sure where they stood, and she'd prefer to be alone with him in a situation where it wasn't a possibility that she might throw up in his lap.

"She may have had an agenda," Sarah said awkwardly.

"She really likes you," he said quietly.

Her heart was about to explode. "Marissa's such a great kid."

"She's going to miss seeing you every day at the B&B," he said, staring at his hands on the bar.

"It's going to be weird for me, too. But I'm still there if she wants to visit when she gets back from camp," she said. At least for a few extra days, until the reunion was over.

He nodded. "Yeah, I'm sure she will," he said, his eyes meeting hers. "She's gotten attached."

Her heart echoed in her ears, and her breath caught and held in her chest. He was staring at her lips as though he wanted to kiss her, and there was no denying the longing in his voice. She swallowed hard and moved a little closer, letting him know that she wouldn't refuse if he wanted to go for it.

A rough shake of the safety bar had her straightening as the kid glanced at them. "Thumbs-up?"

"Thumbs-up," Wes croaked as she half-heartedly gave the sign.

"Fair warning. I may throw up," Wes said as the kid went back to his post and gave the safety instructions.

"I may beat you to it," she said as the ride started rotating slowly. If it stayed at this speed, she'd be fine. But within seconds, the car was being flung from one side to the other, circling around the other cars, just narrowly missing them as they passed, the repetitive carnival ride jingle echoing in her rattled brain. Sarah struggled to remain on her side of the seat, but the force had her sliding into Wes.

He didn't seem to mind as he wrapped one arm around her.

They started to lift off the ground, and Sarah thought she might have a heart attack. She clutched the safety bar and pressed her feet into the floor as the scenery whizzed past outside the ride—one big blur of bright lights and people.

Wes's hand covered hers, and she closed her eyes and buried her head into his shoulder as the ride continued to twist and turn and jut and twitch all around the platform. It was hard to appreciate the contact when she was so freaking terrified.

"Don't worry, I got you," he whispered into her hair.

The ride went higher and faster, and she let go of the bar, her hands tangling in his shirt instead. She moved as close to him as possible, and his arms went around her as he held tight. The force of the gravity made it difficult to hold her head up, so she buried it in his chest and forced several deep breaths as her stomach rippled.

Oh my God, *this* was how she was going to die.

But out of all the ways to go, this wouldn't be the worst.

A long, excruciatingly terrifying minute later, the ride started to lower back toward the ground and the speed started to slow. As the ride came to a stop, she reluctantly released Wes's shirt and moved away.

His gaze met hers, and her heart pounded even more viciously than it had while the ride was throwing them around like rag dolls. Adrenaline was coursing through her, and the near-death experience only enhanced the sexual tension thick on the air around them.

"You okay?" Wes asked.

She nodded, not trusting her voice.

"Arms up," the kid attendant said, arriving at their cart.

Sarah looked away and raised her arms as the bar lifted and they were free. Wes climbed out and extended a hand to her. Hers shook slightly as she placed it in his, heat radiating through her arm all the way to her core, and climbed out on trembling legs.

"Well...that was fun," Wes said as they made their way to the exit where Lia and Marissa were waiting.

"That was terrifying." In more ways than one. Her feelings were growing for Wes...or maybe just returning from a place where she'd kept them buried for years. They were back with a terrifying intensity now.

"That was so amazing," Marissa said, her cheeks flushed from exhilaration.

"Yeah, amazing," Wes mumbled.

"What's next?" Lia asked, looking even more excited than the kid and not at all concerned that her hair was messy and windblown.

Who was this woman? And how did Wes and Marissa bring out this side of her?

Sarah shook her head. "I'm definitely done with the rides." Her vision was still struggling to focus, and her stomach wasn't surviving another one of those experiences.

Wes nodded his agreement. "Yeah, these are all yours," he said, handing the ride tickets to Marissa.

"Well, there's really no point in you two standing in all these lines with us," Lia said casually, but there was a hint of mischief in her eyes. "Marissa and I will just go, and you two can hang out…"

Marissa smiled. "Great idea."

Wes stared at her as though waiting for her to respond. "Um…okay," she said.

"Sounds good," he said. Then to Marissa, "You sure?"

"Absolutely," she said, taking Lia's hand and rushing off toward the next ride.

"Don't feel like you have to stick around," Lia called out, walking backward through the crowded fairway. "Just text me if you leave and we'll Uber it back to your place later."

Yep, they'd definitely been set up.

And Sarah had never been so grateful for Lia Jameson's interference in her entire life.

Wes turned to her and shrugged. "Well, we've been ditched."

"Looks that way." She shifted from one foot to the other, looking everywhere but at him.

"Walk on the beach?" he asked.

Her surprise had to be reflected on her face, but she nodded. "Sure." A walk on the beach with the man who'd always held her heart seemed like a much better way to spend the evening than surviving more amusement rides.

Though she suspected her emotions were about to go on a ride of their own.

• • •

The sand was still warm from the heat of that day's sun as they walked barefoot down the beach. Everyone had abandoned it for the fairgrounds, and the farther they moved away from the bright lights and noise, the more alone they were. Walking along in silence, the waves rolling up on the shore was the only sound.

Wes reached across and took Sarah's sandals from her, carrying them in one hand with his.

"Thank you," she said, sounding suddenly shy.

He hadn't anticipated how intimate this would feel. The two of them alone, just the glow of the moon reflecting off the water...

"So is everything ready for the reunion?" he asked, immediately regretting the casual, non-intimate question. Slipping back into friend territory wasn't the objective, but he wasn't sure how to do this. It had been years since he'd dated, and this wasn't just some woman—this was Sarah.

They had a shared history, and they knew each other really well, even better since she'd been back in town... it was different with her. And after the kiss fiasco, he suspected he might only have one more shot at this. He wanted to get it right.

"Yes, I think so," she said. "Everything's booked, guests are confirmed, the B&B is ready...thanks to you."

"Are you looking forward to heading back to L.A. once it's over?" He didn't know why her answer mattered so much all of a sudden. He knew she was going back, but a small part of him hoped she was at least a little bit sad about leaving.

"Not as much as I thought I'd be," she said, looking at him.

Their eyes caught and held. She was so incredibly beautiful, he couldn't look away. Especially the way the moonlight caught in her eyes. Her dark hair blowing around her bare shoulders and the curve of her gorgeous body had his body betraying his common sense to take things slow.

"We will be sad to see you leave," he said. "*I'll* be sad to see you leave."

She looked as torn as he felt as they stopped walking. He turned toward her and dropped their shoes into the sand, taking her hands in his and moving several inches closer. He heard a heart beating and he couldn't be sure if it was hers or his.

"Sarah…I don't know what's happening the last few weeks, but I want you to know how grateful I am for everything you've done for Marissa."

She nodded, looking slightly disappointed. "Grateful."

"More than grateful." He released one of her hands and touched her cheek. "I've also liked spending time with you…even if I didn't always agree with the choices you were making regarding the upgrades."

She laughed, and the sound warmed him to his core. "I've enjoyed spending time with you, too," she said. She stared up at him, and the questioning look in her gaze was one he had no answers to. All he did know was that he wanted a do-over on that kiss.

He tangled his hand into her hair and slowly

lowered his head to hers. She smelled like the salty sea air around them, and the nervous way her eyes flitted between his eyes and lips had him wanting to kiss her even more.

"I want to try that kiss again," he said.

He saw her gulp. "You know you don't deserve another shot at it, right?" she asked, but her tone belied the words. It was full of longing and desire.

"I do know that, but I'm hoping you'd be willing to forgive and forget?"

She swallowed hard as she nodded.

He lowered his head even closer, and she stood on tiptoes to close the gap between them. Her mouth was warm, soft...and this time, he was prepared.

He grabbed her hips and pulled her closer, their feet sinking into the sand. She wrapped her arms around his neck as she deepened the kiss, savoring his mouth. The flavors of mint and vanilla mingled together—his gum, her lip gloss...and they tasted good together. They felt good together, the way their bodies molded into each other, the perfectly in-sync rhythm of the kiss. It wasn't just chemistry or lust...it was something deeper. Something a lot like love.

Which had him absolutely terrified but all in. He'd always been intimidated by her. She was so far out of his league. Still was, but right now he didn't care...he just wanted her.

Picking her up into his arms, he knelt on the sand and carefully lowered her onto it. Lying on his side, he rested her head in his hand as he continued to kiss her more desperately. He felt his entire body come alive. It had been so long since a woman had him feeling this way.

Breathless, he pulled back to look at her. "Sarah, I…"

"Me too," she said, reading his thoughts.

He wanted her, right there on the beach. There was no one around, but anyone could walk by. Thickening in the front of his shorts was begging for him to think of something, and the look of pleading desire in Sarah's expression just added that much more pressure.

"I bet the ocean's warm," she whispered against his lips.

Holy hell…could they actually do it? He studied her expression to see if she was serious, and she grinned. "Unless, of course, you're not up for it."

"Oh, I'm up for it," he said, getting to his feet. He unbuttoned and removed his shirt. Sarah's appreciative gaze made him feel that much more confident. She obviously liked what she saw. He'd caught her checking him out over the last few weeks.

"Your turn," he said. He wasn't going all in alone. He extended a hand to her and pulled her to her feet.

She didn't even hesitate as she removed her tank top, slowly lifting it up over her body and tossing it to the sand. Her body was amazing — smooth, toned, soft-looking. It took all his effort not to reach out and touch her.

"You're up," she said.

He undid his shorts and removed them, standing there in only his boxers. He hoped the darkness helped to hide the bulge in the front of his underwear. He motioned for her to continue disrobing.

She hesitated only a fraction of a second before sliding the flowy skirt down over her hips and wiggling out of it.

He swallowed hard at the sight of the lacy white thong she wore. Low across her stomach and cut high on her hips, elongating her stomach and illuminating the hourglass shape. Damn, she was smart *and* sexy.

"I didn't think geniuses wore sexy undergarments," he teased, because otherwise he was going to grab her and take her right there on the sand. He didn't care who was watching.

"Common misconception," she said, nodding toward the underwear. "Off."

He hesitated slightly. "Maybe we should move into the water first."

"You afraid you might disappoint?" she asked, the teasing glint in her eye driving him wild.

"Yes," he said with a laugh, taking her hands and walking backward toward the ocean. The first cool waves hit the back of his legs, and his breath caught. "It's cold... You sure about this?"

She released his hands and ran farther into the waves before diving into them.

"Holy shit." She was all in. No backing out now.

He took a deep breath and dove in after her. The cool saltwater chilled his body, but as he resurfaced next to her, he was immediately hot again. Her long, dark hair wet, pushed back away from her face and hanging down her back, was sexy as hell. The fabric of the white bra, now wet, was virtually see-through, and the shape of her breasts and the peak of her hardened nipples were on full display.

Her inhibitions, her confidence was seducing as hell.

He moved toward her and wrapped an arm around her waist, drawing her into him as the ocean waves cascaded around them. He kissed her hard, and her arms encircled his neck. His cock throbbed as she pressed her body even closer, wrapping her legs around his waist.

"Sarah, you are so hot," he said, his hands caressing her waist, over her rib cage, down along her hips and ass.

"You sound surprised," she said.

"It's not just this body, which is amazing; it's everything about you—your confidence, your strength, your kindness…"

She reached behind her body and unclasped the bra. She slowly lowered the straps down over her arms and tossed it onto the shore.

His hands gently massaged her breasts, and she moaned as his thumbs rolled over her nipples. He lowered his head to the crook of her neck and tasted the salt on her skin. So delicious. So tempting. He hardened even more, and she reached below the water to grip his cock.

He groaned and bit her neck gently as she stroked up and down. "You're killing me."

She removed her hand and ground her hips against him, rubbing up and down the length of him. Her breathing grew labored as she increased the speed and intensity.

"It's been a long time…" He wasn't sure why he was warning her.

"Me too," she said. She kissed him as the ocean waves splashed up around them and he gripped her thighs as he felt himself getting close to the edge. His five-year celibacy combined with the weeks of sexual tension mounting between them had him on the verge of coming far too fast. He closed his eyes, and a second later, she was gone.

Hearing the splash of water around him, he opened his eyes and frowned. She was swimming back toward the shore. What the…?

"Sarah?"

She kept going, suddenly at the speed of an Olympic athlete, until she reached the sand. Then, climbing out, she gathered all their clothes into her arms. "Thanks for a fun night!" she called out to him.

His mouth dropped. "You're leaving me stranded out here? Naked?" And stealing his clothes, if appearances could be trusted.

"I guess now we're even," she said as she jogged away down the beach, putting her own clothes back on as she went.

He bobbed in the waves, watching her disappear as the first of the carnival fireworks exploded across the night sky. Vibrant colors of red, yellow, and orange burst across the dark night sky, the glow reflecting on the ocean around him.

Now they were even? What the hell did she mean?

One thing was certain. This new memory of skinny dipping with Sarah Lewis was definitely going to rival the old one.

CHAPTER NINETEEN

Sarah towel dried her hair an hour later in her bedroom, still grinning over her actions. It had taken all her strength not to give in to Wes in that moment. Her body had come alive from his touch, his kiss, his desire for her... She'd wanted him just as badly as he'd clearly wanted her.

But he'd totally deserved it.

Maybe leaving him stranded without his clothes had been a little overkill, but years of repressed feelings mixed with self-preservation revenge fantasies had overshadowed any guilt. She'd needed to set their record straight. He'd rejected her—twice. If he wanted her, *really* wanted her, he had to work for it.

A loud banging on the inn door had her heart racing.

Shit. There was no questioning who that was.

Heading downstairs, her legs felt slightly unsteady and she stopped on the stairs, seeing him enter, using the key she'd given him during the renovations. The laugh that escaped her at the sight of him in a women's beach cover-up was uncontrollable, and the look on his face when he turned toward her made her laugh even harder.

"You think this is funny?" he asked, advancing toward the stairs.

She nodded, struggling to compose herself. The thin, flowy fabric with the brightly colored flower pattern did little to conceal his body underneath. "Little bit," she croaked out before another fit of laughter.

"I had to flag a nice lady down and beg her for her cover-up, then I had to catch a taxi on the boardwalk looking like this, and then I had to agree to fix the understanding driver's fence for free in exchange for fare because someone stole my wallet," he said, climbing the stairs. His hair was still damp, and she could smell the salty ocean lingering on his flesh.

"Well, it serves you right," she said, crossing her arms across her chest in her thin silk bathrobe. She swallowed hard, but a lump seemed to be stuck in her throat.

He stopped on the stair below her, and his gaze burned into hers. "What did you mean, *now we're even*?"

She swallowed again, then cleared her throat. "That night in the water…before graduation. You set me up." She hated admitting that his actions that night had stayed with her over the years, that he'd had that much control over her teenage heart back then, but it was the truth. First heartbreaks were the deepest.

He frowned. "No I didn't."

"That's not how I remember it," she said, her pulse racing. And she'd thought about it to an unhealthy level over the years.

"Well, your memory must be a lot different from mine," he said, his voice slightly husky. "Because I remember a moment when I wanted to kiss you."

Her mouth gaped. So all this time, she hadn't been imagining that connection. That moment. He'd felt it, too. That put her overthinking mind at ease a little, but he wasn't off the hook. "But then you left."

He released a deep sigh. "My friends showed up. What was I supposed to do?"

"Not leave me bobbing alone, naked in the ocean, to become a joke for your friends?"

The sting of that humiliation had followed her for the weeks leading up to graduation. She'd felt her peers' eyes on her, heard the whispers. She didn't think Wes had perpetuated the gossip or rumors, but he certainly hadn't been affected by them the way she had. Maybe if it had been someone else, someone she hadn't been so in love with, she could have laughed it off. But having her hopes dashed in such a public way by him had left a scar.

He lowered his head, and remorse was apparent in his expression when he looked at her again. "I freaked out, okay? I was super attracted to you that night. Why do you think I dared you to do it in the first place?" He moved up a step until his face was level with hers. "I liked you, Sarah."

Her heart raced, and her mouth was dry. "Well, why didn't you say something? Why didn't you tell me? Why did you leave?"

"Because you were this amazing genius, and I was just a dumb jock. You had all these amazing plans, and I had football. We were worlds apart back then. I wasn't good enough for you."

That's how he saw things? "That's not what I remember," she said softly.

He reached out and cupped her face. "I liked you, Sarah. I still like you," he said, pulling her face toward his.

She could barely breathe as she moved toward him. "You do?"

"Yeah, I really do," he murmured against her lips. "And I'd really like to finish what we started in the water."

Oh my God. She didn't trust her voice, so she nodded. She desperately wanted that, too.

In half a heartbeat, he swept her into his arms and headed back upstairs to her bedroom. They fell onto the bed, and Wes rolled them so that she was on top. His lust-filled gaze when he looked at her surprised the hell out of her. No other man had looked at her like this before. Especially not one as hot as Wes.

His train of thought seemed to echo hers.

"Having a body this hot and a brilliant brain on top of it should be illegal," he said, his hands working fast to ditch the cover-up and untie her silk robe. His gaze drank her in. "You are certainly intimidating, Sarah Lewis," he said, massaging her bare breasts.

She was intimidating? He was the one built like a god. He was the athletic one. The one good with his hands...in all kinds of ways. The charming and charismatic one. On top of that, he was an amazing father and driven to make a great life for himself and his daughter.

If anyone should be intimidated, it was her.

"I feel like I'm punching above my weight here," she said, her hands caressing the tight six-pack and the broad, muscular shoulders. If someone had told teenage Sarah that one day she'd be lying naked on a bed with an equally naked Wes Sharrun, she'd never have believed it.

This went further than just a teenage fantasy come to life. This was the most unexpected thing she could have predicted five weeks ago arriving in Blue Moon Bay, grieving the loss of her grandmother and conflicted over the future of the inn.

He stared at her as though she'd lost her mind. "I'm just a small-town blue-collar worker trying to keep his head above water."

He was so much more than he gave himself credit for. Her feelings for him years ago were based on how cute he was, how nice, how popular and good at sports. He was the polar opposite of her, and she'd been intrigued by him. Now, her resurfacing feelings were based on so much more.

She flipped their position so that she was on top. In control. And then lowered her body toward him, inching her ass farther down his body, until she could feel his erect cock between her legs. He closed his eyes, and a low moan escaped him as she slowly grinded her hips back and forth over him.

It took almost nothing for her to get wet. Turning him on was proving to be a major turn-on for her. In the boardroom, online, at work, lost in a computer program, she knew what she was doing…but outside of that, in real life, she often felt like a fish out of water. Never quite good enough, never having just the right thing to say, not enough confidence to go after what she wanted.

But with Wes in this moment, she felt empowered in

ways she never had before. He brought out a side of her that she hadn't known existed.

With him she felt sexy and strong and confident... She wanted to feel the way he made her feel all the time.

She lowered her mouth to his and kissed him hard. Pulling back slightly, she ran her tongue along his bottom lip, capturing it with her teeth as desire welled up inside her.

His fingers dug into the flesh at her waist as he pushed her down closer on his cock.

She lay back onto him, skin to skin, her breasts against his chest as she wiggled her hips back and forth over him.

He reached a hand between them, his fingers sliding along the length of her wet folds, and he swallowed hard. "Damn, that's hot. I love how wet you are."

Her breath caught as his finger dipped inside her body, and she clenched her muscles tight around it. It felt so good, but she needed more. Needed him to fill her. "Condom?" she asked.

"In my wallet. In the shorts you stole on the beach."

She giggled as she climbed off him to retrieve the shorts.

Wes leaned on 'his elbows, watching her as she opened the wallet and took out the condom. "You're not even the least bit guilty, are you?" he asked with a grin.

"Nope," she said, climbing back onto the bed and straddling him as she tore the plastic open and slid it down over his erection. He lay back against the pillows, and his eyes closed at her touch. She raised her body slightly and lowered herself down over him. The sensation of him filling her, the tightness between their two bodies had her panting slightly.

He cupped her ass and slowly, carefully lifted her up and down over him. "Sarah…Sarah…" The sound of her name on his lips only amplified her need for him. She could listen to him say her name forever. Feeling desired was a new, intoxicating sensation for her. Feeling desired by *him* was everything she'd ever wanted.

She gripped the headboard with both hands as she continued to ride him up and down. Faster and faster until he flipped them suddenly, gaining the top position. He wedged himself between her legs. Taking both of her hands in his, he interlaced their fingers as he raised her arms above her head on the pillow. He lowered his mouth to her neck, and she turned her face to the side as he kissed and savored the taste of her.

"You are so incredible," he whispered in her ear as he plunged even deeper into her body. "I haven't wanted anyone so badly in a very long time."

She knew the feeling. She not only wanted him; she craved him.

She squeezed his hands tight as she felt her arousal mounting. His thick, big cock driving in and out of her body increased its urgency and her legs trembled on either side of Wes. She craved release as her muscles tightened and released over him with each thrust…but she didn't want this feeling to end.

"Wes, I'm so close," she said, arching her back, driving her pelvis forward to get even closer to him.

He reduced his pace to an excruciatingly slow rhythm, pulling the full length of his cock out to the tip, then slowly sliding back in...

He raised his head to look at her, and his eyes locked with hers as he continued the teasing of her vagina with his cock.

"Wes, please..." she said, her panting growing more desperate.

"What do you want, Sarah? Tell me what you want."

Him. All of him. She always had.

"I want you," she said. How she felt about him was on the tip of her tongue, but while she gave her body completely, she held back on the emotions. For now.

He groaned as though his actions were torturing himself as well. "Say it again," he said, pumping slightly faster.

"I want you, Wes," she said. Gripping his hands even tighter as he started moving faster, harder. Diving into her body as though he couldn't get deep enough...

Her orgasm peaked, and ripples of pleasure had her calling out as her entire body trembled.

He plunged in hard. Deep. And held it. He released his own grunt as he came; then his body relaxed on top of hers.

He fell forward, his head dropping onto her chest as he released her hands and used his to support his weight above her.

She cupped his head between her hands and kissed

the top of his head, breathing in the scent of his slightly sweaty hair and enjoying the feel of their two bodies still connected.

• • •

An hour later, she slipped quietly out of bed and, wrapping her robe around her body, she went out onto the deck. Of all the upgrades she'd made to the B&B, the decks off the bedrooms were by far her favorite addition. But if someone had told Sarah three months ago that she'd be standing on one enjoying the view of the ocean waves at midnight while Wes Sharrun slept in a bed in the room behind her, she'd have told them they were insane.

Yet that was her reality.

She took a deep breath and stared out at the view. This place was truly incredible and the longer she stayed, the harder it was to think about leaving, giving up the B&B...and this time with Wes. But what did it mean? Their attraction had definitely been growing these past few weeks, her feelings for him were more real than ever, and now they'd taken their relationship from friends to...what?

His arms wrapped around her and she jumped. She hadn't heard him get up. "Hi," he murmured against her ear. His warm breath against her skin made her shiver, and he wrapped his arms even tighter. The feel of his bare chest and abs against her back had her heart picking up its pace.

He was real. His touch was real. This wasn't just one of her fantasies, and she wasn't dreaming.

"Did I wake you?" she asked. She couldn't sleep. Partially his fault and partially the overwhelmingness of the whole situation. She'd had sex with her high school crush. She'd had sex with Wes Sharrun. No matter how many times she repeated the thought to herself, no matter how long she lay there staring at him, she could hardly believe it.

"I wish you *had* woken me," he said with a smile, turning her sideways to hold her and kiss her, while still enjoying the view of the moon reflecting on the ocean. His lips were the best thing she'd ever tasted. "You okay?" he asked, scanning her face as he pulled back slowly.

She smiled. "Yes. Great... Just, um, this"—she gestured between them and to the unmade bed inside the room—"was unexpected."

He looked slightly nervous as he asked, "In a good way?"

"Definitely in a good way." She kissed him again and pressed her body into his.

"If you're done admiring the view, I'd like to take you back to bed," he said against her lips.

"I'm not sure," she teased. "This view is kinda spectacular... Think you can compete?"

The flicker of challenge reflected in his blue eyes and Sarah's breath caught as he scooped her up into his arms and carried her back into the room.

CHAPTER TWENTY

Wes's knee bounced as he waited in the lobby of the bank the next day. He pulled at the tie around his neck and glanced around at the quiet office. He hadn't realized how much he was hoping for this loan to come through until he was seated there waiting on the verdict.

This could help change his future for the better. If he could get the office space, it would be the first step in expanding his company. Having a place—not in his home—to meet with clients and design new building developments would help motivate him to push forward with growing Sharrun's Construction.

And the night before with Sarah only confirmed how much he wanted to start building a new future for himself and Marissa. Taking that chance with her, putting himself out there and going after what he wanted, had been the best decision he'd made in a long time.

Holding her, kissing her, making love to her had felt so right. Unexpectedly right. There was no remorse or doubt lingering in his mind. Which surprised him but also gave him a sense of relief. He wanted to be with Sarah Lewis. The high of this new connection with her was almost enough to ease his anxiety over the meeting.

"Wes, come on in," Shawn said, appearing in the lobby with his file in hand. He barely glanced at him as he entered, and Wes was desperate to read the guy. The last meeting, the man had barely been able to contain his fangirling. But that day, the manager wasn't giving anything away as he gestured for Wes to take a seat, and then he sat behind the desk.

Good news? Bad news?

Wes sat back in the chair and crossed one ankle over his knee…then he sat forward again.

"So, we've reviewed your application and all the supporting financial paperwork…" Shawn paused. His professional demeanor that day was freaking Wes out. Was the guy nervous about telling one of his former idols bad news?

"Come on, man. Just tell me. Did I get the loan?"

Shawn's wide smile reappeared as all pretenses vanished. "You got the loan," he said, sounding almost more excited for Wes than Wes felt himself.

Wes's heart pounded in his chest as he tipped his head to the right. "Sorry, you know I have trouble hearing in one ear. I thought I heard you say I got it?"

Shawn nodded. "You heard right. Congratulations, Wes. I know you've been struggling to get things back on track in recent years, so I'm happy we were able to help you with this part."

Wes released a sigh of relief. "Thank you."

"We just have a few trees to sign, and then you can be on your way," Shawn said with a chuckle, opening the file.

"None of this is electronic yet?"

"Maybe in big city branches, but here we're still old-school."

"I've been accused of that myself," Wes said, accepting the pen to sign the documents.

Twenty minutes later, he left the bank, feeling as though he were floating down Main Street. An amazing night connecting on a physical level with a woman he was crazy about and now the first real steps at achieving his career goals.

He reached the office space for lease and, taking out his cell phone, he dialed the broker's number on the FOR LEASE sign. With any luck, he was getting his office space back, and this time, he wouldn't lose it. No matter what sacrifices it took.

Three rings and then voicemail.

Wes left a message and then texted Sarah.

Loan was approved! Be ready at six. We're going out to celebrate.

He beamed as he headed toward his truck. Life was certainly looking up.

• • •

Three hours later, the three of them sat at a table on the upstairs patio of Surfboards on the pier. The sun set on the ocean, and the light cast a warm glow reflecting off their glasses as they cheered a toast to Wes's good news. Champagne for the adults, sparkling water for Marissa. Sitting there with them, being invited to their special celebration that evening, warmed Sarah's heart. To be included, to feel like she belonged there with them, was a good feeling. She'd expected a little awkwardness the next day after their night together, a bit of questioning, an adjusting… But everything felt right that evening.

Marissa was positively beaming as she glanced back and forth between them. "So…how was your night?"

Sarah blushed and choked on the bubbles, and Wes grinned. "We made the best of it after you ditched us," he told his daughter.

The little girl just laughed, looking proud of her involvement in the two of them getting together.

Sarah was more than a little grateful for the matchmaking skills of the nine-year-old. "When will you hear back about the space?" she asked Wes.

"Hopefully by next week. The leasing agent is out of town at some real estate convention, but I've put in my offer, so we'll see…"

He looked excited but nervous, and Sarah reached across the table and touched his hand. "It'll work out. I know it will."

His gaze locked on hers, and she immediately wished they were alone back in her room at the inn, but they'd already discussed their plan of not leaving the bedroom once Marissa left for camp the next day.

So for now, Sarah shifted her focus to her. "Are you excited about camp?"

Marissa shrugged. "Not really, but it'll be nice to see old friends." She toyed with the edge of her napkin; there was definitely something on her mind.

"Is there anything we still need to buy?" Wes asked her.

She shook her head. "I think I have everything."

"We should probably pack tonight," he said.

Marissa nodded. "Sounds good."

Wes glanced at Sarah, and she returned his concerned look. Marissa was obviously wanting to say
something, and it was a rare occurrence for the little girl
not to speak her mind. Sarah's palms sweat a little. Was
she concerned about the two of them together? She'd
wanted it to happen before, but maybe now she was
conflicted?

Wes leaned toward her. "Hey, everything okay?" He
paused. "Is this…the three of us having dinner together
okay?"

Marissa's eyes widened as she nodded emphatically.
"Yes! Definitely. About freaking time," she muttered and
Sarah relaxed. "I just wanted to ask…Friday is parents'
day at camp…" She turned toward Sarah. "Do you think
you could come?"

Sarah's eyes widened, and she looked at Wes. Marissa
wanted her to attend parents' day at camp. She'd love to
go and support Marissa, but she didn't want Wes to
think she was getting ahead of herself with regards to
their relationship. They'd only spent one incredible
night together…

"I think it's a great idea. If you're free," he said, his
gaze filled with all the love and affection she'd always
dreamed about. He squeezed her hand across the table
and looked almost as nervous waiting for her answer as
Marissa did.

He wanted her to go. Marissa wanted her to go. Her
heart felt like it might explode out of her chest as she
nodded. "Yeah. Absolutely. Wouldn't miss it," she said.

CHAPTER TWENTY-ONE

A blast of wind whipped Sarah's hair in front of her face as she walked along the nearly empty boardwalk toward the blown-glass hut the next day. What a difference from two weeks before, when locals and tourists had filled the air with sounds of summer. But the current rain and windstorm had tourists staying indoors.

That upcoming long weekend would be the official shutdown for the season.

On the ocean, the fierce waves appealed to only the most hardcore surfers, and even they looked to be calling it a day as the yellow caution flag was replaced with a red warning on the lifeguard tower down the beach. All the market huts had dragged their outside tables inside, and the dark-gray clouds made it feel as though it were evening despite it only being a little past noon.

Since reading the latest journal entry, she'd been putting off picking up the decorations she'd ordered. It was odd knowing that this man had meant so much to her grandmother and not feeling as though she could bring it up or ask him about it. It was none of her business, but she was dying to know why he'd treated Dove that way. Walked away from her and the love they'd once shared. Yet she hadn't been able to read further.

Reaching the shop, she struggled against the wind to open the heavy door and hurried inside, shaking her wet hair away from her face. The forecast had predicted the storm, but she'd expected to be back at the B&B before it hit.

Either way, she'd needed to pick up her order. She didn't want Mr. Harrison to think she no longer wanted it.

"Hello?" she called as she walked toward the back of the shop. "Mr. Harrison?"

"Be right with you," she heard the older man say, followed by the sound of terrible coughing.

She waited, but the coughing continued. Deep, throat-tearing noises that sounded really unhealthy.

Finally, he emerged, with a white napkin, wiping his mouth. His eyes were watery and slightly bloodshot. Somehow, he looked older than he had before. "Oh, hi, Sarah…"

He looked surprised to see her. "Hi, Mr. Harrison. You okay?"

He waved a hand, tucking the napkin into his pocket. "Fine. Just a little lung cancer is all."

Her mouth dropped. "I'm so sorry. I had no idea you were sick."

"Not sick. Dying. Finally," he said with a grin.

"I'm so sorry to hear that…" Despite his casualness, her knees felt slightly wobbly as she gripped the edge of the counter. He was sick. He was dying.

"Sweet girl, when you get to be my age, it's almost a relief to know your days are numbered. I've lived through wars, depressions, technology changes, and teenagers wearing their jeans around their knees. I was starting to think nothing could take me out."

Sarah gave a small smile. At least he was in good spirits, and the man was in his nineties…and alone. In a sad way, she could appreciate his acceptance of the end of his days.

"You were in the military?" She knew he was, but she wasn't ready to admit just how much she knew. Yet. Not in a rush to leave, and thinking he might like the company, she pulled up a stool at the counter and sat.

"Enlisted at eighteen. I'd always been fascinated by planes and bombers, so I went into the air force. I loved flying a jet. I flew my P-51 Mustang over Japanese airfields near Tokyo for ten months before I was captured, held as a prisoner of war in a Japanese war camp for eighteen months."

"Oh my God—that's horrible."

"I learned a lot about the people we were fighting in that time. I learned the language and the culture, got to understand their world. Had me questioning a lot of things. Good and evil. Right and wrong. Made me realize there's two sides to every story."

She nodded. Two sides. She'd only read one. She was desperate to hear his, to know why he did what he did. Why he broke her grandmother's heart. She refused to come to her own conclusions. Life and love were complicated. She understood that right now better than anyone.

"So what happened after you returned?" She cleared her throat. "Did you marry? Have a family?" He was all alone here now, but that didn't mean he didn't possibly have family somewhere.

His eyes smiled as he shook his head. "I'd only ever loved one woman, and she deserved everything I couldn't give her. I was a different man when I came back. The things I saw, the things I did changed me. It took a long time to come to peace with my part in the war. I was better alone."

Sarah's throat tightened. "But if you loved her…"

"I loved her enough to let her be happy. She married soon after and had children. I saw her almost every day…until the day she died, and seeing her smile and knowing she was living a wonderful life, that was enough for me."

Tears burned the backs of Sarah's eyes. But her grandma hadn't been completely happy. Not without him. How could she tell him that? Would it matter? Or would it only make him sad to know that Dove's heart had broken with his rejection? That she'd never fully gotten over him?

He snapped his fingers, making her jump. "You came for the bulbs," he said, pointing to his head. "Nothing wrong with the old brain, in case you were afraid I'd forgotten."

Sarah laughed, feeling the tension from the moment dissipate slightly. "Guilty." *She'd* practically forgotten the reason she was there.

"Wait right there," he said, going into the back room, where another terrible-sounding coughing fit took over.

"Do you need help?" she called. Not waiting for an answer, she pushed past the curtain to his work area. Several wooden benches were set up with various paint cans and sections of glass on top. In the corner was a furnace where the clear glass was melted, and on the other side of the room was an annealing oven, used for cooling finished pieces.

The shop extended farther than she'd realized. Behind the work area was a small living quarters. She could see the bachelor-style suite with the kitchenette, small living room, and a cot in the corner. Dated but comfortable-looking furniture and a small television and not much else.

He lived here, too.

I was better alone.

He'd spent his entire life alone. Her heart ached for him and for her grandma and for what never had the chance to be.

Seeing a row of pictures along the wall, she stopped to look at them. Jack in his air force uniform with two other men. One she didn't recognize...but the other was definitely her grandfather. In the next picture, there were the three of them—her grandmother in the middle with her arm around each man, her smile lighting up the black-and-white picture. The photos had to have been taken before the men had left for war. They all still looked young and hopeful.

"Recognize that beauty?" Jack asked, coming up behind her with a large box in his arms.

She took it from him quickly, and her arms sagged under the unexpected weight. "My grandma. She was...?" She couldn't finish the sentence, turmoil and a desperation to keep her grandma's confidence making her say instead, "Thank you for getting these made so quickly. I really appreciate it."

"You're more than welcome." He led the way back into the front of the shop, holding the curtain for her. "Looks like the storm is blowing over."

A solitary beam of sunlight pierced through the dark sky and streamed in through the open blinds at the window. Sarah shivered, an eerie chill washing over her she couldn't explain.

She set the box on the counter and reached for her wallet.

Jack shook his head. "No charge."

"I have to pay you."

"Sarah, chances are I won't live long enough to spend the money I already have. Take them. A gift to Dove's granddaughter."

She released a deep breath, knowing there was no point in arguing with him. "Thank you, Mr. Harrison. This is very kind of you."

The beam of sunlight moved across the floor and retreated into the clouds as new rain—big, heavy-sounding drops—started pelting against the window.

"Looks like we're not out of the woods yet. You better hurry back to your car. Let me get the door for you," he said, opening the shop door.

She eyed the ominous-looking sky as she stepped outside. "Bye, Mr. Harrison," she said, hoping it wasn't the last time she'd see him.

• • •

Wes glanced at Marissa in the passenger seat of the truck as they drove along the coast toward Camp Crowley. Dressed in her Girl Guides uniform, her oversize duffel bag at her feet, she looked slightly nervous as she turned her cell phone over and over in her hands.

"You okay?" he asked.

"Yeah, fine…"

She didn't seem herself that morning. Quieter, more withdrawn as she'd finished packing her things, eaten breakfast, and they'd headed out. Was she really hating these summer camps? Maybe forcing her to go wasn't the right thing to do. She usually enjoyed them once she got there, and by the end of the week, there was always a teary farewell to friends she'd reconnected with.

He cleared his throat. "I was thinking next year, we can skip this one and try that STEM camp instead." She'd be ten then, and it was time to start giving her more freedom and independence. She was growing up, and that terrified him, but he suspected he'd worry about her when she was forty. That didn't change for parents as their kids got older.

She nodded, her gaze lost out the window. "Sounds great, Dad."

Okay, something was definitely up. "Hey, are you okay with…the whole Sarah and me thing?" She'd been pushing them together before, and she'd seemed excited about it at dinner, but maybe now she wasn't feeling so great about it. Maybe she felt her own friendship with Sarah would be challenged if he and Sarah were spending more time together. Or that she'd lose part of his time and attention.

But she turned to him and gave the first real smile that day. "Yes, Dad. I think you and Sarah together is great."

He reached across and touched her cheek as he turned onto the gravel road and the gates of Camp Crowley came into view. She sighed in the seat next to him, and he stopped the truck and put it in park.

"What are you doing?" she asked.

"If you don't want to go, you don't have to go," he said. He was done encouraging her to do things she hated. She'd gone to this camp for three years. She'd given it a try. If she wanted to skip it, that was okay with him.

"It's fine, Dad, really," she said with what he knew was forced enthusiasm. "I'm looking forward to seeing my friends. I guess I'm just nervous."

"You sure?"

"Yes," she said with exasperation. "Come on, I'm going to be late for check-in."

Wes drove through the camp gates and parked next to the other cars in the lot. Parents hugged their kids and collected their overnight bags. Most kids looked eager to hurry off and join their friends, and most of the parents looked just as eager to see them go after the long summer.

Climbing out, he waved to several parents he recognized, then turned to Marissa. "You got everything?"

"Yes, Dad."

Now was the hard part. "Electronics?" he said, holding out a hand for her phone.

She kissed it, then handed it to him. "I'll see you and Sarah on Friday?"

He nodded. His heart was still full at the thought. She liked Sarah enough to invite her to parents' day, and Sarah had agreed to come. The way she'd fallen so perfectly into their lives still surprised him, but it made sense. Sarah offered both of them so much, and Wes only hoped he could give her everything she deserved.

He hugged Marissa tight. "Have a great time at camp. See you on Friday." He stood there and waved as she dragged her duffel bag toward the check-in desk.

Unfortunately, he couldn't shake the nagging feeling that something was up with his daughter.

. . .

Hanging the last of the blown-glass bulbs in the guest rooms, Sarah stood watching the sun reflect off the various colors. They were the perfect addition to the rooms, and now whoever bought the inn, she'd feel as though there was still a part of her in it. A part of Mr. Harrison, too. It felt right somehow to honor her grandmother's first love in this small way.

"I hope I'm making you proud, Grandma," she said.

Her cell chimed with a new email notification, and her heart raced seeing the subject line from her boss. The last few days, she'd completely forgotten about work. With the new revised proposal approved by Gail, she'd let herself relax until the pitch. Spending time with Wes and Marissa, she'd barely given it a second thought.

Opening it, she held her breath as she read, *Pitch meeting for SmartTech has been moved up to this Friday at nine thirty a.m. They loved the proposal and don't want to wait until after the long weekend. Need you here.*

A month before, she'd have been jumping in her car and heading back to the city immediately, letting Whitney take over the event and putting the inn on the market from a distance, but now it wouldn't be as easy to walk away from her hometown.

What the hell was wrong with her? This was her career. Her promotion was riding on this pitch. This was what she wanted.

Friday.

Oh no! That was Marissa's parents' day at camp.

Sarah bit her lip as she stared at the message, unsure how to reply. Maybe she could ask Gail if they could keep the original pitch time. Or maybe she could do the pitch in the morning and still make it back in time for the camp event. Marissa said it started at noon. It would be tight, but as long as the pitch was only an hour, like most… Either way, she knew she had to be there.

She squared her shoulders and, hitting reply, she typed, *Of course I'll be there.*

But guilt immediately washed over her as she hit Send. She'd promised Marissa she'd be there for her as well. Disappointing the little girl had Sarah's chest tightening. But this was work. It was important. And she wasn't actually a parent…

Her stomach twisted. If she was going to be with Wes, be in their lives, she would be a parent. She'd need to step into that role for Marissa. Surprisingly, the idea didn't scare her. She loved the idea of being in their lives, and she knew she could be a great friend to Marissa and hopefully eventually the stepmom she deserved.

Would she understand if Sarah didn't make it to camp that Friday? Would Wes?

Sarah sighed. There had to be a way she could do both. She would hate to have to make a choice, but staring at the sent reply to her boss, she felt like she already had.

• • •

As Wes turned into the driveway of the B&B that evening, he couldn't help the sense of pride at seeing the newly renovated inn. It had all its original charm but was stronger and sturdier to last another hundred years or more. He climbed out and headed up the path toward the front door.

Seeing Whitney standing on the lawn snapping photos on her cell phone, Wes shook his head. Always on the clock. Whitney probably dreamed of her to-do list when she slept. He'd never met anyone who worked harder than that woman. He stopped next to her. "Hey, Whitney, how are you?"

"Oh, hey, Wes," she said with a smile. "This place looks incredible."

"It really does. I'm happy Sarah decided to renovate,"

he said. He wasn't sure if Sarah had told her friends about them yet. They hadn't really defined or labeled what was going on between them, but he knew he wanted a real relationship, and he sensed she did as well.

"Where's Marissa?" she asked.

"Girl Guides camp," he said. "Just dropped her off." He was still concerned about her mood at drop-off, but he was desperate to trust her. If she said she was okay being there, he'd try not to let it worry him that week. It was only five days, and he was looking forward to the alone time with Sarah before she headed back to the city.

"I hear she and Sarah really hit it off?" Whitney asked, a grin on her face. One that said she suspected Marissa wasn't the only one.

"Yes. Fast friends." He sighed. "She'll miss her once she heads back to L.A."

Whitney eyed him. "Yeah…I suspect we all will." She snapped several more photos and shook her head. "After all this time and money, I just hope Sarah's efforts work to preserve the place."

Wes frowned. "Why wouldn't they? I'm sure someone will be interested in buying it."

Whitney tucked her cell phone into her dress pocket. "I'm not worried she'll be able to sell it; I'm just not sure the new owner will have the same attachment to it."

Wes's gut tightened. It was true. Dove's Nest meant a lot to the residents of Blue Moon Bay, but an outside investor might not care. "Have you expressed your concerns to Sarah?"

"No. I don't want her to feel pressured into not selling. She's gone above and beyond to give the inn a fighting chance against a big chain, but I know she wouldn't be happy staying here and keeping it just to save it." She checked her watch.

He couldn't expect that of Sarah, either, and he didn't.

"Anyway, I have to run. Let Sarah know I'll call her later," Whitney said with a wave as she headed toward her yellow convertible.

Wes stared at the inn a minute longer before heading inside. Sarah descended the stairs, hearing him enter, and she immediately hurried toward him. "How did drop-off go?"

"Good," he said. He wouldn't worry her over his own uneasiness. His hands cupped her face, and he pulled her into him. "I've been waiting all day to do this," he said, his mouth crushing hers.

Her hands slid beneath his T-shirt and roamed over his abs and pectoral muscles, her fingers tickling his ribs. Her tongue explored his mouth, and her breathing was labored when she pulled back. "It was so hard not to do that with Marissa around."

"Tell me about it." But they were taking it slow and being respectful around his daughter. She may like Sarah, she may even like the idea of the two of them together, but too much, too soon might have her feeling differently. Sarah was the first woman to come into their lives since Kelly died, and Wes still needed to be careful of his daughter's heart...

Even if there was no saving his own.

Taking his hand, she led the way into the den, where her computer was set up. "I just need to finish this code real quick; then I'm all yours," she said, sitting on the sofa and picking up the laptop.

"I like the sound of that," he said, sitting next to her. He kissed her cheek, then her ear, then her neck.

She giggled as she gently pushed his face away. "That's distracting."

If she thought that was a distraction…

He slid a hand over her bare thigh in her jean shorts. Moving higher and higher and then dipping his fingers below the fabric. He inched them higher until they reached her underwear.

"Wes…" She continued to type, but her breathing grew heavier and she opened her legs, giving him better access. She moaned and closed her eyes as his fingers moved higher to massage her mound through the thin lace. She stopped typing.

"You're supposed to be working," he murmured against her exposed shoulder in her tank top.

She sucked in her lower lip as his fingers moved the fabric aside and he plunged two into her already wet body. She took several shallow breaths as her fingers flew over the keyboard.

"It's so damn sexy watching your brain work so fast," he said, taking her hand and placing it over his erect penis, straining against the front of his shorts.

"It doesn't take much to get you going, either," she whispered, squeezing her hand around him.

"Are you kidding me?" he asked, moving his fingers

in and out and massaging his thumb over her clit. "Damn, Sarah…you have no idea what you do to me."

He kissed her neck again as his fingers moved quicker in and out of her body. He felt her tighten, and he desperately wanted to feel her body clenching around his cock.

"The coding can wait," she said, setting the laptop aside and turning her full attention to him.

"I'm sorry," he said with a grin. "Should I stop and let you work?"

"Not a chance." She unzipped his shorts and slid her hand through the opening of his underwear to grip his penis in her hand. It was already rock-hard, and the throbbing sensation at her touch was almost painful. She was incredible; the way she made him feel was incredible.

She started to stroke him up and down, rolling her thumb over the tip of him, then coating the length of him with his precum.

He put another finger inside, and she sucked in a breath as her grip tightened on him. "Does this hurt?" he whispered in her ear.

"Only in a good way," she said, her voice strained. "Faster, please," she begged, picking up her own pace on his cock.

He plunged in and out, deep into her body as her legs trembled and he felt her orgasm erupt. Her body convulsed, and she closed her eyes and suppressed a deep, satisfying moan on a kiss.

He grinned as he slowly slid his fingers out of her

body. "Better than working?"

She nodded. "Much better," she said, removing her hand from his body and getting up off the couch. He watched as she knelt on the floor in front of him and pushed his knees apart.

Oh, Jesus.

She wiggled in between his legs and, gripping his penis with one hand, she lowered her head to his lap.

Wes's head fell back against the sofa as Sarah's mouth wrapped around him. He couldn't remember the last time he'd had a blow job. The feel of Sarah's wet, warm mouth sucking and licking him was torture. Sweet, delicious torture.

He closed his eyes as her tongue slid the length of him and circled the top… Her hand at the base of his cock massaged his balls, and he stifled a moan as the pleasurable sensations flowed through him.

She sucked harder, and he was dangerously close to the edge. "Sarah…" His voice held a note of warning, but she didn't stop. A moment later, he gripped the fabric of the sofa cushions and threw his head back as he came, the overwhelming sensations stealing his breath.

She slowly removed her mouth from him and, getting up off the floor, she sat on his lap. He wrapped his arms around her and kissed her hard. "You're so incredible," he said, brushing her dark hair away from her face.

"You're not too bad yourself," she said. She smiled and kissed him again, but then her gaze lowered. Her expression darkened slightly and she bit her lip.

"Hey, everything okay?" he asked, placing a finger under her chin and tipping her face up to look at him.

"Yeah." She paused and shook her head. "Actually, not really."

His heart thundered in his chest. First Marissa, now Sarah. "What's going on?"

"The pitch meeting with SmartTech Kids was moved up…to this Friday," she said, looking disappointed.

"Okay…"

"The same day as parents' day at camp," she said.

His chest tightened. "Oh."

"I'm so sorry, Wes," she said quickly. "I'm still going to try to make it. My meeting is at nine thirty, so as long as it doesn't go longer than an hour, I can get back here in time."

"Hey, if not, it's okay," he said reassuringly. They'd just started getting serious; it would be unfair to expect Sarah to choose a camp day over a big pitch meeting she'd been working hard on for months. Her promotion was riding on it.

"No, it's not. Marissa will be disappointed if I'm not there," she said. "I promised her."

Wes kissed her forehead. She looked truly pained by the conflicting schedule, and her concern made him fall that much harder for her. "She will understand," he said.

Sarah still looked worried. "I really want to be there."

He nodded. "I know." He really wanted her to be there, too. "But if you can't, that's okay."

Sarah sighed as she snuggled into his chest. "I'm going to try my best."

CHAPTER TWENTY-TWO

The L.A. boardroom was already set up for the meeting that Friday morning when Sarah arrived at the office. SmartTech products sat in the center of the table, and the large flatscreen at the front of the room had Sarah's presentation slides ready to go. Coffee and a dessert tray were laid out, and Sarah paced the room, flipping through her presentation notes.

She checked her watch. It was just after nine.

Camp parents' day was scheduled to start at noon. Her meeting started in ten minutes... How fast could she talk? Could she get through this pitch in an hour, then hit the road? It normally took two hours to get to Blue Moon Bay...if there was no traffic. If she drove really fast, she might be able to make it and only be a few minutes late.

She took a deep breath.

She'd never had to juggle her commitments before. She'd only ever had to think about herself. Her own future goals. What she wanted, and it hadn't affected anyone else if she worked long hours, weekends, pulled all-nighters, and poured all her attention and energy into work.

Now there were others to think about.

The relationship with Wes was new, but she already knew she was in love with him. In love with *them*. Her life was already different after the last few weeks, the last few days especially. She felt different.

This was the first real challenge of how they could make a long-distance relationship work. It was a test of sorts for her.

Wes had reassured her again that morning when she'd been reluctant to leave that this was fine. He understood. Marissa would understand if she couldn't make it. But Sarah was suddenly struggling with what she could only assume other parents faced every day—the internal battle of choosing family over career. Of balancing two desires, lifestyles, to try to make things work.

So far in her career, the only way she'd succeeded was by giving it 100 percent. Could she give it 50 and still achieve her goals? It wouldn't be fair to Wes and Marissa if she tried to maintain her workaholic pace, putting them last on her priority list. They certainly weren't there in her heart.

She sighed, then tried to appear completely focused as her boss entered the room.

Donning her usual black power dress—square neck, cinched at the waist, just below the knee—and four-inch red heels, her short white hair slicked back and airbrushed makeup on her thin face, Gail was success personified. For so many years, Sarah had looked up to her mentor. She'd wanted to be just like Gail.

Suddenly, her own suit and heels felt confining. She longed to change into the sundress and sandals in her car.

"You ready?" her boss asked as she checked the monitor cables on the table.

"Absolutely," Sarah said. This was what she wanted. This was the setting she was comfortable in. This was what she was good at. She needed to push everything else aside and show Gail that she deserved the promotion. Maybe if she was working on her own projects and not having to jump whenever Gail called, she'd have more time for the other things she now knew she wanted in her life.

"Great. Let's run through it," Gail said, sitting at the head of the boardroom table. She crossed one leg over the other and folded French-manicured hands on her lap.

Sarah frowned, checking the time. "I don't think we have time." The executives from SmartTech Kids would be arriving any minute, and she didn't want to be in mid-presentation when they arrived. That wouldn't exactly look professional.

Gail waved a hand. "The meeting's not until noon. We can run through this a few times to make sure we nail it."

Heat rose on Sarah's neck. Noon? Her boss had told her nine thirty. She'd told Wes she would be back as soon as possible to try to salvage part of parents' day if she could. She hadn't promised him and he wasn't expecting her. But she'd been planning on trying her best to be there for at least part of the day. Now that wouldn't be possible.

"Why did you tell me nine thirty?"

Gail looked surprised that it should even matter. "Because I wanted to make sure you were here on time."

When had she ever let her boss down? Sure, in recent weeks she'd been divided in her focus and not as available as usual, but her work hadn't suffered at all for it. In fact, Gail herself had admitted that the time away had helped.

"Is there a problem?" Gail asked when she continued to stand there.

"Um…no," Sarah said, squaring her shoulders and taking a breath. It didn't matter. She was there now. There was nothing she could do. And her boss was right—a few run-throughs made sense. She hadn't really had time to do much prep work herself…

She reached for the television remote and stood at the front of the room. She smiled and scanned the empty room as she would later that day when the seats were filled with the executives. "Welcome, SmartTech Kids. I'm Sarah Lewis and this is… This is…" She stopped, glancing down at her note cards; then she shook her head. "This is not where I need to be," she said, letting her hands fall to her sides as her gaze met Gail's confused one.

"What's going on?"

Sarah blew out a breath, then said, "I thought the meeting was this morning. I actually have something else…something important I need to do this afternoon." And if she left now, she'd make it in time for the entire parents' day event. Marissa wouldn't have to be disappointed. For the first time, she'd have a "mom" present for the mom and daughter scavenger hunt. And all of a sudden, finding hidden items using a compass she had no idea how to use was the only thing that mattered. She wanted to be that person Marissa could depend on and trust. She could be that mom the little girl was missing. Her heart nearly burst at the thought.

"What are you talking about?" Gail was clearly not impressed.

"I have to get back to Blue Moon Bay."

"This is about that old inn?"

Sarah shook her head. "Not exactly." She wouldn't try explaining it to Gail. There was no point. Her boss had given up the idea of having a family years before, choosing her career. It worked for her. It made her happy.

Gail's life wasn't the life Sarah wanted.

She packed up her things, and Gail stood. "You're leaving?"

"Yes."

"What about the presentation?"

"Here are my notes. Everything is on the slides," she said. Her boss had everything she needed to handle this without her.

"Sarah, this isn't funny."

"I'm not kidding." She grabbed her purse. "I'm sorry, Gail. But I think I'm finally realizing that I'm never going to have the flexibility working here that I need to do the things I want to do...to have other opportunities that will make me happy."

Gail scoffed. "Happy? Life is not about being happy, Sarah. It's about working hard, building something meaningful..." She gestured at the office around her.

Sarah smiled as she moved past her boss, out of the boardroom. "That's what I'm hoping to do." With the inn. With her own business. With Wes and Marissa.

CHAPTER TWENTY-THREE

Wes paced outside the Camp Crowley gates just before noon. He'd told Sarah that her not being here was okay and he meant it, but now he was really hoping she did. At least for a little while. When Marissa saw just him there that day, she would be so disappointed. But this would be the way it would be if they all moved forward in a relationship...as a family.

Sarah's life was in the city. She'd never said she would move back to Blue Moon Bay, and with his new lease space and office plans hopefully coming together, he had no intentions of moving to the city.

But couples made long-distance relationships work all the time. They'd figure it out.

He scanned the cars driving up the dirt road. Still not hers.

Hearing a chime, he reached for his cell. But it wasn't her. It wasn't even his phone. Another chime. He frowned.

Must be Marissa's cell phone. He retrieved it from his pocket and stared at the lock screen. He knew her password. That was a condition of having the phone, but he'd never used it before. Trusting her, not wanting to violate her privacy. But another chime had his heart racing. Who was sending multiple messages to his nine-year-old? Most of her friends were at camp with her without their phones right now.

He punched in her access code, and a picture of the

two of them appeared on the screen. It was one taken their day out on the boardwalk when they bought the glass bulb for Sarah. He scrolled to her messages and saw ten new ones.

He hesitated, hating to violate her privacy, but someone was desperate to contact her and if it was innocent enough, then it wouldn't matter if he read the messages first.

He was playing the parent card on this one.

He opened the text messages and frowned, seeing the unknown number. Maybe it was some telemarketing thing or an election text service or something. He clicked on the number and images started to load. He squinted to see a man's chest…stomach…the next photo had his face immediately blazing with heat.

Who the hell was this? He winced as he filtered through the messages until he reached the last one sent. *CyberStud480 downloaded your app and wants to chat.*

CyberStud480 was going to die.

Enraged, Wes struggled to calm his breathing. His hands clenched at his sides; he'd never wanted to tear someone apart so badly in his life. Not even in his football days had he felt this rage out on the field. But this was so different. This was his daughter. And some middle-aged creep was sending her inappropriate messages and pictures? Some of the messages were from Monday, when she'd left for camp. This must be what had been bothering her. She'd been receiving these disturbing messages but had been too worried to tell him.

He paced in front of the gate, his shoes kicking up the dirt at a breakneck pace. What did he do? Did he respond to the guy? Block the number, obviously. Was there a way to block any incoming messages? Right now, he was tempted to destroy the phone. This creep had found Marissa's contact information on her app. Her personal information was out there. To be exploited by assholes like this one.

He swallowed hard, but his heart was still in his throat. If she'd had her phone that day and had seen these images...

Seeing Sarah's car approach, his anger dissipated slightly. She'd made it. Good, someone to talk this through with. Calm him down before he threatened to find this guy and beat the life out of him. But then his anger returned. Unfortunately, she was also to blame for these messages on his daughter's phone. She'd helped Marissa get this app online in the first place, when Wes had always been against his daughter being active on the internet.

She climbed out of the car and rushed toward him, pulling on her sandals as she went. "I made it!" she said, stumbling over the gravel. "I think I may have a few photo radar tickets in my future, but I'm here!" Her wide smile faded, seeing his expression. "Hi?"

He forced a breath, but it caught in his chest, not making it to his lungs. "Hey...I, um..." How did he even start this conversation? What exactly did he say? He cleared his throat. "So, Marissa's been getting these." He handed her the phone. It wasn't pleasant to look at, but if Marissa had had to endure them, Sarah should see them, too. See the danger she'd opened his daughter up to.

Sarah frowned as she took the phone; then her hand covered her mouth as she saw the images. "Oh my God."

He nodded, his arms folded across his chest. He was practically vibrating out of his skin right now. If the guy were standing in front of him, he couldn't be held accountable for his actions. For the first time in his life, he understood the insanity plea.

"This person is disgusting. How did he even get her number?"

His voice was tight as he fought to control his anger. "The app you created for her. It has her contact info."

Sarah shook her head, but then her eyes widened. "Shit, it must have gotten hacked. Her info was only on the secure seller's page."

"Obviously it wasn't very secure."

"Unfortunately, there's only so much you can do when things are online," Sarah said, sounding remorseful but as though this couldn't have been prevented.

He stared at her. "That's why I didn't want her online."

Sarah's gaze registered his anger, and she seemed to retreat slightly. "Right, but this hardly ever happens…"

"It happens often enough," he said, his voice cold. "This is exactly the kind of thing I was trying to protect her from."

Sarah scoffed, but her voice was gentle when she said, "Wes, technology is part of the world now. It's everywhere. You can't shield her from it."

She was arguing with him? "I *can* shield her from it. It's my job as a parent to protect her from this shit as long as possible. She's *nine...*" His voice rose, and he lowered his head. Getting upset with Sarah wasn't his intent. This was his fault. He'd allowed it to happen.

Sarah sighed. "I'm sorry, Wes. You're right. I guess I wasn't thinking about the dangers of her information being in there."

"No, you weren't. And it's not your fault. You're not a parent. You don't get it."

The moment he said the words, he wanted to pull them back. But he couldn't, and ultimately, it was true. He didn't expect Sarah to know how to be a parent when he was still struggling with it himself, and he was doing it full-time.

But his daughter's safety came first.

"You're right. I'm not," she said. A long, awkward silence fell between them before she cleared her throat. "I should probably go."

Damn it. She'd made it in time for the camp day. That in itself just made everything so much harder. Marissa wouldn't have to be disappointed... But how could he hang out with her and act normal when he was so conflicted and torn? Marissa seeing them at odds would only ruin the fun day even more. Not that he'd be having much fun. Having to have a conversation with her about this asshole contacting her would be brutal.

"I'll let her know you really wanted to be here," he said quietly. Defeated.

Sarah's hurt expression tore him apart, but maybe they'd moved too quickly. Protecting Marissa had always been his first priority. It was one of the reasons he'd never gotten into a new relationship. The moment he let his guard down, let someone into their lives, this happened.

It wasn't Sarah's fault. He should never have let her talk him into this technology freedom for Marissa when he was against it.

"Tell her I said hi," she said before turning and walking away.

And as much as he wanted to go after her, for his own sake, his own heart, he was far too conflicted. He had no other choice than to watch her go.

CHAPTER TWENTY-FOUR

Just forty-eight hours and all of this will be over.

Balancing on the top rung of a ladder, the one that specifically said, Do Not Stand Here, Sarah reached as high as her arm would allow to change a burned-out light bulb in the dining room chandelier. The reunion was the next night, and then she could figure out what she was going to do with the inn and get the hell out of Blue Moon Bay.

The day before had been a disaster. She'd essentially quit her job...or had she been fired after walking out on her boss? Either way, the termination letter she'd received the evening before from Gail had solidified the fact that she no longer worked at Digital Strategies.

She wasn't sure how she felt about it yet. She didn't regret her decision walking out on the pitch, but not having a job was slightly terrifying. It had been her life for a long time.

And she thought she was at least trading the stressful workaholic lifestyle for something more...something better, a balanced life with Wes and Marissa in it. But she'd lost that, too.

Wes's anger the day before was completely justified. She hadn't even thought about the fact that Marissa was a minor and putting her info online could be dangerous. She dealt with cybersecurity and breach attacks all the time. It was just another element of doing business on the internet for her. But for Wes, this was one of the most terrifying things he had to deal with regarding his daughter.

Sarah had never claimed to have maternal instincts before, but even she'd wanted to find out who that disgusting waste of space who was texting Marissa was and beat the life out of him. She just hoped Marissa was okay. Driving away from the camp gates the day before had broken her heart.

"Sarah!"

Lia's voice calling her name nearly caused her to fall off-balance. Descending the ladder quickly, she looked for a place to hide. Lia, Malcolm, and his parents had arrived earlier that day from Napa, and the other woman had returned to her unbearable self. Almost as though her bitch switch had been activated by the presence of her perfect husband.

For two people so much in love, the couple had seemed to have an odd tension between them when they'd arrived at the B&B with his parents in tow. They'd been tense and awkward toward each other when she'd shown them to their room for the weekend. She'd shuffled things around to give them the biggest honeymoon suite room. Lia should have been thrilled, but instead she'd just looked slightly terrified.

Maybe it was an in-law thing. Maybe Lia didn't get along with them, or maybe the pressure of trying to impress them was making her extra controlling.

Either way, Sarah would be happy to see them all leave two days from now. Clearing her head and figuring out next steps for her future was going to require space and quiet.

"There you are," Lia said, appearing in the dining room dressed in a slim-fitting suit, her hair pulled back in a tight bun. Sarah couldn't even picture the carefree woman with flushed cheeks and messed-up hair enjoying an amusement park ride a week ago.

"Here I am," Sarah said. Lia and Malcolm had gone into their room an hour ago. By now, she'd assumed they'd be naked and having perfect, successful-people sex. Apparently not.

"Everyone else will be arriving in the next few hours, and I want to go over any last-minute stuff," Lia said, checking her to-do list on her phone.

Sarah suppressed a groan. Why, oh why couldn't she be upstairs making Sarah jealous with sounds of lovemaking coming from the room? It would be easier to take than her micromanaging. "Just about everything is ready downstairs, and the guest rooms are good to go." She'd finished putting the little boxes of expensive chocolates Lia had custom ordered for the reunion on the beds an hour ago.

"Well, I'm sure we've missed something."

Translation: she was sure Sarah had missed something.

Well, news flash! Planning events wasn't exactly Sarah's forte.

"Okay, just give me a sec to put the ladder away and I'll meet you in the den." She took her time going out to the shed, going over all the details in her own mind. Everything was covered. Hopefully this tête-à-tête with

Lia would be quick and put the woman's mind at ease. She had her own life to sort out.

In the den, she found her pacing.

"Hey, relax, everything is going to be fine." It was a family reunion, not a wedding or a funeral. If there was a mishap or two, it wasn't the end of the world.

"No, Sarah, everything's not going to be fine." She sighed. "Malcolm's grandmother was too sick to travel. A fun fact no one bothered to mention to me when I organized this event, and now the only thing Malcolm and his parents can talk about is how much she'll be missed, how tragic it is that we're doing this without her."

Lia reached into the pocket of her sports coat and retrieved a chocolate bar. A real one, not the chalk-looking protein things she'd been consuming before. She ripped it open and took a bite.

"Well, how sick is she?" Sarah asked.

Her mouth full of chocolate, Lia stared at her like it was a ridiculous question. "I don't know, Sarah—too sick to travel."

Sarah sighed. Patience. "I'm asking because if she's not completely bedridden, I may have a way that she could still be at the reunion."

Lia stopped pacing. "You mean virtually?"

"I installed some virtual conferencing equipment in the larger event room…" It would mean moving the event into that room instead…moving the decor and the tables and the centerpieces and everything that they'd just finished setting up in the smaller room, but if it would mean that this event could be considered a success, if it would appease Lia, then it was worth doing.

Her self-esteem and confidence could use one thing going right that weekend.

Lia nodded slowly. "Malcolm's aunt decided not to come so that someone would be there with Grandmama...she could definitely help her with a laptop." Relief started to appear on Lia's face as she nodded. "That might work."

It would definitely work; it just meant a lot more work for Sarah.

"Well, go. Get started," Lia said. "We only have a few hours."

Sarah's back teeth clenched. "I'm on it."

Just forty-eight hours until all of this is over.

Hours later, exhausted and barely able to keep her eyes open, Sarah collapsed on her bed. Downstairs, all of Lia's and Malcolm's family members had checked in, gotten settled in their guest rooms, and were mingling with their wine and cheese reception. Loud voices and laughter drifted up the stairs toward her room, but Sarah was happy to be away from the crowd.

Her gaze settled on her grandmother's journal on the table near the armchair. Worried about that day's event, worried about her own future plans, and hurt over her argument with Wes, she hadn't slept the night before. Instead, she'd continued reading the entries in the journal.

Her grandmother's heartache over Jack's refusal of her love had spilled from the pages, and Sarah's own tortured heart hadn't found the reassurance she'd been hoping for. Instead, it had only made her heartache that much worse. She hesitated before picking up the journal to read it.

Unfortunately, she had to know how it all ended back then for Dove and Jack.

The date on this last entry was a full year after the previous one.

Dear Jack,

I got married today. You know that because you were there, ever so briefly, watching from the beach at a distance.

Did you see the dress—so different from the one I'd planned to marry you in. The truth is, I needed to hide my pregnancy, and this gown was the only appropriate choice. Though it seems fitting that I wouldn't get to wear the dress I'd always dreamed of today on this special day.

I love Martin. He's a good man and he's been there for me, when you wouldn't or refuse to be.

As I walked down the aisle today, our last conversation played in my mind. Maybe not appropriate to be thinking of another man while I was about to pledge forever to his good friend and comrade, but the mind wanders where it will.

Mine wandered to you.

Do you remember the conversation?

I said, "Where did you go, my love?"

And you replied, "Somewhere so dark that love cannot exist."

You were different. You are different now.

Unfairly, my feelings are the same. Nothing—not time,

not distance, not your coldness—can change that.

But I will move on and be a good wife to this man I now call my husband. I'll be a good mother to his child I carry, and we will have a future we could only dream of together.

I wish you peace, if love forever evades you.

Know that the purest, kindest part of your soul is safe in my memory. Now and for always.

My last letter to you, my past love,

Dove

Sarah closed the book with a small sigh. Their love story had ended with Dove's final journal entry.

Now what did she do with the journal? Putting it back on the bookshelf in the den didn't seem right when she was planning to sell the B&B. And she wasn't sure it was something she wanted to keep.

What would her grandmother have wanted her to do?

The blown-glass bulb—the gift from Marissa and Wes—hanging in her window reflecting the glow of the moonlight, a kaleidoscope of color shooting across the hardwood floor, gave Sarah her answer.

• • •

"Are you and Sarah fighting?" Marissa's voice drifted over the changing room door the next day as she tried on new clothing for school starting the following week.

Marissa's question was a good one. One Wes wasn't sure the answer to as he paced outside, waiting for her to emerge. They weren't exactly fighting; that would require communicating. He hadn't spoken to her since the day before, when he'd been so angry about the app being hacked and Marissa's safety being put at risk that he couldn't even remember the conversation clearly. All he remembered was the anger and the hurt. Her driving away and the instant remorse he'd felt.

"No, we're not fighting," he said. Catching his reflection in the mirror, he almost did a double take. That day, he was feeling every one of his thirty-two years. The stress and the pressure of his new love-life conflict had dark circles appearing under tired-looking eyes. And the gray strands appearing along his temple hadn't been there six months ago. They were no doubt courtesy of CyberStud480.

"We just haven't seen her in a few days," Marissa said, emerging from the changing room in a pair of jeans and hoodie that had cat ears on the hood and a tail hanging down the back.

"That's cute," he said. "What do you think?"

She shrugged. "It's fine. Don't change the subject."

He sighed. Marissa had been incessant the last two days, wondering where Sarah was, asking if they should bring her a surprise at the B&B…flowers, a coffee… His little girl had a million suggestions. But Wes insisted that Sarah was too busy to hang out.

He still hadn't manned up and told her about his accusing Sarah of exposing his daughter to the dangers of technology. "We will see her at the reunion," he said casually. Truthfully, the idea terrified him. He had no idea where they stood now or where he wanted them to stand. Inviting someone into his and Marissa's life hadn't been easy. Trusting hadn't been easy. And then to have things turn out the way they did…

"So things are okay?" Marissa asked, still looking unconvinced as she studied him.

He sighed, sitting in a chair outside the changing room and pulling her closer. The day before, he'd asked her about the messages and luckily she'd only received one…mildly inappropriate text from the guy. She'd been too nervous to tell him about it, knowing he'd shut down her access to the online app store. But it had definitely been one of those teachable moments parents always talked about, even if it was uncomfortable.

"Look, Sarah came by yesterday," he said.

"Our house?"

"Camp. She came back from L.A. in time, but I'd just found out about the hacking, and things didn't go so well." He ran a hand through his hair.

Marissa frowned. "She made it back in time but didn't come? What did you say to piss her off?" She clamped her lips together at her slip of inappropriate words.

Wes let it slide. He had in fact said some hurtful things. "I may have suggested that it was her fault. For putting you at risk online like that." His chest heaved as he sighed. "Sarah just doesn't have kids, so she doesn't get it."

Marissa was looking at him like he was the bad guy. She folded her little arms across her chest and glared at him. "You blamed Sarah?"

He nodded. "There was no parental controls or anything…"

"Dad, it's the internet. It's not safe even if you do everything right."

"That's why I didn't like you using it," he said. This incident should be illustrating his point perfectly.

"It was just pictures, Dad, and I would have talked to you about it, but I knew this was how you'd react. I knew you'd take this one example of the internet being evil and use it to stop me from making new apps."

"Marissa, there are predators online…"

"There are predators everywhere," she said, touching his shoulder. "This wasn't Sarah's fault. Blaming her wasn't the right thing to do."

Marissa's expression said she was clearly disappointed in him as she disappeared back inside the changing room and slammed the door.

Fantastic. Now his daughter was mad at him. And even worse: she was right.

CHAPTER TWENTY-FIVE

The next morning, Sarah hurried down the boardwalk toward Harrison's Blown Glass, the journal tucked beneath her arm.

The door to the shop was locked. Checking the hours sign, she saw that it opened at ten. It was only nine thirty, and she couldn't wait. Lia would be losing her mind by now wondering where she was. She'd snuck out when she knew the woman was in the shower. Reunion guests were self-entertaining that day, but the local family and friends would be arriving in five hours for the event, and the caterers would be there to set up in three.

She contemplated knocking, but she wasn't sure what she would even say to him. She just knew that the journal didn't belong anywhere else. It was filled with letters to Jack, for Jack.

She walked around the side of the building, noticing a second entrance to his living area. She clutched the journal tight to prevent the news clippings and pictures from falling free.

This was the right thing. She wouldn't second-guess the decision. This journal held her grandmother's deepest secrets that had nothing to do with their family. No one else deserved to have this book except for Jack.

And it would be up to him if he decided to read it or leave the past in the past.

She hesitated before knocking, then listened for the

sound of footsteps or anyone inside, but she didn't hear anything.

She bit her lip. Leave it? Or bring it back tomorrow?

She wasn't sure she'd get the courage again. And Jack was living on borrowed seconds.

Reaching into her purse, she grabbed a notepad, tore off the top sheet, and scribbled her own note:

I thought you should know…

Love, Sarah

Opening the screen door, she placed the journal inside, securing it between the inside and outside doors, and closed it softly. Then she wiped a tear from her cheek as she left her grandma's secrets with the only other person who should ever know them.

. . .

Hours later, the reunion was going well. People seemed to be enjoying themselves. As she set up the virtual conferencing equipment for the surprise appearance of Grandmama, Sarah scanned the room. Food still looked good… Everyone had drinks.

Wes and Marissa hadn't shown up yet, and her palms sweat thinking about how she was supposed to act around them. Had Wes told Marissa about their argument? Did the little girl know Sarah had actually made it to the parents' day?

"Sarah." Mayor Rodale's voice as she approached behind her made her turn. Dressed in a pale-blue suit, white blouse, and sensible but stylish two-inch heels, the woman was small-town elegance.

"Hi, Mayor Rodale, nice to see you." The older woman had been the mayor in Blue Moon Bay for almost thirty years. She'd seen a lot of changes in that time, and Sarah held her breath now.

"Darling, this place looks amazing."

She breathed a sigh of relief. "Thank you."

"Seriously, dear, I'll be honest—when Whitney told me that Lia was holding the reunion here, I didn't have high expectations. But you truly did something incredible. Dove is smiling down; I just know it," the older woman said, patting Sarah on the shoulder before moving on to rejoin her family.

Sarah swallowed the lump in her throat. Mayor Rodale's praise of the B&B gave her an unexpected, overwhelming sense of accomplishment. She'd brought the B&B back to life.

With Wes's help.

Catching his eye now as he and Marissa entered the crowded event room had her hands fumbling with the cables of the virtual conferencing equipment. He looked amazing, dressed in charcoal pants and a pale-blue dress shirt, opened at the collar. It was the first time she'd seen him in anything formal. The shirt sleeves were rolled, displaying his tanned, muscular forearms, and it took everything she had not to rush into those arms.

She'd missed him so much the last few days.

Unfortunately, his simple head nod in greeting was completely unreadable. Was he as nervous about being there as she was having him? Or had he completely just disregarded everything they had together? One mistake and it was over? Albeit it was a big mistake. One she was still anguished over.

Next to him, Marissa scanned the room but didn't see her, so instead she headed toward several other kids sneaking treats from the dessert table. Sarah sighed. She'd missed Marissa, too. She was dying to ask her about camp and talk to her about her plans to design her own apps...

Would she get a chance to talk to her? Would she talk to Wes? This event wasn't exactly conducive to a great conversation.

She connected the cables to the projection screen and motioned for Lia to join her at the front of the room.

"Is it ready?" Lia asked. She was clutching a champagne flute, and the glass looked ready to shatter under her tight grip.

Everyone else was having a good time, but Lia had been tense and on edge all evening.

"Yes," she said, handing her the remote. "Your aunt texted and said Grandmama is all set. Just hit Connect whenever you're ready."

Lia took a deep breath and actually looked nervous as she clinked her glass and the crowd turned their attention toward her. "Hi, everyone. Thank you all for coming. I love that we were able to be together like this." She paused. "Unfortunately, there is one very important member of our family who wasn't well enough to travel."

She turned to glance at Malcolm, and Sarah couldn't

quite decipher the look that passed between them, but Lia seemed even more uneasy than Sarah felt, trying to avoid looking at Wes.

Lia continued, as though a lot was riding on this surprise for her husband. "So, we brought her here the best way we could." She hit Connect on the remote, and a second later, Grandmama's smiling face appeared on the large projector screen in the front of the room.

Malcolm's look of surprise gave way to one of affection as he glanced at Lia, and Sarah's sigh of relief seemed to be in sync with the other woman's.

Lia's grateful smile in her direction had some of the tension melting away. She'd done it. She'd pulled off the event. She'd impressed the great Lia Jameson. And more importantly, she'd impressed herself. She hadn't given up on the inn or its legacy. Her grandmother's legacy.

"Thank God for technology, am I right?" someone in the crowd said, and Sarah shifted her gaze to Wes. He was looking at her, his expression torn. Conflicted and strained. Should she go talk to him? Should she avoid him? Her heart raced and the air around her felt stale, thick...

It was impossible being near him and not wanting to rush into his arms. Knowing she may never have a chance to be with him...and Marissa ever again had her chest tightening and tears threatening to appear.

She hurried out of the dining room and into the foyer, looking for an escape. Several guests lingered at the base of the stairs. She'd have to interrupt them to head up to her room, so instead, she took the stairs down to the wine cellar; yanked the big, heavy door open; and slipped inside.

Tears welled in her eyes, and she pressed her fingers to her lids. She would not cry. Not right now, anyway. She had to make it through the next few hours.

She forced several deep breaths. She'd just focus on making sure everything ran smoothly and after dinner escape to her room. Lia would be gone the next day, and she could focus on the next steps.

The cellar door opened behind her and she turned quickly. Wes?

Lia. "There you are," the other woman said.

She wiped her eyes quickly and cleared her throat. "Did you need me for something?"

"Yeah, I, uh…" She moved into the cellar, letting go of the door.

"Maybe don't let the…door shut," Sarah said with a sigh as it closed. She hurried toward it and gave a quick tug on the handle, but it wouldn't budge. "Damn."

Lia's eyes widened. "What?"

"This door has been sticking lately, so it's safer to leave it ajar."

Lia immediately reached for the handle and pushed with all her strength. It wouldn't budge.

Sarah pushed with her.

Nothing.

"Please don't tell me we are trapped in here." Lia's breathing immediately shallowed.

Sarah glanced at her. "Stay calm."

"I'm claustrophobic."

"It's not exactly a small space." Sarah continued to push on the door as Lia started to pace.

"Still, it's a creepy-ass cellar. And I'm trapped inside." She clutched her chest above the white silk blouse tucked into a thin, knee-length black pencil skirt. "Air. I need air."

"Don't panic," Sarah said. "You have your phone on you—call someone to come down and yank the door open from the outside." Her own phone was in her bedroom charging.

"Right. My phone." Retrieving it from the pocket of her skirt, she scrolled through the contact list.

"Come on, Lia—just pick someone. Almost everyone you know is upstairs."

"I'll try Wes," she said, hitting Dial.

Sarah's cheeks flushed again at the mention.

Lia eyed her with amusement, her panic momentarily forgotten. "So, Marissa said you two have been joined at the hip lately."

Not anymore. But her heartache wasn't something she wanted to discuss with Lia. She still hadn't even talked to Whitney or Jessica about everything yet. She desperately needed some girl time with her besties. They'd help her figure out what to do next.

"Is he answering?" she asked, nodding toward the phone.

"Why won't the call connect?" Lia asked as the call refused to go through.

"Try again."

She did, but once again the call wouldn't work.

Lia glanced at the display screen. "No bars. There's no service down here." Her staggered breathing returned. "Do you have your phone?"

"No."

"Oh my God…"

Sarah grabbed her shoulders and moved her back toward the cellar wall. "Deep breaths. It's fine. I'm sure someone will come looking for us when we don't reappear upstairs."

Lia nodded. "You're right. Okay. So what do we do in the meantime?"

Sarah shrugged. "Wait, I guess." Sliding her back along the stone wall, she sat on the floor. This actually wasn't so bad. She'd needed an excuse to get away from everyone; she just wished she were alone.

Lia surveyed the concrete floor, contemplating the likelihood of getting dirty, then shrugged and sat next to her. She hit Redial, attempting the call again, then set the phone on the floor next to her when it once again failed.

"I'm sure you'd rather be stuck down here with Wes," Lia said.

"He probably wouldn't want that." Sarah rested her head against the stone wall and crossed her ankles out in front of her.

Lia turned to face her. "Why not? You two were practically all goo-goo eyed for each other that night at the fair, and I'm sure things heated up with Marissa at camp last week."

Oh, they'd heated up all right. Then they'd fizzled out fast.

Unfortunately, Wes may be able to just walk away from the connection they'd had, but Sarah couldn't just turn off the emotions. She'd fallen hard and fast for her former crush, and the last few weeks had only reinforced her desire to have other things in life besides her career—a relationship, a family…

"Things are complicated."

"Life always is," Lia said. She paused. "I'm sorry if I was a huge pain."

"You really were," Sarah said wryly. Though right now, her high school frenemy was the least of her concerns. It was silly to always have compared herself to Lia in the first place.

"Well, I have to give you credit. The way you were able to save the day with Grandmama's virtual presence might have saved my marriage."

Sarah looked at her as though she were talking a different language. "What are you talking about? You have an amazing marriage, along with the perfect career…a penthouse in New York…"

Lia scoffed. "My career is slowly killing me, if my husband doesn't do it first, and the penthouse in New York is beautiful but lonely."

Sarah blinked as she stared at her. "Wow. I had no idea." Social media really did make it easy for people to portray their lives in any way they wanted. No one really knew what was happening beyond the internet connection.

"That was on purpose," Lia said. "I'm always trying to give the illusion that everything is wonderful. But it's actually exhausting."

"So why does Malcolm want to kill you? Is he... abusive?" The man had been slightly standoffish and high and mighty, but he hadn't seemed dangerous.

Lia shook her head. "No. I didn't mean it like that. He's just as fed up with me as the rest of you." She hesitated. "We've had our issues over the last few years, and they've driven a wedge between us."

"You both work long hours; that has to take a toll on a marriage," Sarah said.

"It's worse than that." She paused. "I kissed my boss about a year ago."

Sarah's mouth dropped.

"It was after a big court case win; we were all out celebrating...Malcolm and I had been arguing about starting a family, about where my career was heading, about everything, it seemed. And one thing led to another. It just happened. Nothing more—just one kiss. He can't forgive me. I can't forgive myself. My marriage was definitely heading south. That's why I planned this reunion. A last attempt to save it."

"Do you think it worked?" Sarah asked, feeling sympathetic toward Lia for the first time now that the facade, the mask Lia always hid behind, was gone.

"Maybe. Malcolm actually smiled at me...like a real smile. The first one I've seen in a long time. That's a start."

They sat in silence for a long moment until Sarah

said, "Hey, we could be stuck here a while. Wine?"

"Wine opener?"

Reaching above their heads, Sarah felt along the edge of a deep stone cutout in the wall and retrieved one. "Grandma left one here for wine cellar tastings she used to hold years ago."

"Your grandma was a genius."

Sarah looked at her hands. "That's why it will be tough to sell the B&B."

"Then why don't you keep it?" Lia asked.

"I don't think I'm cut out to run a B&B. This whole thing is so far outside my comfort zone." And could she really stay in Blue Moon Bay now without being with Wes? Staying in town, seeing him and Marissa, and not being part of their lives would be torture. But without a job to return to the city for, maybe staying was the right thing. She certainly felt more connected to her hometown now more than ever.

"What about you and Wes?"

The million-dollar question. "We're friends." Or they were.

"Look, this is the cellar of truth, so stop lying to me and yourself. You've loved him since we were kids."

"Fine. I loved him. I still love him. I walked out of the most important pitch meeting of my career because I love him and Marissa, but that doesn't matter because he doesn't feel the same way."

Lia frowned, her head spinning toward her. "Wait. You left the meeting? The one you were preparing for for months?"

Sarah nodded. "Yep. Marissa invited me to the camp's parents' day, and there was a scheduling conflict. I basically quit...or I was fired. I don't know." The logistics didn't really matter. She no longer had a job.

"Does Wes know that?"

She shook her head. "It doesn't matter. I realized the job no longer made me happy anyway."

"So what happened?"

Sarah launched into the details of the hacked app and her own failings to keep Marissa protected online.

But Lia shook her head. "That could have happened to any of us. No one's perfect when it comes to parenting." She scoffed. "I think you need to talk to him. I haven't seen him this happy in a long time, and he needs to get out of his own way and give himself another chance at love."

"No, he's right. He has to think about Marissa."

"Marissa adores you. You'd be really good for her. For both of them."

"You mean all that?" Sarah asked. Lia knew Wes and Marissa so well...if she thought Sarah would be a good fit for the family...then maybe there was some truth to it. But it was hard to get her hopes up when she had no idea where they stood now.

"Like I said—cellar of truth," Lia reminded her, gesturing to the room around them. She stood and grabbed a bottle of red in one hand, white in the other. "Anyway, back to the wine—red or white? I drink both."

"Both sounds great," Sarah said. Maybe the answers she was seeking weren't at the bottom of an expensive vintage wine bottle, but she had to start looking somewhere, right?

Lia smiled as she rejoined her on the floor. "I think for the first time since second grade, we just agreed on something."

$\cdots$

An hour after arriving at the event, Sarah had disappeared. Wes had seen her briefly in the dining room when she'd been setting up the electronics for Lia's surprise for Malcolm's family, but then she'd vanished.

He needed to talk to her. They couldn't just let everything end after one argument. He'd been angry and he'd said things he hadn't meant. A few days to cool off had him realizing that Marissa was right. He couldn't protect her from everything, all the time.

His daughter's silent treatment the last few days had helped him come to that conclusion. It was torture, her being upset with him and not communicating with Sarah. Ignoring problems never solved anything. And this reunion might not be the ideal place to talk, but he suspected it might be his only chance if she still planned to head back to the city the next day.

Unfortunately, he couldn't find her among all the mingling guests. Maybe once the event had started, she skipped out. Her conflicted expression before she'd escaped the dining room an hour before continued to haunt him.

"Hey, Dad!" Marissa came toward him with several

other kids around her age. Blue frosting ringed around her mouth, and the way she was practically vibrating meant she'd consumed way too many sugary desserts.

"What's up?" At least she was talking to him.

"We were playing on the cellar stairs and we heard noises from the wine cellar," she said, eyes wide, looking sufficiently freaked out.

"It's the ghost of the woman who used to live here," one of the older kids, a teenage boy with a fauxhawk, said, holding his arms up in a ghostlike position to frighten the younger kids.

Marissa hid behind him. "Is it Dove, Dad?"

"Of course not," he said. Someone must have gotten stuck in there. That old wooden door was a hazard, one he'd forgotten to fix. His hope rose a little. Could be a great excuse to come back the next day before Sarah left...talk to her then. "Come on. Let's go check it out," he told the kids.

They all made their way down the cellar stairs, and he motioned for two of the bigger kids to help him pull on the door. On three, they pulled, and the sound of giggles and voices made his pulse race.

Inside, Sarah and Lia sat against the stone wall, an open bottle of wine next to each of them. High heels off, completely unfazed to be trapped in the cellar, they were laughing hysterically at something. The laughter of two slightly tipsy women. He couldn't help the grin that spread across his face. For years, the two of them had struggled to get along, always competing for top spot in everything at school. Seeing them this way warmed his heart.

"Hey…" he said, entering the cellar. "You two having your own party?"

Sarah's eyes widened as she saw him, and she quickly ran a hand over her hair. Her cheeks flushed slightly, but then she lifted her chin defiantly and, ignoring him, she turned to Lia. "So I hired a contractor to renovate this place and he neglects to fix the cellar door."

Seriously? Wes sighed. "I'll fix it tomorrow."

Lia shot him a look. "We could have died in here."

"Well, you didn't. Free to go," he said.

"Hey, Sarah!" Marissa ran into the cellar and wrapped her arms around Sarah's neck.

His chest tightened as Sarah hugged her back and looked just as happy and relieved to see her. His actions at the camp had been assholic. He knew that now.

"I'm sorry I missed parents' day," she said to Marissa with a quick glance his way.

The little girl gave him the side-eye. "Dad told me it was his fault."

All three women glared at him. Okay, time to break this up before he was the one locked in the cellar all night. "Okay, everyone can head back upstairs."

Marissa ran off with the other kids, and Wes extended a hand to Lia and Sarah to help them up off the floor.

Sarah ignored it and Lia swiped it away. "We are two grown-ass, independent… Whoa," she said, reaching for the wall behind her as she swayed off-balance.

"Need some help with these two?" Malcolm's voice in

the cellar doorway was a relief.

Lia beamed at the sight of her husband. "Hi!" she said, as though she hadn't seen him in weeks. Malcolm approached and wrapped one arm around her. She clung to him like a life preserver, but Wes suspected she was using her slightly inebriated state to get close to him.

"You got the other one?" he asked Wes.

Wes glanced toward Sarah, who looked slightly unsteady on her legs. "Yeah."

Lia jabbed a finger at his chest as she passed. "Be nice to her. She gave up her career for you and Marissa."

Wes's pulse raced as he frowned. What? As his friend and her husband left, he turned to Sarah. "What did Lia mean just now?"

Sarah stared at the wine bottle in her hands and shrugged. "I don't know."

He moved closer. "Sarah…"

Her body swayed slightly, and he reached toward her. Obviously now wasn't the time to talk. "Hey, can I help you upstairs to your room?" The buzz from a full bottle of wine in an hour would take a little while to wear off.

She eyed him. "Fine, but don't get any ideas, buddy," she said, her words slightly slurred as she allowed him to wrap an arm around her waist. He bent to pick up her discarded heels and escorted her out of the cellar. The feel of her body next to him and the sweet smell of vanilla on her skin had his mouth watering and his heart thundering in his chest.

He probably deserved the warning, as he wanted

nothing more than to get all kinds of ideas. The temptation to kiss her and hold her was strong, but she was definitely not in a consenting state or mood.

He helped her up the B&B stairs to her room and opened the door. She moved away from him as she entered. "I'm good from here," she said as she lay on the bed.

Damn, he didn't want to leave her. They needed to talk.

Now wasn't the right time, but he hoped she'd give him the opportunity the next day when he came by to fix the cellar door. He'd been wrong, and Lia's words had him questioning just how very wrong.

He set her high heels on the floor and reached for a blanket from the chair, then softly draped it over her as she hugged a pillow and her eyes flitted closed. His hand rested just a minute on her shoulder as he stared down at her gorgeous, sleepy face.

He was falling in love with her.

There was no doubt that she was the only woman he wanted to be with, wanted to be a family with. He'd screwed up. Could he make things right? Either way, he needed to know. "Sarah, did you walk out on your pitch meeting?" he asked softly.

She didn't open her eyes as she nodded. "Yep. And I'd do it again," she mumbled as she drifted off to sleep.

He swallowed hard, his emotions overwhelming him. She'd done that for Marissa. For him. He was more than a little touched by the gesture. He had to find a way to make things right.

CHAPTER TWENTY-SIX

"To a successful event," Whitney said, holding her wineglass in the air on the outside patio of the inn the next day.

Sarah forced a smile behind dark sunglasses as she and Jessica raised their own drinks. Hers was sparkling water, as she never wanted to see a glass of wine again. "To not killing my client," she said, but she was kidding.

She couldn't claim to remember all the fuzzy details from her time locked in the wine cellar with Lia the night before, but they'd definitely put their past feuding ways behind them. She'd been actually a little sorry to see her leave earlier that morning.

The three friends clinked their glasses together.

"Seriously, Sarah, I'm so proud of you," Jessica said. "Dove's Nest looks better than ever."

"Thanks, Jess," Sarah said, sitting back and taking in the view of the ocean in the distance. The inn did look great…and more than that, it was starting to feel like home. One Sarah wasn't sure she was ready to let go of.

Should she tell her friends about her out-there idea? She'd been mulling it over in her mind the last few days and that morning, and the more she thought about staying in Blue Moon Bay, the more her conflicted spirits lifted. She took a deep breath. "So, wild idea, but what if I kept the B&B?"

Jessica's mouth dropped, displaying her obvious surprise, and for once, Whitney ignored her phone chiming constantly with new messages on the table as she lifted her sunglasses over her head and stared at Sarah. "For real? You want to run a B&B?"

"Honestly, no. Not in the traditional sense anyway. I was thinking more of turning it into an event center for special occasion rental and corporate retreats...that sort of thing." Sarah didn't love the idea of different guests checking in and out at different times and having to keep the place fully occupational year round, but hosting events once or twice a month wouldn't be so bad.

Whitney nodded. "That could work," she said slowly. "The property is amazing, and the structure of the inn is unlike any others we have here. The main dining room could hold at least a hundred people—perfect for smaller weddings, corporate events, especially with the twelve guest rooms. The Seaview Inn only has half the space you have. Your backyard is big enough for outdoor events, and the kitchen could easily accommodate large dining requests."

Her friend was already designing the event venue brochure in her mind, Sarah was sure.

"But do you think I could generate enough business? Is Blue Moon Bay a place people will want to host events and retreats?" Sarah said.

Whitney shuffled her chair closer. She pulled out her phone and opened her Outlook planner for city events. "Look. Four businesses this month will be hosting corporate retreats here—at Seaview Inn." She scrolled. "Another three in October... Two in November... And then the Christmas season blows up. I won't even show you the calendar because quite honestly, it gives me heart palpitations thinking about the work I have to do."

"Things are starting to pick up around here," Jessica said. "*Young and Trendy* magazine listed Blue Moon Bay as a dream destination for hipsters because of the surf conditions and laid-back environment."

Whitney pointed to herself. "That was me. *I* did that. A half-day photoshoot with some local wave stars and a press release." She dropped an imaginary mic.

Sarah laughed. "We've already established that you're a rock star." She turned to Jessica. "What do you think?"

Jessica beamed at her. "I love the idea," she said, then paused. "But I want you to be happy in whatever you decide. What about your career?"

"I think I'm going to go out on my own. Finally start designing my own apps. I can do that from here, and the B&B business could keep me afloat financially." Without her steady income in the city, her apartment would be far too expensive anyway.

This made sense. This gave her an opportunity to take a chance on herself.

"Really?" Whitney asked. "You truly want to stay?"

She really did. Sarah nodded. "Yeah, I truly want to stay."

"Then yes, of course I think this is a great idea," Jessica said. "And you know I'll help any way I can. Free dessert catering for a year."

Whitney pointed a finger at her. "You can't do that.

You are both small business owners. No freebies."

Jessica laughed. "Sorry, Sarah… Family discount," she whispered.

Sarah's heart felt lighter than it had in weeks as she looked at her two best friends, confident that with their help and support, there was nothing she couldn't do. Unfortunately, it didn't help ease the ache of knowing that staying meant having to see Wes and Marissa and not being a part of their lives.

Running into them at the reunion the night before had only made it clearer just how much she cared about them, and when Marissa had hugged her…Sarah hadn't wanted to let go. Maybe they could still be friends, and even if things hadn't worked out with Wes, Sarah could still be there for Marissa. In whatever way that looked like.

She sighed. It would never be enough, but unfortunately, the choice didn't seem to be hers.

Wes helping her to her room the night before was fuzzy in her memory, but she knew not to read anything into the gesture. Once again, he'd just found her in an embarrassing state and had come to the rescue.

Her head still pounded, and she needed something to dull the ache in her brain at least, even if she couldn't dull the ache in her chest. "I'll be right back," she said. Getting up from the Adirondack chair, she headed into the inn, but her heart stopped as the front-page headline of the local newspaper laying on the porch caught her eye.

Celebrated War Hero and Local Entrepreneur Jack

Harrison Passes Away Peacefully in His Sleep

"Oh no." Sarah's hand shook as she picked up the paper and continued to read.

Found the previous morning by his vendor neighbor who checked in on him each morning. *"Make sure I'm still breathing," he'd tell me,* the neighbor's quote read.

He'd died. Jack was gone. Had he found the journal? Had he read it?

"You okay?" Jessica asked, coming up next to her.

Sarah nodded, but a teardrop hit the page in front of her.

"Oh no, Mr. Harrison died?" her friend said, reading over her shoulder.

"Yeah," Sarah said, wiping her eyes.

A ceremony of life is scheduled to be held on the beach this weekend by the local vendors who called him a friend. He wasn't survived by any family, was how the article ended.

"Did you know him?" Whitney asked, looking concerned by her tears.

"My grandmother loved him," Sarah whispered. "At one time. A long time ago." And their love had never been. The thought made her chest ache so hard, she thought her heart might actually be breaking.

"No kidding? Wow," Jessica said, wrapping her arm around Sarah's shoulder. "I'm sorry, Sarah."

"He was such a sweet man," she said.

"Do you think you'll go to the celebration of life?" Whitney asked.

Sarah didn't know. "He may have died never

knowing the truth about how my grandma felt about him."

"Maybe he did know," Jessica said. "And maybe he's finally with her now."

"Maybe," Sarah said as she sighed. Her grandmother and Jack had always loved each other, but they'd never found a way back to each other after the war tore them apart.

Could Sarah find the courage to go after the love of her life?

CHAPTER TWENTY-SEVEN

If there was an award for how bad a person could mess something up, he had to at least be in the running for it. Wes ran a hand over his exhausted face as he turned into his driveway the next morning after meeting Lia for a quick coffee before she'd left to head back to New York. She'd confirmed what she'd alluded to the night before. Sarah had walked out on her pitch meeting, essentially quitting her job in the process to be there for Marissa.

He didn't deserve Sarah.

She was amazing and kind and beautiful and for the first time since Kelly, he'd felt something. Something real. And he'd panicked and messed it up. He'd been afraid and unsure and he'd let his own hesitation get in the way of something incredible. The last two days, all he could think about was her.

She was still in town. He'd noticed her car parked at the inn when he'd driven past. He'd been tempted to stop, but he'd also seen Whitney's vehicle in the driveway and hadn't wanted to interrupt. Obviously the friends were getting together before Sarah left town. He'd stop by later to fix the cellar door, and maybe she'd give him a chance to at least apologize for being an asshole.

His cell rang, and he glanced at the unknown number on call display before answering. "Hello?"

"Hi, is this…Sharrun's Construction?" an unfamiliar female voice asked.

"This is Wes Sharrun," he said.

"I was wondering if your company did rebuilds of cabins as well as B&Bs?" the woman asked.

A rebuild of a cabin? "Is it your personal cabin?"

"No, I'm sorry, I should have introduced myself. My name is Awilda Melendez and I own Melendez Cottages. We were forced to shut down after weather damage from a storm last year, but we are hoping to reopen next summer. Unfortunately, there's significant work that needs to happen before then."

Wes was too stunned to answer. Melendez Cottages were along Highway 1 and they'd been there for years. He remembered staying there himself on a fishing and hunting trip with his father when he was a teen. There was at least forty cabins in the area, and they'd been shut down for a while. They'd suffered excessive damage in the hurricane-like weather they'd seen on the coast the summer before.

"Mr. Sharrun?"

"Oh, yes, sorry, I'm still here."

"So, would your company be capable of a job that size? Do you have time to give us a quote?"

Absolutely. He cleared his throat. "Yes. I can and I do. Tomorrow too soon?" His aunt would kill him for acting eager, but he was beyond eager. Opportunities like this didn't fall out of the sky every day.

She laughed, obviously taking his urgency as a good thing. "Sure. I'm in San Diego right now, so I could drive in and meet you out there tomorrow at noon?"

"Perfect. That's perfect."

"Thank you so much, Mr. Sharrun. I look forward to meeting you."

"Likewise..." He paused. "Excuse me, Ms. Melendez, but can I ask how you heard about my company?"

"Your website. I just loved the Dove's Nest renovations. The combination of modernization while maintaining the original charm was really incredible. We'd like to have that same sort of aesthetic moving forward with Melendez Cottages. Guests these days want to unplug...until they don't," she said with a laugh. "We'd like to appeal to all campers, not just those who want to lose themselves in nature."

His website? She'd seen the Dove's Nest renos? "Yeah...I totally understand," he said. He hadn't until Sarah had proven that tourists really could have the best of both worlds and why should they have to choose. Everyone's idea of a vacation was different.

Damn, she'd been right about so many things.

"Great. So I'll see you tomorrow at noon," she said.

"I'll be there."

Disconnecting the call, he pulled into his driveway a few minutes later, still in a daze. His website. What was she talking about? She'd gotten his cell phone number right, so she must have found it somewhere. But he'd never gotten around to making a website. Always thought it unnecessary.

Going inside the house, he sat at Carmen's desk in the quiet, empty kitchen. He opened a search engine and typed in *Sharrun's Construction*.

A new website loaded with the name of his company

on top. First website listed on the search, and not in the shady sponsored-ads section. He scanned the site, and there was no question that it was meant for his company, complete with photos of the B&B renovation.

Holy shit. It looked professional. Not like the one-page, poorly designed one he used to have through some free local business site before the free trial expired.

He scrolled through the pages and clicked on the About Us page... A picture of him and Marissa loaded onto the screen. One taken a few months ago on the beach. One of his favorites.

A local company with heart, Sharrun Construction can accommodate all your construction needs big and small... Specializing in B&B rebuilds... Our motto is "Don't tear it down, save it"...

Wes's chest tightened the more he read, and a lump formed in his throat as he scrolled past the list of past projects and quotes from locals he'd done work for, praising his skill and craftsmanship. Someone must have contacted all these people to get these quotes.

Not someone. Marissa.

This had to be the surprise she'd been working on.

Getting up from the desk, he headed down the hallway toward her bedroom. Clearing his throat, he knocked on the door with a shaky hand. "Hey, it's me."

"I know, Dad; I'm coming!" she called through the door. "I'm just trying to find my cleats."

He opened it slowly. "Actually, I was thinking maybe we'd skip soccer today." He'd call Dustin and ask his assistant coach to fill in for him at practice. His daughter deserved a special day together, and she also deserved the option of quitting the team.

He scanned the room, stunned to see that it was clean. Was she applying for a daughter of the year award? Because there wouldn't be any contest.

"Skip soccer?" she said slowly. "You okay?"

His laugh was a strangled sound. "More than okay. I'm actually the luckiest dad on earth."

She frowned, studying him. "Okay, now you're scaring me."

"I just got a call to quote a job about an hour down the coast... The lady said she found my info online on my website."

Marissa's eyes widened even more. "Don't be mad. I was going to tell you. Actually, Sarah and I were going to show you together, but..."

But he'd made a mess of things. Right. All of this was his fault, and he wasn't the only one suffering for it. Marissa hadn't said much the last few days, but he could sense her disappointment over not seeing Sarah. "Mad? What are you talking about?" He moved closer and wrapped her in a hug. "I am so proud of you." He pulled away and looked at her. "That website was fantastic."

"Sarah helped," she said with a huge smile.

Sarah. Another kick to the gut. He needed to find a way to make it up to her.

"We wanted to surprise you... Guess the marketing worked too well, huh?"

He hugged her tighter. "Just well enough." This new job opportunity with Melendez Cottages might be the one he needed to get his company…his life back on track, and he wouldn't have it if it weren't for his genius daughter and the woman he was in love with.

He cleared his throat. "Hey, you wouldn't happen to have an app that could help me go back in time and stop myself from doing something stupid, would you?"

Marissa raised an eyebrow as she looked up at him. "Nope. Unfortunately, you're going to have to make it up to Sarah the old-fashioned way—by groveling."

Groveling. Right.

• • •

The ceremony of life on the beach was the perfect send-off for Mr. Harrison. All the local business vendors along the boardwalk had closed early that evening to say a final farewell to a man who'd meant a lot to all of them. One by one, they'd helped spread his ashes into the ocean and shared a memory of the man they'd gotten to know over the years.

Sarah had only recently gotten the chance to know him, but he'd always hold a special place in her heart. She hoped he'd finally found peace.

As the sun set on the ocean, everyone slowly dispersed, leaving Sarah alone on the beach. She stared out into the waves and fought to calm her conflicted emotions. Her grandmother and Mr. Harrison had never gotten their second chance, despite the love they had for each other.

Maybe some things just weren't meant to be.

Years ago, Dove's Nest had helped her grandmother cope with heartache and loss, and now this new event venue would help her heal from her disappointment as well.

She wiped a tear from her cheek as she silently said her own goodbye to the man who'd meant so much to her grandmother; then she turned to head back.

Her cell phone chimed with a new email from Whitney, and Sarah smiled to see the new reopening brochure her friend had redesigned for the inn. Sarah gulped. This was it. She was doing it. She was staying in her hometown and taking a chance at her own dream, while preserving her grandmother's.

Climbing into her car, she took her time driving along the coast toward the inn. For so many years, she'd been desperate to leave. She'd always felt out of place in the small town and hadn't thought she could accomplish the things she wanted living there. She'd been wrong. She'd just needed to carve out a place for herself and let the community embrace her.

Just like they were embracing the new Dove's Nest.

She pulled into the driveway, and seeing Wes's truck parked in front, she swallowed hard. He must be there to fix the cellar door. She hadn't really seen him since their argument, and the idea of seeing him now had her chest tightening even more. Staying in Blue Moon Bay and not being with him was going to be torture. But she'd made her decision.

Checking her reflection in the rearview mirror, she climbed out of her car and slowly made her way to the front door. A deep breath and she entered.

The ominous sound of the buzz saw had her eyes widening as she entered the foyer. She frowned as she moved in farther and glanced up the stairway to the guest bedrooms.

Wes stood on the top step, dressed in his jeans and paint-splattered T-shirt, his utility belt on his waist as he used the saw to cut into the landing where she'd fallen through. What the hell was he doing? Destroying the place? Her heart raced as she hurried up the stairs toward him. "Wes!"

He continued to work, cutting a huge piece of wood out of the landing.

"Wes, what the hell are you doing?" She'd just decided to keep the inn and now she'd have to pay him to repair the landing again?

He finished cutting and turned off the saw. Removing his safety goggles, he turned to face her. "Hi," he said, looking nervous.

He should be nervous. "Hi?" How about an explanation for destroying her newly renovated staircase?

"So, I heard a rumor that you've decided to keep the place," he said, his thoughts on the subject undecipherable.

"So, naturally you decide to destroy it?" Her pulse raced. He looked so freaking good and despite the situation, she had to hold herself back from rushing toward him.

"I'm not destroying it. I needed to show you something," he said, bending to lift the piece of wood from the landing. He turned it around and handed it to her.

With a slightly shaky hand, she took it. Then frowned as she flipped it over. He'd written something on the plank of wood.

"A lot of builders like to leave their mark somewhere in their builds and renovations. A little signature on the drywall…a family photo…"

Sarah squinted to read what he'd written.

The incomparable Sarah Lewis was here.

Her laugh was more of a half sob as she stared at it, feeling new tears well in her eyes.

Wes put the saw down and moved toward her. "So it's true. You're staying?"

She nodded. "Yes. I've decided this…place, Dove's Nest, is too important to let go of," she said, fighting to keep her emotions from overwhelming her.

The last few days had taken their toll, and as ready as she was to move forward with her plans, she was still as conflicted as ever.

"So this decision to stay had nothing to do with me? With us?"

Her heart pounded. Was he saying there was still a chance for them?

Just days before, he was willing to let her go. She refused to let her guard down so quickly this time, but she couldn't lie to him. "It wasn't *not* because of you…of us," she said quietly, glancing at the piece of wood in her hands.

He took several strides toward her, and his chest rose and fell as he took several deep breaths. "I was wrong, Sarah. About everything. You were right about Marissa needing freedom and space to be who she is…and about me needing to let go of the past and tradition and embrace the new."

She shook her head. "I understood you being angry about the app. I should have been more careful—"

"Parents learn as we go. We all make mistakes along the way, but what you did for Marissa this summer…" He paused, emotion written all over his handsome face. "What you did for me with the website—I can't thank you enough."

"That was all Marissa," she said. "She's so incredible. The before and after pictures, the quotes from locals, and creating the website design…all her." Man, she missed the little girl as much as she'd been missing Wes.

"She is incredible," he said. "And so are you. I've always thought so, and these last few weeks, my feelings for you, my attraction—has only grown."

He paused, and she held her breath. She felt the same way, but doubt and fear held her back from saying anything. She'd put herself out there too many times already. Maybe he still wasn't ready…

"Sarah, I'm sorry." He stepped closer. "And I'm hoping you'll give me one last chance to prove to you how I feel about you. This is what I want. Sarah, I want you here with us." He took her hands in his and pulled her toward him, his gaze locked on hers.

She stepped into his arms, desperate to believe that this was the right decision for all of them. That everything was going to work out. She was in love with him, and she loved Marissa, and she wanted this new start.

Blue Moon Bay was her home and she wanted to be here. With them.

He touched her cheek, then cupped her face in his hands as she stared up at him. "I love you, Sarah. I'm *in love* with you," he said.

The words were everything she'd been wanting to hear. "It's only ever been you for me, Wes."

His gaze burned into hers with a look she'd never seen before—desire, affection, attraction. No sign of hesitation or uncertainty.

She swallowed hard.

"Sarah, kiss me. I promise you I won't hurt you this time. Or ever," he said, tracing his thumb along her bottom lip, his eyes darting back and forth between her eyes and her mouth.

She released a deep breath as she raised her arms to encircle his neck, drawing his head lower. "Say my name again," she whispered.

"Sarah," he said against her lips as their mouths connected and she let everything go—her fears, her reservations, her doubt. She clung to him as they stood on the broken staircase, feeling as though all the pieces were finally put together.

She could feel her heart opening a little more with each second and the stress of the last few months evaporated in the hot California sun.

Starting over wasn't looking so bad after all.

Her breath caught in her chest, and all the happiness and hope in there made her feel like she might explode as she pulled back to look at him. "I'm in love with you, too," she whispered. "But you know you need to fix my staircase again, right?"

Wes grinned at her as he held her close. "I was counting on it. At the very least, it gave me an excuse to come back here."

Sarah kissed the man she loved again, knowing everything was going to be okay.

Thank you, Grandma.

EPILOGUE

A month later…

Wes could barely see the top of Marissa's head over the stack of boxes she carried from the truck toward the office space on Main Street. They were finally moving back out of his kitchen and into a real office.

And he owed that to Sarah.

The woman he was in love with more and more every day.

The past month together, growing closer, growing stronger as a couple, as a family had been better than he'd ever imagined. They were good together. They worked so well as a team. He couldn't imagine his life without her. Couldn't imagine *their* life without her.

He was a lucky man.

He unlocked the door and held it as Marissa entered. She set the boxes down on the floor and looked around. "Wow, it's even bigger than I remembered."

She'd been little the last time he'd been in the space. Being in there again now felt good. It felt right, like he was moving in the right direction.

"We're going to be busy." He'd hired two assistants to help run the office as Aunt Carmen had officially retired, and thanks to his new website, he had work booked into the summer of the following year. Life had changed in what felt like the blink of an eye. But in the best possible way.

Sarah's car pulled up outside and she climbed out, carrying a box of her own.

Damn, the sight of her always had his heart pounding out of his chest. She was so beautiful and so amazing. He didn't deserve her, but he was ready to spend the rest of his life trying.

"What's this?" he asked, taking it from her and kissing her as chastely as possible with Marissa watching.

"A new system for the boardroom for virtual meetings with clients," she said.

He laughed as he shook his head. "You're really going to bring me into this century, huh?"

"That's the plan. After all, I did it with the B&B. *We* did it with the B&B, so anything's possible," she said.

He set the box down and wrapped one arm around her, leaving a gap for Marissa to join in the group hug. "So, we'll do all of this…together?"

"Together," Marissa and Sarah agreed.

Marissa nudged him, and he glanced down at her wide-eyed, eager expression. *Ask her*, she mouthed.

Wes's heart beat out of his chest, and his palms were immediately sweaty as he took a deep breath. Marissa was right. Now was the perfect time.

He reached into his pocket and took out a tiny box, the local jewelry store logo visible on top. He'd been carrying it around for a week, waiting for the right time. A month seemed fast, but they'd known each other their entire lives. And why put off what they both wanted? He loved her, and he could feel her love for him and Marissa every day.

Sarah's mouth dropped as he slowly got down on one knee.

Beside him, Marissa could barely contain her excitement, ready to burst out of her skin any moment. If he didn't ask quickly, his daughter would take over the proposal herself.

"Sarah, I'm in love with you. I can't imagine my life—*our* life"—he smiled at Marissa—"without you in it. Will you make us the luckiest family ever and be my wife and Marissa's stepmom?" he asked, swallowing back his own emotions.

Tears welled in Sarah's eyes as she glanced back and forth between them. She nodded quickly. "Yes! Yes. A million times yes," she said over a strangled-sounding laugh.

Wes stood and took her hand in his shaking one. He gently slid the engagement ring on her finger and kissed her softly.

Marissa clapped and hollered as she watched on.

"Really?" Sarah asked, the look of surprise still on her beautiful face. "We're really going to do this?"

Wes nodded. "The three of us forever." He kissed her again. "So make sure you leave a date open at that busy B&B of yours for the wedding."

Sarah smiled. "Any date you want."

He'd marry her that minute if he could. "I love you, Sarah."

"I love you," she said. "And I love you," she said to Marissa.

Opening his arms once more, Wes held the two most important people in his life tight as he released a deep, satisfied sigh. The best things in life really did happen when you least expected them.

ACKNOWLEDGMENTS

Thank you to my agent, Jill Marsal and my editors, Lydia Sharp, Liz Pelletier, and Stacy Abrams for all the insightful feedback and edits. Thank you to the entire Entangled team for the breathtakingly beautiful cover and all the marketing and promotion efforts. A big thank you to my husband and son for surviving this deadline as we also planned a move across the world while I was writing lol! And a big hug to all my readers who continue to support me and my stories! Thank you for allowing me to do what I love and call it "work". XOXO

*A brand-new small-town romance proving
sometimes fake dates can turn into forever.*

forever
starts now

USA TODAY BESTSELLING AUTHOR
STEFANIE
LONDON

What happens when two people who've given up on forever
find it in each other…?

Single men are as scarce in Forever Falls as a vegetarian at
a barbecue. That is, until Ethan Hammersmith moves in.
After his fiancée gave him an ultimatum, he left Australia
and never looked back. He isn't in America to find a new
girlfriend, though. He's searching for the father he never
knew. But now it's like he has a flashing sign above his head
that says "available." Thankfully, the manager of the local
diner is willing to give him cover—if only she weren't so
distractingly adorable.

Monroe Roberts, town misanthrope and divorcée,
knocked "forever" permanently off her wish list ever since
the love of her life skipped town with the cliché yoga
instructor. And good riddance. She's got this struggling
diner to keep her busy, trying anything to boost sales…until
a hot Australian strolls in and changes everything. Monroe's
restaurant is packed full of women who aren't there to order
food, unless Ethan is on the menu. This could sink her
business faster than ever. So—light bulb—what if they
pretend to be together?

It sounds like the perfect plan. Until they realize there is
some very real chemistry in this fake relationship. But is it
enough to heal two hearts that have been so deeply
wounded?

AMARA
an imprint of Entangled Publishing LLC